Sam's control snapped.

"If you don't stop looking at me like that, I'm going to give you what you want."

"What are you talking about?"

"You want me to kiss you."

"Give me a break." Dallas laughed with just the right note of disgust and disbelief.

"Liar," he said softly.

She swallowed. "Whatever we had—whatever that night was—is gone."

He suddenly, fiercely, wanted to thrust his hands into her hair, pull her to him and ravage her mouth until she surrendered. Until she admitted that he, Sam, was in her head. Then he would turn away from her, the way she had from him. "Are you sure about that?"

"Yes." Uncertainty flickered in her eyes.

He raised one eyebrow. "Really."

"Positive." And Dallas hoped she was telling the truth.

Dear Reader,

Happy holidaze! The holiday season always does pass in a bit of a daze, with all the shopping and wrapping and partying, the cooking and (of course!) the eating. So take some time for yourself with our six Intimate Moments novels, each one of them a wonderful Christmas treat.

Start by paying a visit to THE LONE STAR SOCIAL CLUB, Linda Turner's setting for *Christmas Lone-Star Style*. Remember, those Texans know how to do things in a *big* way! Then join Suzanne Brockmann for another TALL, DARK AND DANGEROUS title, *It Came Upon a Midnight Clear*. I wouldn't mind waking up and finding Crash Hawken under *my* Christmas tree! Historical writer Patricia Potter makes a slam-bang contemporary debut with *Home for Christmas*, our FAMILIES ARE FOREVER title. Wrongly convicted and without the memories that could save him, Ryan Murphy is a hero to treasure. Award winner Ruth Wind returns with *For Christmas, Forever*. Isn't this the season when mysterious strangers come bearing…romance tinged with danger? Debra Cowan's *One Silent Night* is our MEN IN BLUE title. I'd be happy to "unwrap" Sam Garrett on Christmas morning. Finally, welcome mainstream author Christine Michels to the line. *A Season of Miracles* carries the TRY TO REMEMBER flash, though you'll have no trouble at all remembering this warm holiday love story.

It's time to take the "daze" out of the holidays, so enjoy all six of these seasonal offerings. Of course, don't forget that next month marks a new year, so come back then for more of the best romance reading around—right here in Silhouette Intimate Moments.

Seasons Greetings,

Leslie J. Wainger
Executive Senior Editor

Please address questions and book requests to:
Silhouette Reader Service
U.S.: 3010 Walden Ave., P.O. Box 1325, Buffalo, NY 14269
Canadian: P.O. Box 609, Fort Erie, Ont. L2A 5X3

ONE SILENT NIGHT

DEBRA COWAN

Silhouette®

INTIMATE™MOMENTS®

Published by Silhouette Books

America's Publisher of Contemporary Romance

SILHOUETTE BOOKS

ISBN 0-373-07899-4

ONE SILENT NIGHT

Books by Debra Cowan

Silhouette Intimate Moments

Dare To Remember #774
The Rescue of Jenna West #858
One Silent Night #899

DEBRA COWAN

Like many writers, Debra made up stories in her head as a child. Her B.A. in English was obtained with the intention of following family tradition and becoming a teacher, but after she wrote her first novel, there was no looking back. After years of working another job in addition to writing, she now devotes her full time to penning both historical and contemporary romances. An avid history buff, Debra enjoys traveling. She has visited places as diverse as Europe and Honduras, where she and her husband served as part of a medical mission team. Born in the foothills of the Kiamichi Mountains, Debra still lives in her native Oklahoma with her husband and their two beagles, Maggie and Domino. She would love to hear from you.

SASE for reply: Debra Cowan, P.O. Box 5323, Edmond, OK 73083-5323.

Prologue

"Dammit, Kittridge! Where are you?" Detective Sam Garrett tried to ignore the hard squeeze of alarm in his chest as he stalked up the driveway, past the For Sale sign in the yard, the moving company's truck and through her front door.

The calm Oklahoma day mocked the churning turmoil inside him. He completely disregarded the stack of boxes he'd seen in the back of the truck, the furniture already loaded and covered, but he nearly tripped over the two suitcases in the entryway. June sunshine slanted through the miniblinds of the living area, pushing strips of light into the now barren room.

His gut told him she was still here. And even if his gut hadn't told him, her spicy, intriguing fragrance would have. That smoky floral scent penetrated his lungs and settled into a hard knot of regret.

He saw her then, standing rigid in the hallway, those normally serene gray eyes freezing him out. She wore her black U.S. Marshals windbreaker over a white T-shirt and faded jeans that molded those long, lean legs like snakeskin.

"That's it," she said to a burly man dressed in jeans and a

T-shirt stamped with the name of the same moving company as on the side of the truck.

"Yes, ma'am." He glanced at Sam, then scurried around him, plucking up the two suitcases and one last box in the living room.

"What the hell's going on?" Sam demanded.

She stooped, picked up a briefcase and a small overnight bag. "If you'd return my phone calls, you'd know."

He winced. In the past two days she'd left at least six messages, but he hadn't been able to make himself face her yet. Not after their night of paradise that had lashed him with guilt ever since.

"I've been busy."

"Uh, yes, I met—what's her name? Mona?"

Mandy. It made him sick to know that Dallas had seen Mandy this morning and known that Sam had been trying to forget what he and Dallas had done.

A tight heaviness sat in the middle of Sam's chest just as it had since they'd made love two nights ago. "Look, I wasn't thinking. I lost my head—"

"Would that be with her? Or with me?" Her cool, too-sweet tone chipped at him like a pick.

"Dammit, Dallas!" His sharp cop's gaze took in the empty bookcases, the soft ivory walls now bare of the delicately framed prints of various city skylines that she collected.

Through the hallway he could see the gleaming wood top of her dresser. The other night it had been littered with scrap paper, dainty crystal perfume bottles, her gold U.S. Marshals badge, and her .9mm Taurus. Now it, too, was empty. There was nothing left in the house that spoke of the soft edginess of Dallas Kittridge.

He clenched his teeth, fighting to keep the anger from gnawing away his control. "After I found out that you'd come by my house this morning, I went to your office. One of the other marshals told me you were getting a transfer."

"Yes."

Rage erupted with a numbing fear, and yet there was also the sting of betrayal. Why hadn't she told him? "The marshals have just as much red tape as the PD. You had to have requested a transfer right after Brad died back in April. You must have known before we made—before we were—" He swore, fisting his hands at his hips. "Why didn't you tell me?"

"I wasn't sure I was going to get it."

"And when you were?"

"I thought about saying no." She started to edge past him. "I was going to talk to you about it the other night."

But she hadn't. They hadn't talked at all, just clutched desperately at each other. He shifted, crowding her against the doorjamb. "You don't have to go. You can stay—"

"That night convinced me I shouldn't." She looked at him then, her gray eyes stormy. "That was the biggest mistake of my life."

"It wasn't the smartest thing I ever did, either," he retorted.

"Then we should both just walk away."

His heart thundered against his ribs. "We've been friends for a long time, Dallas."

Her strong, stubborn chin trembled slightly. "Brad's dead. There's no link between us anymore."

"That's bull and you know it!"

"He's gone, Sam. Things will never be the way they were."

"That's not because he's gone." Sam shoved a hand through his wavy dark hair, fighting panic and a crushing sense of helplessness. "He's always going to be here between us, isn't he? Because of what we did."

"I don't know. I only know that I can't be around you without thinking of him."

The self-loathing in her voice triggered his internal alarms. He tensed, flashing back to the night they'd made love.

He should never have given in to the impulse to hold her. It had led him straight to heaven, then dropped him into hell.

Afterward, she hadn't said a word. She'd just rolled away from him and faced the wall. Even as guilt had slashed through him, he'd felt rejection. And then she'd reached toward the nightstand, for Brad's picture.

That same rejection hit Sam now like a sniper's bullet—vicious, unexpected, nearly disabling. "Who the hell were you thinking about the other night? While you and I were—"

"I need to go." She looked away, positioning the travel case between them like a shield.

"Answer me." Sam grabbed her arm, disbelief and horror crashing in on top of the rejection he felt. "Who were you thinking of that night, Dallas? Him or me?"

She yanked away from him. "I've got a plane to catch."

"Dallas—"

She fixed her gaze on the opposite wall; her throat worked.

He closed his eyes as denial screamed through him. He wanted to shove her up against the wall, kiss her until she melted against him the way she had that night. The air grew thick. Sam couldn't breathe. Searing pain bloomed in his chest, arrowed down his arms, his legs.

He knew she felt guilty about Brad, about what she and Sam had done together. It was his own unrelenting pain and rawboned guilt over his partner's death that had caused Sam to go to another woman, had kept him from facing her, until now. And now it was too late.

He was losing her, just like two months ago he'd lost Brad. And just like with Brad, it was his fault.

He looked up and realized she was gone.

"Dammit!" He raced outside in time to see her pull out of the driveway and peel rubber down the street.

Damn her! Damn her for leaving, for thinking of Brad while she'd made love with him, for ripping out his heart.

She was right. What they'd done the other night was the biggest mistake of their lives. Now he had to live with it.

Chapter 1

Eighteen months later

Less than two weeks until Christmas and he was up to his kneecaps in dead bodies.

Detective Sam Garrett stared at the latest victim who lay limply on beige carpet, and a wave of deep fatigue washed through him. He'd been on the job since four o'clock this morning, but he needed the work. And there was no shortage of it here in Oklahoma City.

In the eighteen months since Sam had requested, and received, a transfer from Vice to Homicide, he'd needed to stay busy. Needed to keep his mind screened from the memories of Brad and the insidious direction those thoughts always took. Not that Sam had been able to shake thoughts of his former partner for a single day. And this month—today—marked the twenty-month anniversary of Brad's death.

Sam had been on the Oklahoma City Police force eleven years, five of those with Brad. And the last twenty months without him. Almost two years.

As always, guilt and regret accompanied his thoughts of Brad. And as always, his efforts to ignore memories of *her* were futile. But Sam was tired and angry and determined not to think about Dallas Kittridge. At least not tonight.

His partner, Virgil "Rock" Moody, an old bull who'd served on the OCPD for over twenty years, was out with the flu, as was half the department. Sam forced himself to stare at the brutal sight of the newest victim's slack features—or rather, the uniform marks imprinted on her throat.

For the first time, he wished he had his partner's callous acceptance of whatever they found. Something about this homicide already chewed at his gut like acid and he wished he could just dismiss it, the way Rock always did.

He rubbed his burning eyes and tucked his notebook into the back pocket of his Levi's. Jamming a stick of gum in his mouth, he sighed, feeling tired and for an instant, hopeless. Hilary Poole, a homicide they'd caught about two months ago, had had marks on her neck similar to the ones on Audrey Hayes, tonight's victim.

Poole had been picked up at a country-western bar called Calhoun's. Sam would start there, see if Audrey Hayes had been at that bar last night.

He turned toward Mark "Hutch" Hutchinson, the medical examiner who was directing the removal of the body, now enclosed in the black body bag. *Poor lady.* Sadness swept through Sam, followed by a surge of determination. He'd find this slime who preyed on women.

If this was the same guy, he'd killed two women in a couple of months. Sam was growing increasingly frustrated. He had no prints, no description, no weapon. Nothing. With a last glance at the instant photo one of the lab guys had snapped, he slipped it into the pocket of his sheepskin coat.

He walked outside, needles of rain stinging his cheeks. He buried his chin in the coat and hurried to his dark blue pickup.

As he reached for the driver's door, sensation fizzled down his spine. It was the same feeling he got whenever he confronted a suspect. He snapped to attention and slid his hand into his coat pocket, feeling the cold steel of the .45 Smith & Wesson he carried as backup to his holstered .357 Magnum.

His gaze raked across the wet pavement to the hazy mist ringing the streetlight, but he saw nothing. He glanced behind him, narrowing his eyes to probe the slippery shadows between the trees and bushes and the eaves of the house. Nothing. He waited, straining to pick up any wayward sound, something out of place. There was nothing. The hum tickling his spine disappeared as quickly as it had overtaken him.

He shook his head. Maybe he'd been up too long. Or maybe Brad's ghost was saying howdy. His lips twisted ruefully.

Climbing into his truck, Sam started the engine and blew on his hands to warm them. After a few seconds, he shoved the truck into gear and drove toward Pennsylvania Avenue. From there, he took I-40 east toward Calhoun's.

Thoughts of Brad and Dallas circled through Sam's mind, but he pushed them away, refusing to have his attention swayed from this case. He cranked up the stereo, losing himself in the throbbing strains of Mickey Gilley's "Stand By Me."

Less than twenty minutes later, he pulled into the parking lot of Calhoun's, which boasted "The World's Largest Dance Floor." It was still early for most of the bar traffic, but the parking lot contained a healthy number of cars. The truck stop across the street was well-lit and packed full of truck cabs and trailers.

He nosed into a space close to the door and slid out of his pickup. The swoosh of passing semis on the highway sounded behind him. From inside, the dull roar of the jukebox blasted the air. The live music wouldn't start for a while.

As he walked, he glanced around the parking lot. It was empty of people. Cars passed by on the street, their lights glimmering against the wet pavement. The icy rain misted his hair and eyes and he ran a hand over his chilled face as he reached the door.

Inside, welcome warmth wrapped around him. A pale blue haze of smoke hung over one corner of the bar. Multicolored lights on a lopsided Christmas tree winked from the same corner. The stale odor of cigarettes undermined the scents of food and perfume. Fishing the photo of Audrey Hayes out of his pocket, Sam walked over to the bar.

After a slit-eyed stare at Sam's badge, the bartender, who identified himself as "Danny," said he'd never seen the Hayes woman. He also told Sam he hadn't worked the late shift last night. Sam needed to talk to Theo, who'd be in after nine. Sam remembered the burly bartender from his previous visit. Only one of tonight's waitresses had worked the night before and she, too, told Sam to speak to Theo.

Resigned to returning in a couple of hours, Sam lifted a hand in thanks and started for the door. His cell phone shrilled.

He pulled it from the pocket of his coat. "Yeah, Garrett here."

"What a coincidence," a familiar voice drawled on the other end. "Here, too."

"Hey, Mace." Sam moved next to the front door, grinning at the sound of his brother's voice.

"Where are you? What's the music?"

"I'm at Calhoun's." Sam's gaze traveled over the sawdust-riddled floor to the stage, which presently stood empty except for several microphones and some loops of electrical cord.

"Calhoun's? Work or play?"

"Work."

"Really?" Mace's voice sharpened with interest. "Are you checking out a lead from that homicide tonight?"

"Yeah."

"You think it's related to the one you caught before?"

"Yeah. Both strangulations with similar marks on the victims' necks. I need to talk to the bartender who was on last night, but he's not here right now."

"Well, come on by. Devon and I want you to have supper with us."

"I was just over there two nights ago," he protested with a laugh.

"For some reason, my wife likes you," his brother teased.

And his sister-in-law was mothering him. Sam's gut twisted. Mace and Devon were well aware that the holidays were bringing up painful memories. They'd tried to include him in something at least twice this week. "Devon's got to be sick of me by now."

"*I* sure am," his brother drawled. "Naw, come on. It was her idea. We're having chili."

"Aw, I was really hoping for week-old pizza."

Mace chuckled and Sam smiled.

"Linc and Jenna are coming, too. We'll see you in about a half hour."

Sam hesitated. In his mind, his partner's death was his fault. He didn't deserve the comfort of his family—tonight or any night. He should be alone; go home and sit in the cold darkness where he couldn't hide from what he'd done to his best friend. Or *with* his best friend's wife.

"We're expecting you, Sam." Mace's voice cut through his thoughts. "We're not taking no."

With that, the line went dead. Sam grinned. Mace had a way of getting things on his own terms.

"Right." Sam turned off the phone and jammed it back in his pocket. As much as he'd tried to dodge the past, the phone call from Mace blew the lock on his self-control.

Standing in the bar, surrounded by a cowboy-cryin'-in-his-beer love song and the shuffle of boots, all the emotion that Sam had tried to corral burst free like water from a geyser.

The whole day had been hell. One endless chain of regret and pain and guilt. An infinite sidestepping of memories of Dallas Kittridge—of what he'd done to her…and what she'd done to him.

Finally he allowed himself to wonder how she was doing today; this month. Hell, how she'd been doing in the eighteen months since she'd left. He knew her transfer had taken her to Denver, but he'd never called her. After all, she was the one who'd left.

Was she working today? Was she remembering? Had she even considered coming back to Oklahoma City and going to the cemetery, as Sam had done? Had she *ever* gone to Brad's grave site?

He muttered a curse and pushed through the door. Sharp air bit at his cheeks. He buried his chin in his sheepskin collar, stalking toward his truck.

He didn't want to think about her. Didn't want to remember her throaty laugh. The way those smoky eyes flashed wickedly. The feel of her long lean legs tangled with his. The soft stroke of her fingertip against his eyebrow.

He shrugged his shoulders against the memories, tried to shove them away. They lingered like her perfume—tantalizing, torturing.

He reached his truck and awareness zapped down his spine like a jolt of electricity—the same feeling he'd had back at the murder scene.

His body tense, he slowly turned, his gaze scouring the parking lot. That little patch low in his back went numb the way it did when he faced an armed suspect. Floodlights from the parking lot danced through the drizzle. Then he saw her.

His breath wedged crosswise in his chest, arrowing pain out to his arms.

Moving from the shadows of the large country-western bar, Dallas Kittridge materialized out of the night like a shimmering mirage. She came slowly toward him. Guarded yet purposeful.

A black leather duster hid legs that he knew were slender and muscular and long enough to rival a supermodel's. Black boots clicked softly on the wet asphalt; fine diamonds of moisture misted her black turtleneck. Even her tawny hair was dark with rain.

She stopped a few feet in front of him and slicked her hair back out of her face, gazing at him head-on. Garish light from the flood lamps skipped over her, gouging deep hollows of shadow beneath her high cheekbones. He thought he saw pain in her gray eyes, a second before they were transformed into flat pools of nothing.

Disbelief shot through him. She couldn't be here! But she was. She looked tired. She was beautiful.

"Well," she said softly. "Hello, Detective Charm."

That crushed-velvet voice wrapped around him, torched the guilt he'd tried to quash all these months. His gut knotted with instant desire—an unwelcome reminder that only his best friend's wife had ever affected him this way.

Because he itched to touch her, to make sure she was real, he crammed his fists into his pockets. "What'n the hell are you doing here?"

Chapter 2

She'd anticipated his surprise, his shock, but not the desire. It flared in his eyes—twin flames of consuming heat—and she felt it hum between them. Need quivered through her and she straightened against it, determined to call the shots, to face him and have it over.

Dallas detested this wanting, this gut-tightening hunger she felt around him, the same need she'd felt the night they'd made love. It was need that was more than physical; it overwhelmed her soul, gave her a feeling of completeness with Sam she'd never had with Brad. And it was wrong. It had been wrong then—her husband had been dead two months and she'd still loved him—and it was wrong now.

The initial surprise faded from Sam's eyes and so did that flash of frank male interest. She was glad. For an instant, he'd looked at her as he had that long-ago night—like he wanted to possess her, *like he already did.* Which scared her more than anger or guilt or resentment.

"Dallas!" He started toward her, his eyes glittering like hard points of steel.

She took a step backward—one step.

He stopped, his eyes guarded, his body going as rigid as hers.

"Detective Charm?" His sculpted features slipped into a blank mask and his voice became cool and steady. "What kind of name is that?"

Dallas swallowed, glad he couldn't see the flush of her skin through the mist of shadows and rain. Her heartbeat ripped through her chest like machine-gun fire. She'd privately taken to calling him "Detective Charm," while trying to get over the betrayal she felt over the glaring truth that she hadn't meant any more to him than any of the other dozens of women he'd slept with.

His normally teasing blue eyes and quick smile marked him as aptly named, but now his eyes had turned the flat silver of a glacier and his mouth had tightened in wariness. Still, he was compelling. Intimidating.

She'd watched him at the crime scene, then followed him to the boot-scootin' bar, giving herself what she'd thought would be enough time to ready herself for this unavoidable contact. But not even her survival training at Glynco could have prepared her for the ambush on her senses—the way his woodsy scent mingled with the rain and caused a kick in her belly, the way his gaze slid down her body like ice over heated skin, resurrecting the ache she'd lived with since that night a year and a half ago.

"Have you already been to the cemetery?" he asked quietly.

Guilt jabbed at her. Valeria's case had overshadowed her plans for the cemetery. "Not yet."

"Then what are you doing here, Marshal Kittridge?"

Braced for an onslaught of emotion, Dallas nevertheless tensed at the grimness in Sam's voice. If he was working on Valeria's case—and it appeared he was—he would find out soon enough what she was doing here. In the meantime, she had the advantage of surprise and she intended to keep it for as long as possible.

"I'm meeting someone." His shoulders were still broad enough to rival a defensive end's, his hips narrow, and there was a taut strength in his six-foot-two frame that made women want to test it, see if they could make him lose control.

Involuntarily, a warmth spread through her. One long ago silent night, she'd felt the release of that power as he'd surged into her. She didn't want to unleash it again. It could consume her, make her regret that she'd left here. And she didn't want to regret it.

He snapped his fingers in front of her face, jolting her out of her musings. "Hey, this person you're meeting—are they from the FTC?"

The Federal Transfer Center, used by the U.S. Marshals Service as a transfer and holding place for federal prisoners, was located near Oklahoma City's airport. And not very close to Calhoun's. "Maybe."

Grudging admiration mixed with frustration glinted in his eyes. "The FBI has nothing on you when it comes to 'tight-lipped.'"

A sharp retort rose to her lips, but she bit it back. She had no desire to trade barbs with Sam. She'd decided to step out of the shadows, using her advantage while she still had it. And she *had* caught him off guard. Now it was time to move on.

"Nice to see you, Sam." She smoothed back her rain-dampened hair and turned to go.

"How are you, Dallas? How have you been?"

The obvious reluctance in his voice sent a pang through her. She schooled her expression before turning back to face him.

"Fine," she said breezily, fighting the urge to grit her teeth. "Just fine."

"I'm glad." He stepped toward her, his boot soles a muffled scrape against the pavement. His lips flattened, as if he were steeling himself for something unpleasant. "Do you have time for coffee? Or dinner—"

''No.'' She cut him off, glancing over her shoulder as she unconsciously moved her hand toward the Taurus holstered at her hip. ''No.''

''Not even coffee?'' His voice deepened, touching places inside her she'd closed off long ago.

She eyed him warily as desperation funneled through her. She had to get away from him before she lost all advantage. ''Nope. Sorry.''

''Dallas, I've wanted to talk to you for a long time. To apologize—''

Apologize? She knew what was coming and dread washed over her in a sickening wave. ''I didn't come here to rehash anything. There's no need for apologies.''

''I want to. I've wanted to since you left, but I couldn't bring myself to call you.''

''Consider it forgotten.'' Her voice was tight with the effort not to scream.

He took a step toward her, his heat pushing away the cold air that surrounded them. ''I can't forget, Dallas.''

The rawness of his voice had her clenching her hands. She couldn't do this. Her hand closed over the Taurus's butt and she gripped it tightly. This was what she could depend on— her job, not Sam Garrett.

She lifted her chin and slid her gaze toward the bar's front door. ''Maybe a drink will help you forget.''

Pain flashed through his eyes and for an instant she hated herself for hurting him. Remembered how she'd hurt him a year and a half ago. Then she remembered how he'd turned his back on her when she needed him desperately. Not even as a lover, but as a friend.

''Can't you spare the time for me to apologize properly? For old times' sake?''

She glared at him. He *would* bring up their past relationship. She didn't want to hear what he had to say, didn't want to feel again that razor-edge of betrayal or be reminded of the savage jealousy she'd felt upon discovering that bimbo,

What's-her-name, in his apartment only two days after they'd… She tore her thoughts away from those memories.

Distance was the one thing that enabled Dallas to keep thoughts of Sam and his lovemaking out of her mind. Distance she wasn't willing to give up.

"I apologize for not returning your phone calls," he began, as if she'd consented to hear him out. "And I very definitely apologize for Mandy—"

"I accept your apology. Let's just leave it at that, shall we?" She hated herself for the way her voice turned soft, almost pleading, but she wanted away from this man who reduced her to one big, throbbing nerve. "They" had been a long time ago. "They" were *over*.

Just this few minutes of contact had sent emotion flooding through her, filling her with the dangerous urge to be held and comforted by Sam. Held and comforted the way he'd done after Brad's death, *before* he had turned away from her. But she was long past deriving comfort from the man who'd betrayed her.

"Dammit, Dallas! I need to explain about Mandy."

She definitely didn't want to hear *that*. "Please don't, Sam. For old times' sake."

Frustration darkened his blue eyes, turning them black and mysterious in the darkness. That familiar stubbornness tightened his features, narrowed his eyes, but finally he nodded. "All right. As long as you know that I'm truly, sincerely sorry for what happened. Especially that you found Mandy there."

"I had no claim on you," she said stiffly.

He glanced away. "I felt bad about what we'd done."

"You think I didn't?" she retorted, wondering how the advantage could have shifted so seamlessly, so *easily* to him.

"Brad was my best friend."

"He was *my* husband."

"You didn't get him killed," Sam said quietly, his gaze shifting to hers.

Dallas froze. "What are you talking about?"

"If that suspect hadn't gotten the drop on me—"

"I have never, *never* blamed you for Brad's death." Dallas trembled with fury and shock. "It wasn't your fault."

"The slimeball shot him with *my* gun."

"It's a risk every cop takes when he responds to a call. Don't carry this guilt, Sam. It's not yours."

He made a choked sound. "Why? Because you say so?" He rolled his shoulders as if trying to escape the memory. "I just want you to understand how guilty I felt, and still do. First Brad, then that night with you. I was trying to forget about you, about *us*—"

"By using another woman. Yeah, I get it. I was just as guilty—maybe more—of cheating. On Brad. He was my husband. But we're talking about us—" Dallas faltered, unsure how to describe what was—what *had been*—between her and Sam. "Our friendship. I didn't dodge your phone calls or go to someone else's bed." She realized she was yelling and lowered her voice to a vehement whisper. "I wasn't the one who walked away from our friendship."

"No, you ran away. And you did it first." The instant the words were out, regret flashed across Sam's face. He stepped back, a tangible wall coming up between them. "I was wrong not to return your phone calls. I was wrong to go to another woman, but I was furious when you turned away from me."

Her gaze held his.

His hands fisted on his hips. "So I suppose you won't apologize?"

"For what?"

Resentment, sharp and naked, glittered in his eyes. "For not telling me your plans, for planning to leave without a word."

She had the distinct sense he wanted to say more, something else. Fury ripped through her. She *had* tried to tell him. That was where Mandy had come in. She clenched her jaw so hard she thought her teeth would snap. "No."

"No," he repeated flatly. "Fine."

"Fine." She bit off the urge to say more. They'd made a

huge mistake. A bunch of words between them a year and a half later wasn't going to fix it.

We can't go back, Sam. I won't go back. Pain sliced through her, nicking the raw place inside her that had never healed since that night she and Sam had made love. Her throat tightened and she knew she couldn't speak without betraying the quiver in her voice that had worked its way up from her belly.

She nodded and turned away before he could see the sheen of tears that suddenly burned her eyes. "I've got to go."

"Sure."

She allowed herself one last look, one last memory of him standing against the truck, a silhouette of sinew and muscle against the sleek lines of the vehicle, his face shadowed by night, his eyes glittering like polished glass.

She read remorse and concern in those features and a strange heat shoved up under her ribs. She turned away, feeling his gaze on her like a steady flame, burning away her anger, burning away the memory of what he'd done to her.

"You look great, Dallas." His voice hung in the cold night air, stroking over her, soft and rusty and final.

Rage. She recognized the heat in her chest now. He was really putting it—*them*—in the past. He could really forget.

She squared her shoulders and pretended she hadn't heard him. She never broke stride, never hesitated, but instead walked on toward the bar, focused on putting one foot in front of the other, holding on to the knowledge that each step took her farther away from him, to safety, to the welcome numbness.

She fought a stirring awareness in her belly the whole way. She wouldn't let him get to her. She wouldn't.

Pushing through the door of the country-western bar, Dallas tuned in to the smooth strains of George Strait's "Easy Come, Easy Go," and headed automatically for the darkest corner. Once there, she disappeared into the shadows as she always did. After a few minutes, she could breathe without feeling that her chest was going to collapse from pressure.

She jammed a shaking hand through her jaw-length blond hair. Anger still pulsed inside her and now she admitted why: she would never be able to forget that night.

From her vantage point, she blankly watched the miniskirt-clad waitresses thread their way among tables and booths. A thin blue cloud of smoke hung in the air; neon glared from the jukebox. She was invisible now. *Invisible.*

That was the thing about Sam. With him, she had never been invisible. He made her feel…exposed, raw. Resentment churned inside her.

Not this time. Hauling in a deep breath, she squared her shoulders. She needed him to help find Valeria's killer, but she wouldn't open herself up to him again. She would keep what distance she had to, do whatever it took to find the murderer. She didn't intend to become a casualty in the process.

She waited for a few minutes, until her heart had quit pounding and her breath had slowed to normal, then she went to the door and pushed it open for a peek outside. His pickup was gone. Other cars and trucks were pulling into the parking lot, their lights slicing through the hazy rain. Dallas walked back to her rented sports car and headed for the crime scene.

Disbelief and shock gave way to burning anger. Sam hated the desire he'd felt on first seeing her, in that split second before the agony crashed back. Before he recalled, with gut-wrenching clarity, how she'd used him as a substitute lover. He'd apologized, tried to move on, blast the memory of Dallas out of his blood. And he'd gotten nothing from her.

What had he expected? A soft apology, a tearful request that they let bygones be bygones and resume their friendship? Not from Dallas.

He wasn't interested anyway, Sam told himself forcefully. She'd turned away from him after they'd made love. She'd looked at Brad's picture. He'd known then that, in her imagination, he had been someone else. He'd been Brad. And when she'd realized that she was with him—Sam—she'd pushed him away.

He couldn't get over how beautiful she was and resented the hell out of it. Just looking at her had reignited the memory. He'd found her crying on the porch and pulled her to him.

"Make me feel something, Sam," she'd whispered that night. *"Anything."*

Sam hadn't spoken at all. Silent and desperate, he and Dallas had come together.

He didn't want to think about her.

He couldn't seem to do anything *but* think about her.

He drove to Mace's, still feeling as if he couldn't quite get a full breath. He didn't like leaving things unfinished with Dallas—*again*—but she seemed to like it just fine. She'd always put him off-balance. Only when they'd made love had he felt they'd meshed on the same plane, at the same time. Not ahead or behind, but together.

If he hadn't run into her outside the bar, he never would have known she was in town. She wouldn't have contacted him at all. Which was how it should be. He'd worked hard to forget her and had succeeded. He didn't need Dallas LeAnn Kittridge screwing up his life again. He wouldn't allow it.

Once inside his brother's house, Sam blurted out what had happened.

"Dallas Kittridge?" Mace stared openmouthed at Sam. "You're kidding!"

"Right," Sam muttered, shoving a hand through his hair. "I think this is real funny."

Devon's eyes lit with curiosity and pleasure. "How is she?"

"Fine," Sam growled, then gentled his tone for his sister-in-law. "I guess. I didn't talk to her that long."

"What's she doing here?"

"Is she moving back?" Devon asked hopefully.

"That's not the impression I got." Sam's lips twisted as he shrugged out of his coat. He tried to tamp down the resentment burning through him, but his efforts were futile. His initial shock and disbelief had exploded into anger, then edged into this smouldering frustration.

Mace shot Devon a meaningful look and they dropped the subject. Linc, a physician, and Jenna, a veterinarian, had both been called on an emergency so they weren't coming. Sam followed his oldest brother and sister-in-law into the kitchen of Devon's home. During the winter, Mace and Devon stayed at this house in the city, rather than their cabin by the lake. Devon had set the small dining table with bowls and glasses and crackers.

Chili steamed in the bowls, emitting the mouthwatering aroma of cooked beef and spices.

They sat down to eat, and for a moment there was only the sound of ice rattling in tea glasses and the scrape of spoons against the side of their bowls.

"Don't forget about Greg's bachelor party tomorrow night," his sister-in-law reminded.

Sam had forgotten all about their cousin's party and upcoming nuptials. He looked up, saw Mace grimace at the same time he did.

"Linc's stopping by first," Mace said. "Want to meet us somewhere for dinner?"

"Sure." Sam shrugged and took another bite of savory chili.

He couldn't shake the feeling that something was going on with Dallas, something more than just her being in town to pick up a prisoner.

Mace interrupted his thoughts. "Did you learn anything else at the bar?"

"No."

Mace slid a careful look at Devon. "But you still think it's the same guy?"

"Yeah." Sam took a gulp of iced tea to dull the burn of the fiery chili.

Devon smiled and rose from the table, reaching for Sam's

and Mace's bowls. "I'm getting more chili. Feel free to discuss the gory details."

Mace grinned and squeezed her leg as she walked past. "Does the medical examiner think those marks on the victims match?"

"Hutch hasn't called yet with his findings, but I think they do. So far, though, the marks are the only things common to these two cases."

"No similarities in hair color or age?"

"Audrey Hayes was a redhead. Hilary Poole was a brunette. I'd say both were in the late-twenties-to-late-thirties range."

"Body type?"

Sam shook his head. "Hayes is petite. Poole was tall."

Mace drummed his fingers on the table. "You know, Lightsey and Palmer caught a homicide about two weeks ago. It was a strangulation, too."

Sam straightened. "Really?"

"I don't know if there were any marks on the neck like the ones you described, but you could call Lightsey. Palmer's out with the flu."

"So is Rock." Sam tugged Mace's cell phone over from the end of the table and punched in the numbers as his brother called them out. There was no answer so Sam left a message on Lightsey's voice mail, along with his own cell-phone number. "I'm pretty sure Hutch will confirm my suspicions. If Lightsey's case matches, we could have a—"

"Don't say it," Mace warned quickly. "The lieutenant hasn't mentioned anything about a serial killer."

Sam nodded, knowing Lieutenant Roberts would be well up on the information involving all three cases.

Devon returned with more chili and the talk turned to basketball games and family; in particular, Linc and his new wife, Jenna.

Sam tried to keep his mind on the conversation, but he kept replaying that scene with Dallas at Calhoun's over and over in his mind.

Then it hit him. That zing of awareness he'd felt upon seeing her at Calhoun's was the same zing he'd experienced at the crime scene.

His breath jammed in his chest. *No!* Dallas couldn't have been at the crime scene. *Could she?*

Denial surged through him, but he couldn't rule out anything that pertained to her. On the other hand, *why* would she have been there? It didn't make any sense.

But neither did her appearing out of nowhere like a ghost after all this time. Now that the haze of shock had passed, he recalled that there hadn't been one iota of surprise in her eyes upon seeing him at Calhoun's—almost as if she'd *known* he would be there.

There was no reason at all why she would have been at the crime scene, but Sam couldn't dismiss the growing certainty and apprehension that she *had* been there, at least for a moment.

He recalled the tension in his back, that split-second sense he'd had that someone was watching him outside Audrey Hayes's house. Had that someone been Dallas?

He shoved away from the table, his chair scraping loudly across the floor.

"Whoa!" Mace looked up, startled.

Sam glanced at his half-eaten bowl of chili, then at Devon. "I've got to go."

Devon nodded, though she looked surprised.

"What gives?" Mace watched him carefully.

Sam shook his head. "Just a feeling. Doesn't make any sense," he mumbled, brushing a kiss across Devon's dark hair. "Thanks for supper."

"You're welcome." She frowned up at him. "Are you all right?"

"I'm fine." He shot her a reassuring smile as he stepped into the living room.

Mace rose, coming around the table. "Is it Dallas? Or the murder?"

Sam shook his head. "If she were really meeting someone from the FTC, why at Calhoun's?"

"Well, who knows why the marshals do anything the way they do?"

Sam shrugged in agreement. "Still... I don't know! Something's not right, here." He pulled on his coat and strode for the door.

His brother followed. "Where exactly are you going?"

"Back to the crime scene."

"Why?"

Sam paused at the door, searching through a jumble of unease and resentment and suspicion. "I don't know. Something feels off. I just want to check it out."

"Want me to go with you?"

Sam considered for a minute, then shook his head. "Naw. It's probably nothing."

Mace's gaze turned steely. "You don't really think Dallas is involved in this?"

"I don't know. I wouldn't bet she's not. Somehow."

His brother stepped onto the porch with him, lowering his voice. "What else is going on?"

"I told you, I just want to check things out." Sam closed his coat against the slicing wind.

Mace shouldered his way in front of him. "I mean between you and Dallas."

Sam paused on the middle button of his sheepskin coat. "Nothing. How could there be? She hasn't even been here."

"Look, you never said, but I know something happened before she left a year and a half ago." Mace leveled his gaze on Sam. "You never talk about her or Brad."

Sam fought the urge to look away. He'd never told a soul about the night he and Dallas had spent together.

"Well?" Mace prompted.

Sam looked out into the night. "I don't want to go there."

After a pause, Mace nodded and his hand descended on Sam's shoulder. "All right, but if you need someone—"

"Yeah, I know." He grinned and walked down the steps. "I'll call you, Dr. Freud."

"Ha-ha," Mace grumbled behind him, laughter tracing his voice.

Sam chuckled.

"Let me know if you find anything at the crime scene!" Mace yelled from the open doorway.

"All right!" Sam reached his truck, his grin fading.

As he turned the key and drove off, he tried to dismiss the dread pinching at his gut.

He told himself Dallas Kittridge had nothing to do with Audrey Hayes. He reminded himself that U.S. Marshals did not catch bad guys; they dealt with the scum once they were sentenced.

But Sam's instincts continued to scream. For the first time since he'd become a cop, he hoped they were wrong. He hoped he found nothing—and no one—at the crime scene. He especially hoped he didn't find Dallas Kittridge.

Raw emotion boiled through her and Dallas resented it. Just one look at Sam had resurrected that crush of physical need and guilt and anger she'd tried to escape by leaving Oklahoma City in the first place.

And that apology! Grudgingly she admitted it had sounded sincere, but it was too late, she told herself. Their relationship had been irreparably damaged, and after a year and a half of silence, one charming little speech wasn't going to make it right.

Resentment and frustration jumbled inside her, bordered with a sly stroke of guilt, edging in, twisting its way through her ambivalence. He'd looked like nine kinds of sin, sounded welcoming and familiar. Even now, a warmth still lingered in her belly, and she hated it.

She'd moved on. She knew how to handle Sam Garrett. She had to remember *that*. Not the way his lips on her body burned away every last restraint, not the way that encounter outside

Calhoun's had revealed a numbness she'd thought long gone. Not the fact that he was the only man who'd ever gotten to her so fast.

She needed him to help her with Valeria. That was all. And she wasn't going to let their past—or the maverick reactions her body seemed to have in his presence—get in the way of that. She was here to find a killer, period.

Dallas fumed all the way back to Valeria's, automatically parking her rented car some distance down the street and moving through the shadows toward the house, avoiding the floodlight. A light rain still fell, misting her face. She flipped up the collar of her black coat and dipped her chin, blending into the night as she slipped up the front walk.

Why did Sam Garrett have to look so good? Why did she want to curl up next to him, get a piece of that warmth, spark that old laughter? She was crazy, that was why.

For months, she'd tried to forget that seductive baritone, those blue eyes that could make a woman beg for mercy. One look at him and she was a walking hormone. Tension knotted her right shoulder and she reached up impatiently to rub it.

Those moments with Sam in the parking lot haunted her, but she reined in her jumbled emotions and focused her mind on the yard as she crossed to the front porch.

If there had been any footprints, the police would have found them. With the rain and all the earlier activity at the scene, Dallas would have no hope of getting a viable print. Instead she would concentrate on the interior of the house.

Glancing around to make sure she was unobserved, she slipped under the yellow police tape and approached the front door. She shone her slender penlight along the frame, but could detect no signs of forced entry. From the corner of her eye, she caught a glimpse of light and doused her own, backing into the corner with her head bowed.

Car lights swept across the street and shone on the yard, then disappeared as the car passed. After a few seconds, she stepped off the porch and walked toward the rear of the brick home.

The marshals operated on a need-to-know basis. As her boss in Denver had so archly reminded her this afternoon before she'd taken some vacation time and hopped a plane to Oklahoma City, Dallas did not have a "need to know."

She couldn't investigate this case—not officially, anyway. It was not the duty of deputy United States Marshals to investigate murder. Dallas was not in the business of gathering evidence.

But this was different. *Personal.* When she'd left Oklahoma City, she'd turned Valeria over to another marshal. The woman might still be alive if Dallas had stayed. If she hadn't run away from what had happened with Sam.

She never let herself think, even indirectly, about the day she'd left Oklahoma City. Sam had asked her a question that day and she hadn't been able to answer it. She still couldn't.

A check of the back door of Valeria's house revealed no sign of forced entry; neither did the windows, which Dallas slowly scanned. Returning to the door, she clicked on her penlight and stuck it between her teeth, aiming the light at the lock. She slid her tension bar and a sheep's-foot pick out of the pocket of her trench coat. Working both picks in unison, she closed her eyes, feeling for the sensitive catch through her fingers.

The lock gave. She grinned and pushed inside, closing the door quietly behind her. She slid the tools back into her pocket, but kept her gloves on, directing her penlight into the murky light. She was in the kitchen.

Light-colored tile gleamed on the floor and countertops. A small glass bowl, filled with wrapped cinnamon candies, sat in the middle of the light oak dining table. Dallas scanned the counters, taking in a small, neat stack of cookbooks, an electric can opener and an under-the-cabinet coffeemaker.

She moved slowly through the room, noting nothing out of order. Stepping into the doorway that led to the living area, she paused, then blackness rippled through the room, parted by the wavering light of the flood lamps outside. Dallas made her way into the room, skirting the couch, which faced the fireplace. She shone her penlight over the carpet and saw a faint indentation in the plush carpet where Valeria's body might have lain.

Guilt surged through her, hot and vicious. She told herself it wasn't her fault Valeria was dead, but Dallas couldn't shake the sense of responsibility. She shouldn't have bailed out on the woman. Knowing Valeria would never have held Dallas responsible only made the guilt more bitter.

And Dallas partly blamed Sam. If he hadn't been such a jerk, she might have turned down the transfer and stayed. Taking in the gleaming wood of the mantel, Dallas admitted that was unfair. She had felt suffocated by memories of Brad— And later she'd been devastated by what she and Sam had done—horrified by the emotions she'd felt while making love with him. In truth, she probably would have left even if Sam hadn't turned to another woman.

Only in the last six months, had the numbness started to wear off. Her house, and Kevin, her next door neighbor, had helped with that. Kevin was fun and easy to be with. They'd dated a few times and he'd helped her lay the new tile in her kitchen.

Dallas shifted her thoughts back to Valeria. She knew the woman had been strangled—Dallas's boss had told her that much. But that was all she knew. She couldn't contact the marshal who now had Valeria's case because Dallas had been ordered by her boss to stay away from the homicide investigation.

Wondering if the killer had used a weapon to first subdue Valeria, Dallas checked the floor and walls for signs of bullets or knives, but found no evidence of any. She wondered if the murderer had used something other than his hands to strangle Valeria. Sam would know.

Tortured by seesawing thoughts of Sam and Valeria, Dallas moved silently through the rest of the house, scanning the walls, the bookcases and finally the kitchen one more time.

She clicked off her penlight, slipped it into her pocket and looked around, sighing.

Drat. She would have to ask Sam what he'd found. Impatient to learn something, *anything,* about Valeria's case, Dallas considered tracking Sam down tonight, squeezing out of him every scrap of information she could. But she'd had all of Sam Garrett she could handle today. After seeing him at Calhoun's, she knew her emotions were too close to the surface.

She'd had the advantage at the bar, and she hadn't needed to worry about him showing up here. Tomorrow she'd be fresh and ready to take him on. She hoped. Anyway, she had another stop to make tonight. The cemetery.

Dallas soundlessly opened the door. And looked straight into the black eye of a gun barrel.

A masculine voice—unmistakably, *irritatingly* familiar—ordered, ''Police! Freeze!''

Chapter 3

A pale thread of moonlight limned the gun's barrel. Sam's heart sank even while rage boiled through him.

Dammit! He'd known she was here. But *why?*

He'd almost missed her black sports car, tucked neatly into a pocket of shadows. But he'd seen a small glimmer of light inside the house—so small, so brief, it could have been a trick of his eyes—and he'd known. Which was why he'd left on the safety of his Smith & Wesson.

He didn't even wonder how she'd gotten in. She could pick any lock, anywhere, usually with the most rudimentary of tools.

As he stared into her gray eyes, which were at first startled, then relieved, his rage settled into icy fury.

"Oh, for crying out loud! Put that gun up," she ordered, using a gloved hand to shove the weapon away. Her smoky voice was steady, as if he'd walked in on a back-room poker game instead of her casing a crime scene.

Sam's blood went from a simmer to a boil. At Calhoun's, she'd acted so damn distant and cool while he'd been torn between kissing her and begging for forgiveness, neither of which he cared about right now. Right now he wanted to throttle her.

"Up against the wall!"

"I will not!"

He stormed into the house, backing her up, kicking the door shut as he moved. A savagery he'd never experienced rose inside him. "Do it!"

He jammed his .45 into his waistband. In one practiced move, she pushed aside the flap on her coat, went for the Taurus at her hip. Instantly, he snagged her wrist.

"Uh-uh. Give me the gun."

"You have no right to take it!"

"You're trespassing!" He pressed forward, forcing her back, ignoring the heat that pulsed from her like sweet summer rain, her spicy floral scent. "You've probably screwed up all kinds of evidence."

"Don't give me that. I know Forensics has already swept this place. Even *your* department can't be that sloppy." Even as she retreated, her gray eyes bored into his. Anger and determination stiffened her body.

He nudged her chest with his, still keeping a tight grip on her wrist. "Hand over your weapon and get up against the wall."

Disbelief flared in her eyes. Her gaze clashed with his— measuring, challenging. He tightened his grip on her and they stood in a silent war, each looking for a weakness in the other. In this instance, rage made him stronger and finally he felt her resistance give. She withdrew her Taurus and held it out, murder blazing in her eyes.

Sam checked the safety, then shoved her gun into the waistband at his back, shifting so that his weight was planted solidly in front of her.

"Now, the wall," he said softly, torn between wrapping his fingers around her throat and slamming his lips against hers.

Her chest heaved against his; her breath burned his cheek.

And her eyes— There was such fury, such betrayal there, he should have felt ashamed. But he'd felt his own fury, his own betrayal too often since that night a year and a half ago. She got to him in ways no other woman ever had. She knew every button to push and she pushed them mercilessly.

Their silent standoff seemed to drag on forever, but Sam knew it was only a few seconds.

"Do it, Kittridge!"

She glared, making a strangled sound of rage as she backed toward the wall. "I don't know what you think you're doing, you big jerk!"

"That's Detective Jerk to you." He matched her back steps with forward steps of his own. "Face the wall."

He could see the debate on her face and when she finally, *slowly,* turned, he knew she was here because she needed something from him. She wouldn't have backed down otherwise.

He was suddenly aware of the darkness weaving around them, the spicy tantalizing heat of Dallas, the sense of intimate aloneness. His blood stirred and he fought it, ordering, "Hands up where I can see them."

"Give me a break," she muttered.

"Now!"

She glared over her shoulder and raised her hands to eye level. He snapped on a cuff over her right wrist, and even as she twisted around with a strangled gasp, he tugged her arm behind her back, forcing her against the wall again. He reached for her left wrist and snapped the second cuff.

"You son of a—" She bucked against him, her hip knocking into his groin. "Get these things off me!"

"Not until I get what I want." He ignored the slow burn inching under his skin, the unmistakable shift from anger to arousal.

"Which is what, Detective Jerk? What do you want?"

"Why are you here, Dallas? Not just in Oklahoma City, but here, at *my* crime scene."

She clamped her mouth shut and looked back at the wall. Clearly, she wasn't about to tell him anything—not voluntarily, anyway. Regardless of what she needed from him.

The realization stoked Sam's anger higher. "Spread your legs."

Her head whipped around. "Just a damn minute—"

"Turn around and do it." He leaned his face right into hers.

Hurt glimmered behind the fury in her eyes and she turned away, her lithe body rigid, unyielding.

"Spread 'em, Dallas," he barked.

Resistance lashed her body. She stood tall and proud, not one ounce of give in her.

Laying his forearm across her shoulders, he flattened her against the wall, immobilizing her, then jammed his thigh between her legs and pushed.

She turned her head, glaring at him. Her breath brushed his cheek. They were so close that if either of them moved, their lips would touch. And he actually thought about it. Then he pressed harder against her shoulders and she faced the wall again.

Anger and resentment simmered between them and as Sam slid his hands beneath her coat and began to systematically run his hands over her body, desire, hot and edgy, clawed through him.

He patted her shoulders and down the taut line of her back, pushing away memories of the bare, velvety skin that he had touched so long ago. His hands moved toward her buttocks and his palms itched to cup them.

As if she'd read his thoughts, Dallas jerked. Fury vibrated in every line of her body.

"Hold still. I'd hate to add resisting arrest to the trespassing charge."

She muttered a strangled curse.

He continued on down, forcing himself to concentrate on finding another weapon, though he knew he wouldn't. If he were honest, he'd admit this search was his revenge on her for showing up here, for coming back into his life. And for leaving in the first place. It—*she*—reminded him of everything between them; of how he'd been useful only as a substitute for Brad, of how she'd cut him to the core.

A breath shuddered out of her. "Sam, this has gone on long enough."

She was right. It had. But he couldn't stop his hand from gliding down the inside of her jeans-clad thigh. He moved quickly and still, heat licked through him in a slow torturous stroke. He grew hard and stepped back, irritated that he'd let his emotions rule him. "Now tell me what you're doing here."

"You can go to hell."

"I've already been there," he said hoarsely, thinking of all the times he'd replayed that night in his head.

She spun, her gaze frigid. "Take these cuffs off!"

He folded his arms across his chest. "Not until I get what I want."

"What is that, Detective?" she taunted roughly. "You've got me cuffed. Wanna play a little sex game with me? You be the big bad cop and I'll be the weak prisoner?"

She infuriated him. It took all his willpower, but he eased down calmly onto the edge of the table. He let his gaze deliberately rake her body. "There's nothing weak about you, doll."

Her jaw tightened so fast and hard he thought it would snap. "Uncuff me."

"Why are you trespassing here? Murders aren't your jurisdiction."

"At the moment, I'm a civilian and I can do what I want."

"That doesn't include breaking and entering."

"I was curious, so I decided to look around."

"A civilian can't 'look around' a murder scene," Sam countered drolly.

She pursed her lips and studied him.

He sighed, weariness fingering through him. "What are you doing here, Dallas?"

''I'd leave if you'd let me out of these bracelets.''

''I know you want something, but what? Why here? Why Audrey Hayes?''

If Sam hadn't known Dallas so well, he might have missed the flicker of pain on her features. And the…*guilt?* Had that been guilt? His gut tickled. ''You knew her, didn't you?''

Dallas stared straight at him, her wide gray eyes revealing nothing, her compelling features blank.

Sam straightened, realization spinning through him. ''She was one of your witnesses!''

Still she said nothing. Just stared at him as if he were the slime she dealt with every day in her job.

Even if Audrey Hayes had been one of Dallas's protected witnesses, it didn't explain why she was snooping around a crime scene.

He relaxed on the edge of the table. If Dallas wanted to stay here all night, it was fine by him. ''You must like those cuffs.''

''All right!'' she exploded. ''I…knew her.''

''You knew her? As in, she was a friend? Or one of your witnesses?''

''A friend.''

Though she didn't hesitate, Sam remembered the earlier guilt that had crossed her face. He gave a rueful smile. ''You're lying. I could charge you with interfering.''

''That's crap!'' She angled her chin at him. ''I haven't done anything to hinder your process here.''

He shrugged. ''Let's see…. Trespassing, resisting, interfering. Those charges'll keep you in jail for a while.''

''You—'' She sighed and her shoulders sagged slightly. ''Yes, she was one of my witnesses.''

''I don't get it. Why would *you* want to investigate her murder?''

''I told you, she's a friend—''

''You have no jurisdiction in a murder case, Dallas. We both know it.''

"Will you take these cuffs off now?"

"Answer my question."

"What are you doing out of Vice anyway?" Resentment darkened her clean features. Turning her back to him, she raised her cuffed hands. "I'm not here officially."

"Meaning your warrant supervisor in Denver doesn't know what you're doing."

"How did you know I was in Denver?"

"Don't change the subject." He hadn't moved and to be honest, he enjoyed the sight of her trim back facing him, the metal cuffs shining in the dim light. "Start talking or I make a call to my lieutenant—and your boss."

"I put her here." Her voice sliced through the room like the prick of a sharp wind. "I made sure she was safe, then I ran out on her."

"Ran out on her? What are you talking about—" Sam stopped, comprehension knotting his gut. "You mean when you left Oklahoma City for Denver?"

She gave a jerky nod.

Sam knew Dallas's strong sense of responsibility—her dedication to her job—and he could see that she held herself liable for this woman's death. He pushed away from the table, stepped toward her and smoothly unlocked the cuffs.

She faced him, her gray eyes glittering in the dim light.

"How can you blame yourself?"

She winced, so slightly he would have discounted it, had it been anyone else. For a long moment, she stared at him, holding the cuffs in one hand, nudging the hem of her glove down to massage her wrist with the other.

Then she said in a low rusty voice, "I should've been here for her."

If there was one thing Sam understood, it was guilt. It didn't have to be logical; oftentimes it wasn't. It sawed at your gut relentlessly, tediously, until you wore it like a scar.

Dallas had left Oklahoma City because of guilt. And Sam

had pushed her away because of the guilt he'd felt over finally having her, after having wanted her for so long.

Yes, he knew guilt all too well. He said gently, "I know your boss couldn't have approved this."

Her features were still sharp with wariness. "I'm taking personal time."

Sam snorted. "Like he bought that. Come on, what did you tell him?"

Her gaze sliced to him and she said testily, "That I was going hunting."

"Which is the absolute truth," Sam muttered, feeling an involuntary surge of admiration—and that old awareness. Annoyed by the gathering heat in his body, he added roughly, "I don't imagine you found much here."

"I didn't." She moved toward him—only a step, but closing the distance enough that he could smell rain and leather and that exotic scent she brandished like a weapon. The cuffs jangled in the stillness.

He watched her carefully, his senses prickling with a mix of anticipation and apprehension as she eyed him the way a hawk would a mouse.

"What did you find, Sam? Anything?"

He grinned. "You know I'm not at liberty to discuss that."

"You can tell *me*."

Sam tried to ignore the frisson of sensation that hummed up his spine, the tingle in his blood as she inched closer. "Civilians can't expect information like that from the police department."

"I'm not a civilian. I'm law enforcement. I need your help, Sam."

The wariness in her voice was gone. Instead, that velveteen voice was soft with sincerity, deep with a plea. Something he knew she would never do on her own behalf.

He shook his head. "You know I can't tell you anything. You of all people should understand the need-to-know rule."

Her face didn't change; her gaze locked with his, revealing

an urgency he found hard to dismiss. "You're my only hope down here, Sam. If I go to your lieutenant, I won't get anything."

"That's right." He still sat on the edge of the table, but his body was tensed as if braced for a blow. He weighed the pleasure of working this case with her against the anguish that same pleasure would cause. "Your hunting trip's over. Go back to Colorado," he said bluntly. "When we get something, I'll let you know."

"I can't. I'm going to find the person who did this and you're going to help me."

"Dallas—"

He rose, but she stepped in front of him, forcing him to sit back on the table. Her coat brushed his jeans-clad thigh, sending a spark of heat to his belly. She didn't touch him, but her spice-scented heat wrapped around him, shocking nerve endings that already vibrated raw from her presence.

Very lightly, she laid the cuffs beside him on the table. The sleeve of her coat brushed his leg and he stiffened. He stared straight ahead, willing her to move away.

She didn't. Her gaze fastened on his face, and against his better judgment, he looked at her.

Her features were too strong to be called beautiful, but they were certainly compelling. Her short blond hair set off to perfection the angles of her face—the strong jaw, the prominent cheekbones, the stubborn chin. Her eyes could be soft, but when they weren't, they defined her as shrewd and streetwise.

Now her voice was misty with memories. "Brad always said you were the best cop on the force. He said no one had instincts like yours."

The air whooshed right out of him. He couldn't believe what she was doing.

"Brad said you were the only one he would ever want to help him out. I agree."

Regret and resentment clashed. Sam surged off the table and pushed past her, putting some distance between him and her damn taunting scent. "You've got some nerve trying to guilt me into helping you."

She turned toward him. "What I said was true."

"What you said was emotional blackmail."

"Which you used yourself, not two hours ago." Her gaze met his, unflinching yet somehow vulnerable. She glided toward him in one long stride and leaned in until her breath brushed his ear. "You owe me, Sam. And you know it."

"Damn!" He grabbed her arm and twisted it behind her back, bringing her up against him. Full breasts pressed into his chest and her thigh burned against his. His gaze dropped to her lips. For one brief, hellacious instant, he thought about kissing her. No, it would be like poison to his soul. "You are one cold piece of work, Dallas Kittridge."

"I ran out on my witness and someone killed her. If I'd been here, that might not have happened. But I left and she's dead, and I'm going to find out who killed her. If you were in my place, you'd do the same thing." She stared straight into his eyes, her own dark with fervor, desperation.

Sam's chest heaved with anger. A perverse desire overwhelmed him to throw her on the kitchen table and rip off her clothes. But sex wasn't anywhere close to what she was thinking. He could tell by the savage intensity in her eyes, the way her breath stilled in her body as she waited, focused and rigid, gauging her next move.

How could he work with her and not be tortured by it?

Yet, how could he deny her? He did owe her, but no more than she owed him. He knew she wasn't asking for his help out of any desire to be close to him, but only because she had to.

Rock had the flu, as did a lot of the department. Sam could use the help. But he didn't know if he could survive being this close to Dallas. "Why would you want to work together? You've made it pretty clear what you think about me."

"I told you, you owe me. And I don't have a choice."

"You don't even trust me."

"I trust you'll find this killer. That's all that matters right now."

"If we're going to be partners—"

"We're not. We're just working this case together."

He studied her for a moment, looking for a crack in her unflinching facade.

"If you really meant that pretty apology back at Calhoun's—"

"I did," he growled.

"Then help me."

Sam relinquished his hold on her and stepped back. Doubt and foreboding churned in his gut. He *did* owe her, but would he have to pay the price with his soul?

He'd finally managed to live with what she'd done to him— as well as what he'd done in return—and now she was here, stirring up all the sludge he'd buried for so long.

"Well?" Her gaze never wavered, though he could sense how much this meant to her. "Do you pay up or not?"

"All right. Let's get started." He stuck out his hand.

The gray depths of her eyes turned cool and unreadable. She glanced at his hand, then moved in a lightning-quick motion to pluck her Taurus from the small of his back.

"Lead the way, Garrett. We've got work to do."

He dropped his hand, his lips twisting ruefully.

She opened the door and stepped outside. He grabbed up his cuffs and followed in the wake of her rain-misted scent, eyeing the silvery shimmer of her hair and the gentle sway of her hips.

Tearing his gaze away, he set his jaw against the old desire that tickled his belly. He'd opened himself up to her once before and he wasn't going to make that mistake again.

She glanced over her shoulder at him. "What have you got?"

"I'll tell you on the way back to Calhoun's." Sam closed the door behind him and caught up with her on the steps.

"Ah, yes. The *other* bartender whose shift starts at eleven."

His gaze sliced to hers. "I knew you were there. I felt it."

"But you didn't see me until I wanted you to," she said smugly.

"No." A reluctant smile twisted his lips. "Not until then."

They walked down the steps and rounded the corner of the house. Sam glanced at her. "So, you think you can trust me to watch your back?"

"I do."

"And that's all?"

"That's all there is. We'll be working together, Sam. Nothing else. If you've got anything else in mind, you can forget it."

She strode off and he stared after her, common sense battling with the gathering heat in his body. He refused to acknowledge that the heat was due to anything other than frustration and resentment. She'd moved on. So had he. And he wasn't going back.

She'd gotten what she wanted. Sam was going to help her. Not because she wanted it that way, she told herself, but because he was the only one who could. Her skin still burned from his touch, and sensation still skittered along her nerves from the confrontation at the crime scene.

Dallas shoved her car into gear and blitzed onto the highway behind Sam, following him to Calhoun's.

Back there in Valeria's kitchen—Dallas couldn't think of her as Audrey Hayes—Sam's hands had gone from efficiently indifferent to blisteringly personal. Dallas had been infuriated by his macho police tactics, but what had driven her crazy was how her body had melted like heated silver when his hand slid between her thighs.

The change in him had been subtle, almost imperceptible, but she'd felt it. His touch had gentled, turned...*knowing*. She'd felt it through her jeans, in the cartwheel of her pulse. An old need had answered with a low tug in her belly.

As much as she resented her body's response to him, Dallas

told herself it was only because Sam had surprised her. First at the door with his gun, then with that rare display of rage. Mr. Easygoing had shown a temper she'd never seen in the six years she'd known him.

He waited for her outside the bar as she eased into a parking space opposite his and crossed the wet pavement to the door. She shoved her fingers through her short damp hair as she joined him.

They both reached for the door at the same time, but Sam beat her, swinging it wide so they could go inside. She preceded him into the smoky interior, where the loud throb of a local band called Foggy Creek overwhelmed the large room.

The song, unfamiliar to Dallas, had a compelling beat—low and insistent—that wound through her, kicking up her pulse. She and Sam made their way to the bar, edging around to the end. When the bartender saw Sam, recognition swept the man's features and he acknowledged Sam with a bob of his head.

As they waited for the bartender to reach them, Sam shrugged out of his sheepskin coat and laid it on a stool beside him. Dallas didn't miss the bunching of muscles beneath the worn denim of his shirt. Immediately she was ambushed by memories of touching those bare, broad shoulders, feeling the power roll through his body as he moved over her—

Slamming the door on those thoughts, she grabbed a handful of peanuts and crammed them into her mouth.

Sam sank down onto a barstool and drummed his long, lean fingers on the scratched wood.

Dallas remained standing, her back to the bar as she scanned the huge room, now crowded with people moving around the scuffed dance floor. The scents of perfume and liquor twined with body heat and smoke. Beneath it all she could smell the rain-spritzed woodsy scent—sultry with an edge—that belonged to Sam.

She could tell by his rigid posture that he was still good and mad. He was also different now. More guarded, reserved.

But only with her, it appeared. She glanced over, saw him flash that careless flirty grin at a couple of waitresses who winked at him. She pursed her lips.

His gaze met hers briefly, then wandered down the line of her black duster. She shifted and directed her gaze back to the people in the bar, but she was all too conscious of Sam.

He was leaner. Harder. She'd noticed that in his eyes earlier tonight, but now she could see it in his other features—the grim line of lips that were saved from being too full by the unforgiving squareness of his jaw and chin, his long straight nose. Even the laugh lines that bracketed his mouth seemed deeper, more serious.

He turned as the bartender walked up. Theo's overdeveloped upper torso identified him as a bodybuilder. His facial features were as hard and set as the weights he lifted. Steroid-induced shoulders and arms strained at the seams of a skintight black T-shirt.

The bald man held out a hand. "Detective Garrett, isn't it?"

Sam shook the man's hand, nodding.

Theo planted his beefy hands on the bar, emphasizing thick forearms more suited to a world heavyweight wrestler. "Have you found that lady's killer yet?"

"Not yet, but I'd like to show you another picture."

Dallas frowned. Sam had been here about another murdered woman? She turned, her gaze assessing the bartender.

The man sized her up quickly and a gleam of admiration lit his eyes, but he dipped his head respectfully. "Can I get something for you, ma'am?"

"Vodka tonic," Sam interjected.

Dallas arched a brow, annoyed that he acted as if nothing had changed, as if that night a year and a half ago hadn't changed everything. "Actually, make that a club soda with a twist of lime."

The bartender grinned. "Coming right up." Theo turned to Sam. "Same for you?"

"No, I'll have a beer. Whatever's on tap."

The man nodded and moved off down the bar to get their drinks.

Sam glanced up at Dallas. "You changed your drink?"

"A lot of things have changed," she murmured. Finally she eased down on the stool beside Sam.

She could feel the heat of him, the light brush of his thigh against hers. His rain-damp woodsy scent teased against her nostrils.

Sam rubbed his chilled hands together and blew on them, looking sideways at Dallas. "Tell me about Audrey Hayes."

"What do you want to know?"

"Anything, Kittridge." Sam half turned on his stool so that his knee bumped hers. His voice was hard, his eyes like tempered steel. "You knew her. Tell me something about her. I've given you more than you've given me and I can't help you if you don't share what you know."

"True."

"Well, then?"

His dark hair was still neatly trimmed at the back and on the sides. The thick waves, as silky and dark as a seal's pelt, spiked endearingly in the front where he'd jammed a hand through them repeatedly. She thought about smoothing that stray lock of hair that flopped over his forehead. Instead, she grabbed another handful of peanuts. "Where should I start?"

The bartender interrupted by setting their drinks in front of them. Sam pulled the instant photo out of his pocket and passed it to Theo, his lean strong fingers tapping the photo. "Do you recognize this woman?"

The burly man studied it carefully for a moment. "No." He returned the picture. "I don't remember ever seeing her in here."

Dallas fought down a swell of disappointment. It was only their first lead, but she'd really hoped it would go somewhere.

"Thanks," Sam said.

The bartender nodded. "Sure. Let me know if I can get you anything else."

With that, he moved back down the bar. Sam stuffed the picture back into his shirt pocket and looked at Dallas. His eyes, which warmed to cerulean blue when he smiled, were hard and laser-bright.

She sipped at her club soda. *Focus on the case. That's why you're here.* ''Why did you come to this bar? Did someone see Valeria here?''

''So, her real name is Valeria. Valeria what?''

''Luciano.''

''Why was she a protected witness?''

Dallas hesitated, then sighed, easing out of her coat. ''She testified against her husband.''

''Who was…''

''A member of the Dixie mob out of Atlanta.'' Dallas took off her right glove and started pulling at the other one. ''It's crossed my mind that her murder could be a hit ordered by her husband.''

Sam shook his head. ''I don't think so.''

''Why not?'' She tossed her gloves on the stool beside her, on top of her coat.

''Because Audrey Hayes and a murder I caught about two months ago had identical marks on their neck.''

''So, you have another victim who was strangled!'' Dallas whipped toward him.

''I didn't tell you Audrey—Valeria—was strangled.''

''I still have *some* connections, Sam.''

Sam nodded, tipping the mug to his lips. ''For the sake of clarity, let's call her Valeria, okay?''

Dallas nodded. ''So, you think the guy who killed her has killed before?''

''Yes.'' Sam swallowed his beer, staring into the murky light that wavered around Theo.

''It could've been a hit.''

''Maybe.''

''But you don't buy it.''

''No.''

He was holding something back. Out of caution? Or because he didn't trust her? "Why don't you believe it could've been a hit, Sam? What are you not telling me?"

"The marks on their necks are too distinctive."

"It could've been a copycat."

"We don't even know what made the marks. Some kind of chain or something. That information wasn't released."

"Hmm. I don't think we should rule out a copycat yet. I still have to notify her husband. I can ask him some questions when I see him."

"You're going to see him?"

She nodded.

"Why don't you just call the prison?"

She shrugged. "I think I'd have a better chance of getting straight answers face-to-face."

Sam took another drink of his beer as Dallas shifted beside him. The longer they sat here, the tighter her muscles became and the more her shoulder throbbed. Still, as long as they stuck to work, she could do this.

"Remember when we used to unwind at your place with barbecue and a beer?"

"Remember that stupid chef's hat Brad always wore?"

"Yeah." Sam chuckled. "And that red-and-white-checked Betty Crocker apron."

She stiffened, even while telling herself that it was only natural that she and Sam would reminisce about Brad. But a sharp ache pierced her chest. She had missed Sam. Only as a friend, she was quick to add.

Still, she hated what had happened to them; what they'd lost. She'd turned to him out of selfish need and they'd both paid the price. She'd hurt him. He'd hurt her. They had to keep things strictly professional now. Anything else would hurl them back to the regret, the pain of the past. "That was a long time ago, Sam."

He nodded. A chill that had nothing to do with the December night lanced the air between them. Dallas didn't know if they could work together or not. Reminiscing with Sam resurrected too many memories of Brad, the guilt she felt over having slept with Sam, the fact that she hadn't yet gone to the cemetery.

He stared ahead, watching the mill of people behind the bar and absently tapping one foot to the moan of a steel guitar.

Dallas recalled the instant in Valeria's kitchen when he'd hauled her to him, the way her breasts had gone heavy, the hard feel of his hip against hers. She'd felt the hunger surge between them, seen the naked desire in his eyes. He certainly appeared unaffected now. Lounging comfortably against the bar, he smiled easily and often as the waitresses sashayed past.

Except for the flex of muscle in his jaw, Dallas could detect no signs of tension in him. He didn't appear any more eager to revisit the past than she was.

"How are you, Dallas? I mean, really."

Well, she'd been wrong about that one. She was quiet for a moment, then asked flatly, "You mean about Brad's death?"

"Yes." Sam sipped at his beer, watching her expectantly.

A sigh eased out of her. She'd been shocked earlier to hear Sam admit that he blamed himself for her husband's death. Whatever had happened between her and Sam, she'd never held him responsible for Brad's death and it bothered her more than she liked that Sam blamed himself. "I've come to terms with it."

"And Denver? Do you like it there?"

"It's cold." She paused, taking a drink of her club soda. "But yeah, I like it there. I bought this darling house and I'm fixing it up."

"That's good." His voice sounded strained, but maybe that was due to the loud blare of music, the constant clink of glasses. "So I guess you won't ever move back here?"

She glanced at him, then looked away. "No."

He turned. "Why not? Your family would like it. Oklahoma's a lot closer to Texas than Colorado is."

She met his gaze, her gut twisting. "There's nothing here for me anymore."

Was that hurt in his eyes? No, it must've been a trick of the neon lights flashing over his shoulder.

He shrugged and stood, grabbing up his coat. "Well, I guess we'll get started in the morning."

"Yes." She rose, too, picking up her gloves and slipping into her coat. "I suppose you'll find me? I'll be at Carrie's."

Carrie Turner was a friend of Dallas's and a woman whom Sam had dated a few times.

Pleasure warmed his features. "How is Carrie?"

"Very well," Dallas muttered, pulling on her gloves.

"Tell her I said hi."

She nodded, shrugging off an inexplicable pang of irritation. "All right."

"See ya tomorrow." Sam pushed out the door without waiting for her.

"Right," she murmured, stepping outside and watching as he got into his truck.

He really did seem to be over the night they'd spent together. He seemed to have honestly put it behind him. Well, so had she. Dallas tossed her head and strode out to her car. Detective Charm had worked his magic on her once. She wasn't giving him another shot.

The night they'd been together had already cost too much. She'd done what she had to in order to survive, but it had meant that she'd run from something for the first time in her life. And Valeria had paid the price. Dallas was determined to find Valeria's killer. She wasn't going to let her history with Sam get in the way of that. Once she finished her business here, she'd go back to Denver. And probably never see Sam again.

Chapter 4

Guilt looked good on her, Dallas decided. That was about all she wore these days. Hammered by it at Brad's grave last night, and haunted by Sam's revelation that he blamed himself for Brad's death.

As she'd lain in Carrie's comfortable guest bed, Dallas's thoughts had seesawed between her visit to the cemetery and Sam's guilt over Brad. It bothered her that Sam was beating himself up over what had happened on that fateful burglary call. It bothered her more than she liked.

The next morning, she sat at a small white-enamel-topped table across from her friend, drinking coffee.

"You got in really late last night," Carrie said, dunking a sugar-glazed doughnut into her coffee. She tucked a strand of shoulder-length mink-brown hair behind her ear.

Dallas still marveled at how her longtime friend could keep her tight, petite figure despite all the junk food she ate. At the thought of all that sugar zapping through her system, Dallas shuddered and sipped at her own straight-black brew. "I went by the cemetery."

Carrie's blue eyes turned soft with sympathy. "How are you?"

"Fine." She sighed, wrapping her fingers around the warm ceramic mug. "It's still so...weird. You know, him being gone."

She'd stood beside Brad's grave until the cold seeped clear through her, until she couldn't feel her toes or fingers or even her legs anymore. She wished the guilt and regret inside her would numb as well, but those emotions were still sharp and cutting. She'd resisted the urge to fall to her knees and beg his forgiveness for what she and Sam had done.

She'd ached for his forgiveness since that night a year and a half ago, and she knew Brad would give it to her. Already had. But she couldn't forgive herself. She'd turned to his best friend for comfort, when she'd still loved her husband. What kind of wife did that make her? What kind of *person?*

Carrie reached across the table and squeezed Dallas's hand, drawing her back to the present.

Dallas smiled at her. "Sorry."

The other woman shook her head. "No need."

Dallas sipped at her steaming coffee. "I miss him."

"So do I."

She knew Carrie really did understand. Dallas counted herself lucky to have such a friend. Carrie seemed like the other half of Dallas, just as she had when they'd first met as freshmen at the University of Oklahoma. Dallas was close to her brother, Austin, but there were some things he didn't understand as fully as her friend.

The first time Dallas had seen Carrie, the petite brunette had been flanked on either side by two great-looking, strapping football players. It still amazed Dallas how Carrie had dated them both at the same time without inciting a riot. She had a gift, Carrie later told her with her self-deprecating humor.

Both from Texas, the two of them had quickly formed a friendship in the dormitory where they lived across the hall from each other. From their sophomore year on, they'd been roommates.

Dallas had begun dating Brad during their junior year and Carrie dated everyone. That was why Dallas had originally thought Carrie and Sam would be perfect for each other. Neither of them had ever found the "right" person. After college, Carrie had begun working for an airline company based in Tulsa and she'd been transferred to Oklahoma City four years ago. Dallas and Brad had set up a double date with them, and the four of them had gone out several times. But things between Sam and Carrie hadn't worked out, for some reason.

Going to Brad's grave tonight had stirred up that memory for Dallas. Along with the ones of how she'd gone around in a daze after his death, not feeling anything for weeks until that night with Sam. She'd felt something then. Something unsettling and exciting and…wrong. Had it been pleasure? Or something more?

It couldn't have been something more than pleasure, because that would mean she had feelings that encompassed more than just friendship for Sam back then; and she hadn't. She'd loved Brad very much.

So had Sam. Dallas told herself that Sam's guilt over Brad's death bothered her so much because she and Sam had once been such good friends. But that didn't explain why Sam's confession had haunted her all last night; why she kept picturing the bleak pain in his eyes when he'd told her.

She'd spent half an hour this morning trying to convince herself it was really all right to work this case with him. She tried to look at it as if they had no history together. As if he were a connection—her only one—to this case.

"I can't believe it's been almost two years since Brad's death," Carrie murmured, nibbling at her doughnut. "Have you seen Sam?"

Dallas narrowed her eyes. "What do you think?"

"I'd say, judging from that bubbly happiness in your voice, you have." Carrie's eyes twinkled. "So?"

"Yes, I saw him. And he's just as—"

"Sexy as ever?"

"Stubborn. Infuriating. Bossy." She swallowed another sip of coffee, the warmth doing nothing to dispel the chill of regret that had burrowed deeper inside her while she'd stood over her husband's grave.

She'd shivered in the late-night cold and mist, fighting resentment the whole time. She couldn't stop thinking about how she and Sam had betrayed Brad. She'd tried to talk to Brad about it—about *anything*—but the words wouldn't come. She'd felt unworthy to be there, yet she hadn't been able to leave. Nor could she get over the fact that Sam seemed to have dealt with what they'd done when she hadn't.

Carrie rose, then paused to put a hand on Dallas's shoulder. "It *will* get easier, Dal. After my mom died, I thought I'd never be able to even talk about her, but time does help with some things."

"I know." She'd never told Carrie or anyone about the night she'd spent with Sam.

Her friend walked to the sink and rinsed out her cup before placing it in the dishwasher. "If you've got time today, we could go to lunch. I don't have to leave until seven this evening."

"I'm not sure." Dallas stood, finishing her coffee. "I'm going out with Sam."

Carrie's dark brows arched.

"It's for the job," Dallas said dryly. "I'll call you if it looks like I'll be free. And thanks for letting me stay here. I'm not sure how long I'll put you out."

"I'm glad to have you. Stay as long as you need."

Just then the doorbell rang and Dallas's stomach jumped. *Sam?*

Carrie flashed a smile as she walked out of the kitchen and toward the front door. "Will that be Sam?"

"Probably." Dallas set her own cup in the sink and shoved

a suddenly unsteady hand through her hair before following Carrie to the door.

The other woman peered through the peephole, then swung the door wide. ''Hi!''

Genuine pleasure lit Sam's eyes and that seductive, so-sure-of-himself grin flashed. ''Hey, Carrie! How's it going?''

''Great. Come on in.'' She stepped back as he walked inside.

Sam's face was flushed by the cold, and his eyes glittered even more blue than usual. He brought inside the scent of winter-fresh air. Broad shoulders, made more bulky by the thick sheepskin of his coat, filled the door. Faded Levi's sleeked down strong thighs and lean calves; the hems brushed the tops of his scuffed ostrich boots. Sensation fluttered in Dallas's chest.

Sam closed the door, his gaze shifting briefly to Dallas. Then he turned to Carrie, a broad smile spreading across his face as he caught her hand and twirled her in a quick little two-step. ''What exotic ports have you flown to since the last time I saw you?''

''Oh, I've been all over.'' She disengaged her hand and waved it dismissively. ''I hear you're working Homicide now.''

''Yeah.'' A sudden tension lashed his words and a muscle ticced in his jaw.

Carrie flushed lightly, but she reached out and touched his arm. ''How have you been?''

''I'm fine. Thanks.'' His voice went soft and warm, as if he and Carrie had been close friends for years, instead of him and Dallas. He looked over her head, his gaze meeting Dallas's. ''Ready?''

''Yeah. I'll get my coat.''

From the other room, Dallas could hear the low murmur of their voices as she put on her holster and Taurus. She came back into the room, sliding her arms into her leather duster.

Sam and Carrie laughed softly at something. They stood

close, their dark heads nearly touching, their elbows brushing as Carrie flipped through a set of photos she'd taken in Hong Kong.

"Are you seeing anyone?" Sam's voice dropped with husky interest and Dallas stilled, her eyes narrowing on the two of them.

Carrie nodded, her thick shiny hair sliding over one shoulder. "A guy I met during a layover in Reno. He rides bulls."

"Ouch!" Sam gave a suggestive grimace and Carrie laughed.

Irritated, Dallas yanked her gloves out of her pocket, her fingers curling into the soft leather. It had been three years since Sam had dated Carrie, but he seemed perfectly at ease with her. He'd been that way with Dallas, once. Now he was uptight and guarded around her, just as she was around him. All because of what had happened between them. Sadness swept over her at the thought.

For the first time, Dallas wondered if Sam and Carrie had ever been intimate. The possibility made Dallas's spine go rigid, but she didn't think they'd ever gotten that far.

Watching them together, hearing Sam's frequent chuckle, caused Dallas's lips to flatten. She'd never given much thought to why Sam and Carrie hadn't dated longer, but now she wondered. Sam obviously liked Carrie, and her gorgeous friend obviously liked Sam.

Something sharp and hot jabbed under Dallas's ribs and she flushed with the memory that she could have kissed Sam last night. She hadn't allowed herself to think about that split second at the crime scene when he'd pushed her into the wall and she'd turned her head.

If they had kissed, it would have had nothing to do with pleasure and everything to do with…anger. Still, she had *wanted* him to kiss her, wanted him to dissolve all her defenses, fill the emptiness inside her the way he had a year and a half ago.

That unwelcome realization spurred a fresh bolt of resentment through her. She was simply missing their friendship. That was all.

"I'm ready, Detective Charm." Dallas's voice was harsher than she'd intended.

Carrie started, turning with a laugh. "I hate it when you sneak around."

Sam glanced over his shoulder, his gaze stripping over Dallas dismissively. He turned, his movements slow and deliberate as he nudged up the hem of his coat and slid one lean hand into his jeans pocket.

Dallas relaxed her clenched teeth and buttoned the two middle buttons on her coat, grinning at Carrie. "Sorry."

Sam opened the door, said goodbye to the other woman and walked to his truck parked in front of Carrie's house. Dallas hugged her friend, promised to call about lunch, and followed him.

The muscles in her right shoulder were already knotted against the prospect of spending all day and possibly the night in Sam's company. She didn't understand this giddy warmth, this ambivalence she felt toward Sam. But she was here for Valeria. She would do what she had to.

Sam didn't like the way Dallas was looking at him. He hadn't liked it back at Carrie's house and he didn't like it now. They rode in his truck, en route to the medical examiner's offices. He'd told Dallas they would stop there first and discuss Hutch's findings on another case.

Dallas kept sneaking glances at him. Her looks were curious, intense. And put him in mind of how he'd almost kissed her last night. He was glad he hadn't. And he wouldn't.

He could keep things strictly professional between them. All he had to do was focus on the leads and ignore the heated looks from her that were starting to linger. And ignore the intriguing scent of her perfume. And the way her long legs looked in those jeans, the way that cranberry sweater turned her eyes to pewter, polished her skin to magnolia velvet. Sure, no sweat.

Last night's rain had stopped, but the day was still gray. Dark clouds, looking swollen and ready to burst, scudded across the sky. The wind blew cold, but the temperature hovered above freezing so the streets were fine. By this afternoon, the streets could ice over. Or it could be sunny and beautiful.

Sam's skin prickled under the weight of Dallas's stare and he slanted a look at her. She glanced away, massaging the muscles of her right shoulder for the second time since they'd gotten into his truck. Dark circles ringed her eyes and her normally golden-toned skin was pale.

"You don't look like you got much sleep last night."

She covered a yawn. "I didn't. I got to Carrie's really late."

Why? Where had she gone? And with whom?

She pushed her hair back. "I went to the cemetery."

Sam snugged his shoulder more comfortably against the door, draping his left wrist over the steering wheel. "They close the gates at dusk."

"Yeah. I rousted the caretaker."

A reluctant grin curved Sam's lips. "I'm sure he appreciated that."

"Hmm?" This time, when she looked at him, the gleam of feminine interest was gone. Instead, she looked distracted. And worried. "I didn't know what to say to him. Brad, I mean."

Nodding with sympathetic understanding, he kept his gaze on the road. "I know what you mean."

"Do you think that means we're forgetting?" Her voice, hoarse and raw, was barely above a whisper. "I don't want to. I don't think we should."

"I'll never forget." Sam's vow sounded more like a curse. He didn't want to admit that he'd feared the same thing. And he would never let himself forget. Not what he'd done to Brad. Or what had happened that silent night with Dallas.

She half turned to face him, the weak sunlight silvering her tawny hair to platinum. "I thought a lot about you last night. Your guilt. The way you blame yourself for his death."

He clamped his jaw tight and hit the blinker with more force than necessary as he accelerated up the ramp and onto Broadway Extension south. The highway's name had been changed to Centennial Expressway a few years back when the state had lengthened the road, but Sam didn't know anyone who called it by the new name.

"Have you seen the department shrink about this, Sam?"

"Yes." His fist tightened around the steering wheel.

"It's not your fault—"

"*You're* not a shrink, Dallas," he said coldly. "And you weren't there when Brad died. I was. So, why don't you just leave it alone?"

"It bothers me that you blame yourself. You're not responsible, Sam. Not in any way."

He didn't want to talk about this with her. Exiting on Northeast Tenth, he ground to a stop at the light.

"I've really thought about this since you told me last night. Maybe it's just your way of holding on. Maybe you haven't let go of Brad at all. Or gotten over what happened."

"Oh, and you have?" he said through gritted teeth as they drove east to Stonewall.

Sadness darkened her eyes and her voice softened reflectively. "I don't know."

"You haven't. That's why you couldn't find anything to say to your husband at the cemetery last night!"

She might have flinched—he wasn't sure—but she angled her chin at him. "I'm not the one who's blaming myself for what happened to him. I'm only responsible for what—"

"Happened afterward?" Sam interrupted brutally, his chest aching.

She turned her head and looked out at the plain brown brick building where they had pulled up to park.

That fast, his anger turned to regret. He didn't want to fight with her. Hell, he didn't want to do *anything* with her, but for now he had to work with her. At least work was a safe topic. "I got a call last night, from another homicide detective. He has a strangulation case, too. About two weeks old."

Dallas's attention locked on him like a rifle on a target. "You mean, there are three of these cases?"

He nodded. "Lightsey's case had no marks on her neck. That's why I want to go down to the medical examiner's office. Ask him a couple of questions."

"Yeah."

"The two most recent murders happened about two weeks apart."

Dallas tapped a finger on the armrest. "What are the dates?"

Sam told her. "One was on a Saturday, one on a Friday. And the one I caught about two months ago was also on a Saturday."

"If it's the same guy, why wait so long between murders?"

"Maybe there's one we haven't found yet."

Dallas frowned. "These last two are thirteen days apart. Maybe that's the pattern."

"Maybe."

"Or maybe the killer is influenced by phases of the moon. I'll check it out."

Sam nodded. He didn't want to voice the bigger dread that had nagged him since receiving Lightsey's call, but he could tell by the sudden strain in Dallas's voice that she was thinking the same thing as he.

They walked into the M.E.'s offices and followed the receptionist's directions past the autopsy room to a fair-size conference room with built-in bookcases.

Hutch sat at a long rectangular table surrounded by a stack of files. The doctor pulled a pen out of the pocket of his white lab coat and scribbled something, frowning.

Sam knocked lightly on the open door.

Hutch looked up, flashing a tired smile as he motioned them inside. "Hey, Sam."

The man's eyes were red-rimmed, as if he'd been up all night. Dark blond whisker stubble shadowed his cheeks and jaw. The muted blues and grays of the walls and carpet gave the room a subdued air.

Sam nodded toward Dallas. "This is Marshal Kittridge. She's helping me out on the Hayes homicide."

Hutch rose and stretched across the oak-veneer table to extend his hand. "Nice to meet you, Marshal."

She shook his hand. "You, too."

"What can I do for you, Sam? I haven't finished with the Hayes woman yet."

"Actually, I had a question about another strangulation. One that came in about two weeks ago. A woman named Mindy Rush?"

"Ah, yes. I remember. I did rule her death as strangulation."

"I heard from Lightsey, the case detective, that she had no marks on her neck."

Hutch frowned, then nodded. "That's right."

"Could you tell me what she was wearing?"

"Let's go look at that file." Hutch stepped around Dallas and led them down a short, carpeted corridor into a utilitarian office. Files covered the desk, but there looked to be some strange organization to the stacks. Filing cabinets lined one wall. A stuffed largemouth bass, mounted on a walnut plaque, hung on one wall.

Hutch walked to a metal file cabinet, dug through a drawer and came up with a dog-eared file. After leafing through it, he eased down onto the corner of his desk. "Yes, she was wearing a turtleneck sweater and corduroy slacks. Boots, underwear—"

"Would that sweater have been thick enough to prevent any marks, if she were strangled with the same weapon as Audrey Hayes or Hilary Poole?

Hutch glanced down at the file. "Yes. The sweater was

heavy cable-knit. In fact, that's probably why it took her longer to die than the other two.''

Beside him, Dallas tensed. Sam grimaced. ''Any sign of rape?''

''There's been no forced sex on any of these victims. Typical strangulation with hemorrhaging behind the eyelids. The guy kills them, undresses them for sex, then dresses them again afterward.''

''He has sex with them after they're dead, then puts their clothes back on?'' Disgusted, Sam shot Dallas a look.

''Yeah,'' the medical examiner confirmed.

''That's sick,'' Dallas muttered.

''Thanks, Hutch,'' Sam said.

''Anything else I can do for you?''

''Any ideas about what kind of murder weapon we're looking for?''

''I'd say a chain, refined, small link.''

Sam frowned. ''Like a necklace?''

''Bigger, but not as thick as a tire chain.''

Sam nodded. ''What about trophies from his victims?''

''He's not taking hair, skin, fingernails or any other body part. Has he taken anything from the victims' homes?''

''Not that we can tell.''

Sam shook the other man's hand. ''Thanks. Just let me know when you finish with Hayes.''

The medical examiner nodded, his gaze shifting to Dallas. ''Nice to meet you, Marshal.''

''Same here.''

Hutch nodded, rising from his desk to walk them to the front door.

''I'm anxious to hear from you, Doc,'' Sam called as they stepped out into the crisp winter air.

''ASAP.''

Dallas walked beside him, her boots scuffing on the asphalt-paved parking lot. Once in Sam's truck, she asked, ''So, are you thinking what I'm thinking?''

"Maybe." Sam still didn't want to admit it, not until he'd spoken to his commanding officer. He shook his head. "We'll—*I'll*—have to speak to Lieutenant Roberts. You'll have to wait in the car."

"Of course."

Her cool tone irritated him, which was just as well. *Cool* was exactly how things needed to be between them.

"A serial killer?" Carl Roberts sat down hard in his creaking leather chair.

It had taken Sam only an hour with his lieutenant. After he'd told the trim, graying man about the similarities between his two cases and Lightsey's, Lieutenant Roberts confirmed Sam's suspicions that Oklahoma City had a serial killer on the loose.

Not quite six feet tall, with a barrel chest and thick neck, Carl Roberts could be tough as nails with his detectives, and soft as marshmallow cream with a victim's family. He was known for the top priority he gave every case. Sam had liked him instantly, the first day he'd reported to Homicide.

The older man sat behind a paper-littered desk, his round sausage-like fingers drumming on the scarred wood. He shook his head, a mix of sadness and anger in his dark eyes. "After the bombing, Oklahoma City doesn't need something like this. Get busy and get me something. *Yesterday.*"

"Yes, sir. What about Lightsey?"

"You take his case. You're the primary from now on. I want some answers before another murder happens." Roberts glanced down at the paperwork in front of him. "Says here in your report that the Hayes woman was a protected witness."

"Yes, sir."

"Have the marshals been notified?"

Up close and personal. "Yes, sir."

"Keep them informed."

"All right." Sam turned to go, breathing a sigh of relief that he hadn't had to lie to his boss.

"Rock's wife called me this morning. He's still down with that flu."

"Yeah, I spoke to her briefly, too." Sam had also spoken to his partner before picking up Dallas and the old guy was so miserably sick he couldn't even get out of bed.

Roberts steepled his index fingers under his chin. "My detectives are dropping like flies, but you can use any of the few I've got left. If you need them."

"I think I've got it covered right now." Sam wasn't about to tell his lieutenant that he had a marshal riding with him, but with Dallas's help, maybe he could find this killer before another murder occured. If the killer stayed true to form, they had only eleven days.

He picked up the manila envelope holding crime-scene photos of his three victims, gave his captain a casual salute and walked out. Information on the murders had already been sent to VICAP—the Violent Criminal Apprehension Program—but so far they'd had no reports of similar killings across the country.

The division secretary promised to add the latest report about Valeria's killing to the Internet site they'd established to advise other law-enforcement agencies about the murders and to solicit any helpful information.

Once in the truck with Dallas, he tossed the envelope to her. "We've got three cases right now. I want to call the surrounding areas and see if we find any more."

He didn't miss the wary relief on her face when he joined her and realized that she hadn't expected him to return. He reflected with some amusement that he hadn't even considered cutting out on her.

As Sam drove to a service station and pulled over out of the way of the gas pumps, she opened the manila envelope. She sat quietly, flipping through the pictures while he used his cell phone to call the police departments in Yukon, the Village and Bethany.

His hope that only three murders had occurred was dashed

when he spoke to the police in Edmond. They'd had a strangulation about six weeks ago. That fell into their pattern of every two weeks. Sam asked if he could come look at their crime-scene photos and Dallas shot him a sharp look, sliding the photographs slowly back into the envelope.

''Another one?'' she asked quietly, her gaze fastened intently on his face.

''Yeah. Her name's Patty Watson.'' He started the truck, his blood humming. He told himself it was because of what he'd learned, but he knew it had more to do with the woman sitting beside him.

Less than thirty minutes later, he was inside the Edmond PD with Detective Rick Groom, looking at photos of a woman with marks on her neck identical to the ones on two of his homicides. Dallas cooled her heels in the truck. He knew it irked her that she couldn't come inside, but there wasn't any way around it. She knew these cops would clam up with any information they knew if she showed her face. The U.S. Marshals Service didn't investigate homicides. Period.

The Edmond detective gave a copy of the crime-scene photos to Sam, then he and Dallas spent the afternoon interviewing people in the apartment complex where Patty Watson had lived. They also checked out a local bar near the highway, The Watering Hole, where Patty had been seen on the night of her murder. No one at the bar could identify any of the victims except her.

Sam stayed focused, but he also noticed Dallas as they questioned the bartender and current patrons. She was good at asking questions. She had a way of being comfortable with herself that made other people comfortable. As tough as she was, she could come across well, and as quite nonthreatening.

She followed Sam's lead, kept her questions short and succinct unless something further was needed. Her attention seemed to be centered on the case only. Still, he felt her…interest.

She wasn't staring all dewy-eyed at him. Inside the bar, she was professional. Aloof. Yet, he felt an indefinable energy pulsing from her. *Between them.* Disgusted with himself, he decided he must have the most colossal ego in the world. He worked hard for the rest of the afternoon to keep his thoughts on the case.

They'd turned up nothing new when he pulled into Carrie's driveway. Dallas's theory about the murders being influenced by phases of the moon hadn't panned out, either. He glanced at his watch and saw it was after five. He had about an hour to get home, shower and change for his cousin's bachelor party.

He put the truck in Park and phoned Lieutenant Roberts to tell him about the fourth victim he'd discovered.

"What did he say?" Dallas asked when Sam hung up.

"'Good work.' And I'd better find a suspect fast." He grinned, tired, but pleased that he and Dallas had managed to spend the entire day working—especially after the way the morning had started.

He hadn't wanted to have to dodge questions and queries about Brad all day. And she hadn't brought up the subject again. He'd managed to mostly ignore her frequent glances, but he'd been very aware of her constantly studying him, as if she wanted to crawl inside his skull.

Tension knotted his shoulders and fatigue settled deep in his bones.

She still looked tired, too, but there was a light in her eyes, an energy that fed on the challenge of finding this killer.

"One common thread seems to be country-western bars," he said. "Tomorrow, we'll start checking out the ones we haven't hit and see if anyone recognizes one or more of the victims."

The approaching dusk shadowed her high cheekbones, softened her stubborn jaw. Dallas nodded, her gaze never leaving his face. "I need to go to Atlanta tomorrow."

"Why?"

"Someone needs to inform Valeria's husband that she's dead."

"Can't the other marshal on the case do that?"

"I know Petey, and I've made arrangements to tell him."

"You can call the prison chaplain."

She shook her head. "I might be able to find out something helpful if I tell Petey in person."

"You can't still think it's a Mob thing? That the guy ordered a hit on her?"

"I just want to be thorough."

At her husky undertone, heat inched under his skin and Sam shifted in his seat, swiping a hand across his burning eyes. "Well, then I'm going, too."

"Why?" She nearly squirmed in her seat. "You've got enough to do here."

Dallas never squirmed, which only made Sam more determined to go. Had she told him everything she knew about Valeria or was her unease spurred by the heat he'd felt simmering between them all day? "The bars won't start hoppin' until nine or ten at night. Besides, this is my case and *I'll* follow all leads."

She looked about to argue, then laughed shortly. Gray eyes scrutinized his face. "All right, Detective Charm."

"All right." Picking up his cell phone, he called Information and waited as the operator connected him to the airlines. After reserving two seats on the earliest direct flight to Atlanta, he hung up. "I'll pick you up about five in the morning and we'll head for the airport."

She nodded.

"You did a good job today, talking to the people at the apartment complex and the bar."

"Thanks." Her voice dropped, stroking over him like crushed velvet, and his stomach jumped.

He rolled his shoulders and told himself he was imagining that warm interest in her eyes. Then her gaze shifted to his lips, and the muscles in his back twitched.

He grabbed the manila envelope and shoved it at her. "Here, don't forget these."

She took the crime-scene photos, her fingers brushing his. "You're sure—"

"You can look them over tonight. Bring them tomorrow so I can see them again."

"Okay."

He glanced over and found her gaze slowly tracing his chest, his hips. She ran the delicate edge of her tongue across her bottom lip.

Though he'd ignored it as best he could, gut-knotting aware-ness had spiked Sam's nerves all day. Now his control snapped. "If you don't stop looking at me like that, I'm going to give you what you want."

"What are you talking about?"

He ruthlessly reminded himself of how she'd thought of Brad while making love to him. That she could be doing the same thing right now. But in his gut, Sam knew better. She was looking at *him,* seeing *him.*

He knew how to make her back off. He clamped one hand on the back of the seat, brushing against her coat. He wanted to intimidate her but his body went hard at the spicy whiff of her infuriating perfume. "You want me to kiss you."

"Give me a break." She laughed with just the right note of disgust and disbelief.

Still, he noticed that she inched farther into the door. "Are you telling me I can't read the signals?"

"I'm not sending any signals—"

"Liar," he said softly.

She swallowed, turning her head to face him. "Whatever we had—whatever that night was—is gone."

He suddenly, fiercely wanted to thrust his hands into her hair, pull her to him and ravage her mouth until she lost that control and surrendered. Until she admitted that he, Sam, was in her head and not Brad. Then he would turn away from her, the way she had from him. "Are you sure about that?"

"Yes." Uncertainty flickered in her eyes.

He raised one eyebrow. "Really?"

Her eyes narrowed, but she didn't give an inch. Oh, no, not Dallas. "Positive."

A year and a half ago, she'd mangled his ego like a bullet ripping through tissue. What kind of idiot would go back for more of that? Still, Sam couldn't stop himself from baiting her. He moved closer. "Shall we try it?"

"Why are you playing this stupid game?"

That fast, his intent shifted from taunting her to breath-knotting anticipation. She hadn't wanted *him* then, only a warm, willing body. He knew that and yet he couldn't stop himself. "Prove me wrong."

"You're ridiculous. And tired." She reached for the door handle.

He reached for her. Even while telling himself to stop, he couldn't. He slid one palm along her nape, the ends of her silky hair tickling the back of his hand.

She stiffened, but didn't pull away. Her skin was soft, warm, inviting. She froze. He caressed her neck, exerting a little pressure, forcing her head toward him.

Her jaw set and defiance glittered in her eyes, daring him to prove his point, *if he could.* Her blatant disdain fired something deep inside him, something hard and sharp.

He leaned in, making his intent clear, his gaze locked with hers in a silent battle. Her breath misted his cheek. "Are you saying if I kissed you, you wouldn't like it?"

"I probably wouldn't feel anything."

"Oh, really? You mean, like a year and a half ago? When you asked me to—"

"Stop it! Just stop." She was shaking and shame blazed in her eyes. Gripping the manila envelope, she opened the door. "I'll see you tomorrow."

"You've been looking at me all day as if you'd like to have a go at me," he growled.

"I would. With my gun!"

Her tart reply snapped his last restraint and he moved in one swift motion. Panic flared in her eyes.

Pure male satisfaction swept through him. She wasn't unaffected, as she wanted him to believe. She wasn't unaffected at all.

He slid his fingers into her hair, cupped the warmth of her scalp. Her breathing quickened; her eyes narrowed.

He gave her plenty of time to push him away, to slide out of the truck. Defiance tightened her features. Her lips flattened and it sparked a savage urge in him to prove that she wanted him. Prove it to himself and to her. He lowered his head.

"Don't even think about—"

He covered her mouth with his and sensation streaked through him. Her lips were warm, moist, drugging. She gasped and his belly clenched.

He tugged gently at her bottom lip with his teeth. Stiff and unyielding, she sat passive beneath his kiss. He remembered this—remembered the resistance, the slow surrender, the hovering memory of Brad. But Brad wasn't here now. It was just Sam and Dallas.

His lips played on hers, soft and gentle and coaxing. His tongue teased the seam of her lips. She didn't open, didn't moan and sag against him as she had that night; didn't yield at all. Angry at her and himself, he ground his lips harder against hers. She sat rigid, unmoving.

Finally it penetrated that she wasn't responding. She wasn't going to return the kiss. No surrender. Not Dallas.

He drew away, painfully aroused, his gaze leveling into hers. He was stunned at his ragged breathing, the sweat that had gathered on his neck, the knife-edged desire twisting his gut.

How could he feel so much while she felt nothing? Her breathing was slightly erratic and that was probably from anger.

Humiliation burned through him and he pulled away.

''See?'' she whispered, climbing out of the truck into the fading light. ''Nothing.''

As she walked to the door, he gripped the seat back, his fingers curling into the soft upholstery. He watched her and mercilessly forced himself to relive the fiery burn of her rejection.

She didn't fumble with the keys or the lock. She smoothly let herself in and closed the door, leaving him in the driveway—blatantly, undeniably aroused. How could he have wanted her so keenly while she'd felt nothing?

The same way he could have made love to a woman who was pretending he was another man.

He swore viciously. Scooting back behind the wheel, he put the truck in gear and rolled out of the driveway.

He'd let her get to him this time. But never again.

Chapter 5

Dallas carefully threw the dead bolt, deliberately slid on the chain, pushed in the knob lock. Knees trembling, she leaned her forehead against the cool wood of the door. Her breath ripped out in shallow pants.

She could still feel Sam's lips on hers, at first soft and coaxing, pulling the strength out of her, turning her bones to powder. Then harder, demanding. Exciting.

She felt nothing, she'd said.

"Liar," Sam had called her. *Liar. Liar.*

Her heart thundered against her ribs and her lips tingled. She could still feel him. Peripherally, she was aware of the sweep of headlights as he reversed out of the driveway. Anger, desire and resentment clashed.

She didn't know what burned her soul more—the brand of his lips on hers or the unfolding realization that she'd liked his kiss. Wanted it. Wanted more.

She'd refused to let herself feel anything during that kiss. She couldn't. Sam's kiss could still turn her inside out, make her forget how she'd betrayed Brad. And how Sam had gone to another woman after leaving her bed.

Pressing her forehead harder against the ungiving wood, she let the darkness flow around her, the quiet of the empty house. A mist of sweat broke over her skin.

Liar.

She pushed away from the door, whirling to flip on both the entryway light and the one for the adjoining living room. Her gloves came off, stuffed into the pocket of her coat. Fighting to ignore the pleasure that rippled through her, Dallas tore off her duster, let it fall to the floor.

Only then did she realize she'd long ago dropped the envelope containing the crime-scene photos. She bent to retrieve it, smoothing the crumpled corner she'd crushed.

Liar. That kiss still hummed through her.

Tossing the photos onto the polished cherry-wood table behind Carrie's plaid sofa, Dallas headed for the guest room, palming her gun and unbuckling her holster. She transferred it to one hand while she pulled her mock-turtleneck sweater over her head.

She laid her weapon and holster on the satinwood dresser, tossed the sweater into a wicker basket in the closet. After toeing off her boots, she shimmied out of her jeans, took off her bra and pulled on a white tank top with baggy gray sweats.

She walked over to the dresser and picked up her billfold. Opening the change purse, she dumped the contents into her palm. One coin. One Eisenhower silver dollar. It had belonged to Brad.

His Grandpa Kittridge had given it to Brad on his tenth birthday. He'd always carried it with him, until he'd given it to her on their wedding day.

It lay cold and heavy in her palm; she closed her fist over it. She'd put the coin away after his death—it hadn't been lucky for him that day.

Being back in Oklahoma City was difficult and not just because of Sam. As she'd waited for him outside the police department, where she'd visited Brad countless times, her chest had tightened with loneliness.

She closed her eyes, tried to imagine that wild impatience on Brad's handsome features, the wicked glint in his eyes, but the picture was fuzzy. Still, it reassured her to have something of his. She opened her hand, stroking the flesh-warmed silver with her thumb, then laid the coin on the dresser beside her badge.

Feeling more steady, she looked up Sam's phone number and left a message on his machine. She would meet him at the airport tomorrow. Even if she had to sit inches from him on the plane ride to and from Atlanta, she wasn't getting back in that truck with him. Not after tonight. She didn't want him going with her to Atlanta at all, but balking would have convinced him that she was affected by him, too aware of him. His ego didn't need any convincing.

Five minutes later, she sat in front of Carrie's gas fireplace, wrapped in a burgundy cotton throw that sported hunting dogs and horses, and holding a cup of hot chocolate. The rich aroma of thick steaming cocoa filled her nostrils and soothed her.

Finally, at last, the prickling sensation began to fade. Her lips no longer tingled from Sam's. Well, only a little.

Dallas crossed her legs Indian-style and dumped the crime-scene photos on the plush pewter carpet in front of her, shifting to escape the glare from the overhead light. Dead bodies. She'd rather look at dead bodies than face the seething arousal she felt. Arousal that reminded her, painfully, that she was still alive and Brad wasn't. Reminded her of the desire, the bittersweet, confusing hunger she'd felt for Sam that night a year and a half ago. And just minutes ago.

Liar, liar.

His voice crawled through her mind and a tight knot of awareness settled in her stomach. She'd been telling herself all along that she missed their friendship, but not the other part—the physical, sweaty part. She had refused to respond to him because that would mean—

Okay, so she was…attracted to him. She jerked and hot cocoa sloshed over the cup, burning the tender skin in the hollow of her thumb. She licked up the liquid, laving the pain for a second.

She felt something for him. This…giddy warmth, this acute awareness was what she'd been dodging all day. No, for the past *year and a half.* That thought sprang out of nowhere, freezing her breath for an instant. Before, she'd always dismissed these feelings as the pleasure one might feel around a friend.

Now she knew it was more. But she hadn't felt like this about Sam after Brad had died, had she? *That* had been only friendship, hadn't it?

Dallas rubbed at the knotted muscles in her right shoulder. She couldn't have felt anything other than that for Sam. She gripped the mug with both hands and focused her attention on a black-and-white glossy of Valeria's body.

Sam probably knew she'd felt something when he'd kissed her tonight, but she hadn't given in, hadn't validated his smug certainty. And she wouldn't. When they'd slept together that once, it had ruined their friendship. This time, she couldn't afford to screw anything up.

Yes, she was attracted to him, but he'd never know it. She'd find Valeria's killer and get the heck out of Dodge—without getting involved with Sam.

Dallas trembled slightly and wrapped her hand around the mug, staring down at the picture of Valeria's lifeless body. She hugged the throw more tightly around herself.

He'd been humiliated. Rejected. *Again.*

Sam didn't like how Dallas got under his skin—quick and sly, like a needle. One minute he'd been taunting her, trying to shatter that cool demeanor. The next minute, he'd let anger—and his ego—take over.

Kicking shut the door to his three-bedroom house, he jerked off his sheepskin coat and threw it across the back of his navy leather recliner. Stalking across the open living room, he halted at the built-in bookcases beside the fireplace.

The picture was there, where he'd left it last night—a single photograph propped against the books on the second shelf. A photograph of him and Dallas and Brad, taken during a weekend cookout the summer before Brad's death. Dallas was in the middle, her arms locked around Brad and Sam's necks in a mock wrestling hold, with Sam and Brad hamming it up for the camera, eyes crossed, tongues hanging out as if she were really choking them.

Even her fake glare into the camera couldn't disguise the laughter in her eyes, the unguardedness of her stance. Her tanned arms were leanly muscled. Her tawny hair gleamed like polished gold in the setting sun. One side of her body molded to Sam's and he remembered the jolt he'd gotten when he'd felt her breast pressing into his shoulder.

The shame had hit him hard, because she was his best friend's wife. And because it had been extremely difficult to forget the feel of her.

The picture blurred. Sam took a cut-glass tumbler and whiskey decanter from the silver tray on the bottom shelf, then strode back to the sofa trimmed in rustic oak. Plopping down on one of the navy-and-burgundy-checked cushions, he unstopped the Scotch, splashed a liberal amount into his glass and tossed it back.

It burned down his throat, simmering in his belly. He glared at the photo, at the completely unguarded smile on her face. Memories flooded back of times they'd shared; laughter, teasing, warmth.

He cursed. She'd practically dared him to kiss her back there in his truck, to thaw the wariness in her eyes. Then she'd frozen him out. But this time it had been different.

A year and a half ago, she'd been listless, completely unconcerned, frighteningly absentminded. Tonight, she'd been controlled, deliberate. Restraining herself. Yes, restrained and angry.

See? Nothing.

Even the memory of her cool silky words couldn't squelch the desire that still hummed through him. Tossing the photo aside, Sam poured another drink, guzzled it down. Sweat peppered his skin. He reached up and tore open the buttons on his flannel shirt, tugging it out of his jeans. He shook his head, rage spilling through him like a backward tide.

Maybe he'd scared her off. Maybe now she'd go back to Denver, leave him in peace.

He laughed harshly. Not Dallas. It would take more than a kiss to chase her out of town.

His hand tightened on the tumbler and he poured, took another swallow of liquor. His mind locked onto the first time he'd come home with Brad and met her. He'd never forget that gut-clutching awareness and then the disbelief, the unease that he was attracted—*very* attracted—to his partner's wife. In all the years the three of them had been friends, he'd never let on, not to either of them. He would never have betrayed Brad that way. And he hadn't. Until after Brad died.

Bile rose in his throat. The decanter clanged against his glass as he refilled his drink. He toed off his boots and pushed them away.

At last, the liquor warmed his insides and he slouched against the comfortable cushions. The Scotch decanter rested on his bare belly. He didn't want to think about her anymore. Not anything about her.

His gaze moved over his comfortable living room, the bookcases stacked with true-crime novels, the *Star Wars* trilogy on videocassette, along with *The Civil War* by Shelby Foote, and his favorite, *How the Grinch Stole Christmas.*

He didn't know how long he sat there, nursing his drink. But now the edge was blurring. The tightness in his chest had eased. He felt loose, relaxed. The image of her steely gray eyes was fading. He sipped his Scotch.

A knock sounded on the door, startling him.

"Hey, Ever Ready! You in there?" Mace called. "Open up!"

Sam struggled to sit upright and blinked a couple of times to clear his vision. Ever Ready. Because he'd always been *prepared* on his dates, his brothers had given him the nickname in high school. And even Brad had picked up on it.

Another fist hammered on the door. "Sam, come on!"

Oh, great, Linc was here, too. Sam groaned, setting the decanter on the solid surface of the coffee table as he pushed himself to his feet. On impulse, he stuffed the photo between the cushions. Clutching the glass to his belly, he walked to the door, bumping into the recliner.

"Sorry," he mumbled, patting the chair.

"Sam!" his brothers called in unison.

"I'm comin'," he yelled, reaching the door and popping the dead bolt. He swung the door open and his brothers walked inside.

Like Sam and their father, Mace had near-black hair and blue eyes, whereas Linc's hair was sandy brown and his eyes were a clear gray like their mom's.

"What's going on?" Mace, three years older than Sam and about two inches taller, closed the door. "Why aren't you ready?"

"You were going to meet us for dinner, remember?" Linc, Sam's middle brother and the one who'd chosen medicine over law enforcement, arched his dark brows slightly at the sight of Sam's unbuttoned shirt, his boots tossed around haphazardly, his coat dangling over the recliner. "You okay?"

"I got in late." Sam moved to stand beside the recliner. "Why didn't you just call me?"

"We did. No answer." Mace's gaze zeroed in on the tumbler Sam held, then shifted to the half-empty decanter on the coffee table.

"We figured you probably forgot anyway." Linc grinned. "Or found some excuse to weasel out of the party."

"Humph."

Mace strode over and picked up the whiskey decanter. "How long have you been at it?"

"Not long." Sam bristled. Being so close in age to his brothers, he'd never been able to get anything past them.

Linc's gray gaze scoured Sam's features. "Hmm, slurred speech, delayed reflexes, red eyes—"

"I'm not one of your patients." Sam turned away, then swayed.

Linc chuckled. "Definitely intoxicated. What's going on? Did something happen?"

"No."

"Something with the case?" Mace frowned, exchanged a look with Linc. "Is that what you've been doing all day? Working?"

"Yes."

"How's Rock?"

"Still sick," Sam said darkly.

"What could possibly— Dallas Kittridge." Mace folded his arms. "She rolls into town and one night later, you're hammered."

"I'm not…hammers." Sam frowned at the glass in his hand. He didn't think he'd had more than one or two drinks. Three, tops. Had he?

Linc's eyebrows shot up and he eased down onto the arm of the recliner. "What's this about Dallas?"

"Nothing."

His middle brother grinned. "How is she?"

"She's back," Mace said.

"Shut up," Sam growled.

"For good?" Linc spoke to Mace as if Sam hadn't made a sound.

Sam's head started clanging like hail on a metal roof. "I don't see anything good about it," he muttered.

Mace slapped him on the shoulder. "Let's go, little brother. Mom will have our hides if we miss Greg's party."

"If she knew there were going to be strippers there, she'd hang us all for going," Sam argued. "I don't want to go."

"If we have to go, so do you." Linc rose from the recliner, giving Sam a light shove on the back.

Sam turned, his drink sloshing onto his bare torso. Cursing softly, he swiped at the liquor. "Y'all go without me."

"Oh, no!" Linc and Mace said together.

"You have to go," Mace insisted with a grin. "You're the only one who can get the strippers to stay and...do stuff. You do have a way with women, little brother."

"Yeah, right."

"Besides," Linc added, "Dallas won't be there. You're safe for a few hours."

"You're *so* funny. This doesn't have anythin' to do with her."

"Oh, really?" Mace shot a look at Linc over Sam's head.

"She... I did not kiss her."

"Whoa!" Linc's voice sounded choked.

Mace chuckled. "Whatever happened, baby brother, you've got to get your clothes on. They're expecting us at Greg's party."

"I hate happy people. They make me sick."

"Me, too," Linc muttered, grabbing one of Sam's arms and slinging it over his shoulder.

Mace rescued the glass tilting from Sam's fingers and grabbed his other arm. "Let's get you sobered up."

"Don't wanna."

"Women are hell, aren't they?"

"No, just her." Sam couldn't make his feet work so his brothers dragged him across the hall to his bedroom.

"You'll feel better after a cold shower."

"Not taking one."

"Oh, yes, you are." Mace and Linc hauled him into the navy-and-white bath off his bedroom. They exchanged looks over Sam's head.

"I hate it when y'all do that."

They both chuckled and as they reached the shower stall, Mace turned on the water. "In you go."

"No!" Sam tried to wrench away from them, but his reflexes were sluggish, his mind fuzzy.

His brothers shoved him inside and frigid water jetted his face. He howled, catching himself on the opposite wall.

The water cleared his head—fast. Before his brothers could move, Sam lunged and grabbed them both around the neck. He stumbled back, pulling them with him.

Mace gripped the shower door and Linc braced himself against the wall. Sam was forced to release them, but not before they'd gotten wet, too.

They stood crammed into the shower doorway, their crisp long-sleeved shirts drenched, their hair straggling across their foreheads.

Sam laughed, the deep sound echoing off the shower walls. For a moment, taut silence boomed.

Then Mace laughed. "You jerk."

"Brat." Linc wiped water out of his eyes and stepped back, grabbing a towel from a brass bar on the wall.

Mace reached in and turned off the water. "So, now do you want to tell us what's going on with Dallas?"

Sam pushed out of the shower stall, unbuttoning his wet Levi's as he squeezed through the door past Linc.

"When did she get back?" His middle brother followed him, dripping water all over the clean white tile and the taupe carpet.

"I don't know. I first saw her last night."

Mace followed them into the room, toweling at his hair. "Was she at your crime scene?"

Sam gave a terse nod of his head.

"No kiddin'." Mace peeled out of his wet clothes and wrapped a towel around his waist.

Linc rubbed at his hair, then unbuttoned his shirt, shrugging out of the soaked material. "What was she doing there?"

"Sticking her nose in where it doesn't belong," Sam answered shortly.

"That would hack me off, too." Mace gathered up their clothes and went down the hall toward the dryer.

Linc nodded, studying Sam carefully. "That's not really why you're mad, is it, Sam?"

Mace returned and Sam glared at both his brothers, then turned to pull on a pair of dry jeans. He stood in front of his dresser mirror, combing his hair. A headache throbbed in the back of his skull and his legs felt unsteady. He sank down on the edge of the bed, its headboard made of the same rustic oak as his dresser and nightstand.

Mace took a cane-back chair in the corner while Linc sat on Sam's bed.

"So are you going to tell us about Dallas, little brother?" Mace asked.

Sam squeezed his eyes shut. He'd nearly managed to forget about that kiss and the burning sting of rejection. But he shouldn't let himself forget. He should never forget the pain she'd caused him.

"Well?" Linc asked quietly.

Sam fell back onto the bed, staring up at the ceiling. "She's here because one of her witnesses was killed."

"That plays into the homicide you're working?" Mace asked.

Linc smoothed back his wet, towel-tousled hair. "She's *working* with you?"

"Not exactly. Not officially, anyway." Sam slanted a glance at Mace.

His oldest brother held up his hands. "Hey, I'm off duty. I ain't reportin' nothing. I heard nothing."

"Thanks." Sam sat up, funneling his fingers through his wet hair.

"How'd you run into her?" Linc draped his towel around his neck.

"Oh, *she* found *me*," Sam drawled.

''Well, that's good, isn't it? I mean, you guys haven't really talked much since she left, right?''

''Right,'' Sam said tightly. He still couldn't confide in his brothers about what had happened between him and Dallas. He surged off the bed and walked into his closet for a clean shirt.

Taut silence weighted the air behind him. He knew his brothers wanted to know what was going on, but no way was he telling them about that kiss. Or anything else. ''We're working together on this case, then she'll be going back to Denver.''

Linc slid a speculative look at Mace, annoying Sam.

Mace eyed Sam. ''Is that what you want?''

Dallas's studied lack of response to his kiss had warned Sam to leave things alone. Not let his ego get caught up in trying to prove that her ''unaffected'' act was just that—an act. He'd been drawn in by her once. He wasn't going there again.

He thought about the photo stuffed between the cushions of his couch. He thought about the night they'd spent together and how they'd suffered for it ever since.

''Yeah, that's what I want.'' But the words sounded unconvincing, even to him. *Especially* to him.

Chapter 6

Seven or eight years had passed since the last time Sam had been through the Atlanta airport. It was larger, but well marked and easy to maneuver. The sun, a fiery gold, dipped low in the sky as he and Dallas boarded their return flight home just after five o'clock. He took the window seat, recalling from the years he'd known her that she vehemently preferred the aisle. A brief flash of relief sketched her features as she sat down and buckled her seat belt. Sam did the same.

They'd maintained a polite, professional distance all day and Sam was relieved. He'd thought about apologizing for that kiss last night, then decided he wasn't sorry. Besides he saw no reason to bring it up. *She* certainly wouldn't. He'd lay money on that.

She'd felt something when he'd kissed her. Anger maybe? Arousal? But not indifference. Whatever it had been, he flatly denied the curiosity that urged him to find out. He refused to be drawn in by her again.

Still, he couldn't seem to stop looking at her. After watching her handle Petey Luciano, Sam had developed a whole new respect for her. Seeing her in action with the Mob boss had spurred a fascination Sam had never felt for her or any other woman. Her tough edginess during the interview hid the heat and softness he'd seen her display often with Brad. Hell, even with *him*.

They sat closer on the plane than he would have liked, but they had no choice. Coach seating was all the department paid for. Dallas's spicy floral scent webbed around him, tickling his nerves. Her knee pressed against his. Their arms touched from shoulder to waist.

She glanced at him, her mouth lifting in a bemused smile.

"What's funny?" he asked, leaning close to be heard over the starting rumble of the aircraft.

She motioned to his sunglasses. "You've had those on all day."

He snorted, looking out the window. Dusk began to settle in layers of red and golden pink.

"Looks like someone had a late night."

He shifted in the cramped quarters, cursing when his ankle hit the metal bar beneath the seat in front of him.

"Looks like someone probably has a hangover."

"Looks like *someone* needs to be quiet," he growled, dipping his right shoulder in search of a more comfortable position.

She chuckled. The whining roar of the jet increased, then leveled as the engines drowned out the words she muttered.

He winced as the noise merged with the dull throbbing behind his ears. He did indeed have a hangover—he'd had it before he'd gone to Greg's bachelor party—but he wasn't admitting it to Dallas.

Folding his arms across his chest, he tried to find a comfortable position. Crammed into the seat like a pop-up toy, he would have a crick in his neck in the two and a half hours it took to reach Oklahoma City. He had no hope of getting rid of this nagging headache. Or the taunting awareness of the woman next to him.

They hadn't spoken much today and when they had, their conversation had remained restricted to the case. Sam had gotten her message last night about meeting him at the airport and had been relieved. After that stupid stunt he'd pulled in the truck, he had no desire to be seated within feet of her. Of course, space on the plane was even more limited, but at least they weren't alone.

Dressing for their trip, he'd worn his camel-hair jacket, white shirt and navy slacks with dress shoes. His navy tie was patterned with a camel-and-burgundy geometric design. Dallas wore plum pants with a thigh-skimming plum jacket, and Sam tried not to notice how the deep purple color warmed her eyes to silver, gave her hair the luster of a newly minted coin.

She glanced at him, then out the window. A flush crept up her neck and he knew she was aware of his regard. She pulled a magazine out of the pocket in front of her and flipped it open. Sam's gaze shifted to the rapid tap-tap of her pulse in the hollow of her throat.

Work. That was where he needed to keep his focus. "You did a good job with Luciano today."

"Thanks."

She kept her nose buried in the magazine, but her easy reply took him aback. It reminded him of the way things used to be between them—uncomplicated, friendly. It made him wish fiercely that Brad were the one sitting next to him. He would give up every forbidden moment with Dallas to have Brad back. Especially when she'd never wanted Sam in the first place.

He scrubbed hard at his face. "What do you think? Did Luciano have anything to do with Valeria's killing?"

"No."

Sam replayed the moment when Dallas had bluntly accused Petey Luciano of his wife's murder. The guy had stood eye to eye with Dallas, but he was built like a bull, twice as wide, twice as heavy as she was.

The middle-aged man had moved faster than Sam would

have thought possible, but Dallas was ready. She had his arm twisted behind him and his face pressed into the wall before he could lay a hand on her. "Now tell me, Petey," she'd said.

The man had denied any involvement, and once he'd settled back into his chair, had given them some background on his wife.

Sam grinned at the memory of Dallas strong-arming the guy. "Yeah, Petey wasn't in on it. I agree."

"You do?" The surprise in her voice brought his gaze to her.

Their heads nearly touched and Dallas's hair brushed his cheek. The scent of flesh-warmed perfume had his throat tightening. They kept their voices low, which created a false sense of intimacy on the roaring jet.

Sam swallowed past a painful lump and nodded.

"Because you'd already pegged Valeria as part of the serial murders?"

"Not only that." He shrugged. "Your instincts are right about him. Petey was furious that Valeria turned evidence on him, but I think he was pretty torn up that she was dead. You never really believed he had her taken out, did you?"

"It was a definite possibility at first." Dallas pushed her blond hair out of her face, away from Sam's cheek. "Now, I think she was in the wrong place at the wrong time."

Her eyes glowed with that excitement again, the thrill of solving a case. He felt it himself every time, but now he found himself wondering what it would be like if she looked at him that way.

"Our tie between all these women is the dancing. And the bars."

"Country-western bars," Sam reminded.

"Right."

Sam figured Dallas would have shared that information if she'd traveled to Atlanta by herself. It was what she wouldn't have told him—what he'd witnessed with his own eyes—that made him doubly glad he'd come.

"Now we have to find this creep who's seen them all."

"And we have to do it pretty darn fast." Four women were dead. Sam didn't want there to be five.

If he hadn't come to Atlanta with Dallas, he wouldn't have seen this whole new side of her. She'd been steel ballet in motion. She'd seemed to know exactly when to back off and when to go to the wall with Luciano.

He'd known she was tough-minded, cool under pressure, but actually seeing her in action was different. It had impressed him, intrigued him. Aroused him.

He shook off the low throb of need that had drummed through his body since he'd seen her dismantle Luciano like a bad engine. She had spine and spunk and she was sexy as hell.

Annoyed with himself, he forced his mind to what they'd learned from the mobster and he realized he trusted her feelings about the man. "Brad always said you had key instincts about people. After seeing you in action, I'd have to agree."

Her smile seemed forced. "Thanks."

His mention of Brad spiked the air with tension, and the past spiraled in. He saw agony flit through her eyes, then she fixed her gaze intently on the ragged seat back in front of her.

She massaged her shoulder. "It's sad, isn't it?"

"What?"

"That Valeria lived in a loveless marriage. I guess a lot of women do. I was lucky."

He barely caught that last. She turned her head away and her words were swallowed up by the roar of the engines. But he did catch it. Even though pain and regret sheared through him, Sam said what he wanted, what he needed to: "Brad loved you very much. The two of you had a good marriage."

"We did." Her voice was tight, hoarse. "And then I—"

He heard the guilt creep in, saw the shame burn in her cheeks. All because of him, because of what they'd done. And if Sam hadn't been responsible for getting Brad killed, he and Dallas would never have spent the night together at all. It made him sick to his stomach. Sam hauled in a breath, bile rising in his throat. "He was lucky to have you."

She turned her head, her eyes searching, uncertain.

Uncomfortable with the need for reassurance in her eyes, Sam shrugged and forced a smile. "He said it often enough."

"He felt that way about you, too. You were a good friend."

Sam clenched his jaw and turned to stare out the window.

He felt her lean over, felt the weight of her breast through his jacket sleeve and desire axed his middle. His face tightened, grew hot. Sweat broke out on his nape.

"That's why he would hate that you hold yourself responsible for what happened."

"Dallas—"

"I know you'd like me to shut up so you can go on punishing yourself, but Brad wouldn't. And he wouldn't want you to blame yourself, either."

"And you?"

"I already told you—"

"Are you saying you haven't once wished I'd been the one who died instead of him?" His mouth went dry; his throat hurt as if he'd swallowed broken glass. This was what he really wanted to know, what had haunted him since the day Brad had died. It was enough that he wished he'd been the one to take that bullet, but if Dallas thought the same thing—

"Absolutely not! No!" She held his gaze, hers compelling, deep, aching; reaching out to him without the guardedness he usually saw in her eyes. "I just wish I knew how to convince you. Am I sorry he died? Yes," she said fiercely, leaning in so he could hear her above the whir of the jet engines. "Am I sorry you didn't? No. And I never will be."

He stared at her for a long moment, wanting to take her hand, kiss her, curse her. Emotion choked him.

"Regardless of what happened between us," she continued quietly, "you're a good man, Sam. Don't let Brad's death change that. He wouldn't want to be the cause of that."

"If only I'd been more alert—"

"Sam, you're a cop. You put your life on the line every day. You do the best you can, *every day*. That has to be enough. If it's not, it's not enough for any of us. And I, for one, have to believe it is."

Astounded by her vehemence, her honesty, he nodded. That Dallas didn't blame him eased the guilt a little. And for the moment, her acceptance quieted the condemning voice in his head, relieved the guilt that rolled over his chest like a tank.

"You were jumped, Sam. It happens. Even to the best of us."

Her justification of his actions suddenly infuriated him. He didn't want her excusing the fact that his actions had caused a death. His partner's death. "You weren't there. You don't know what I did or didn't do. What I should've done differently."

"Like what? Die yourself?" Dallas snapped. She sighed, reached toward him, then dropped her hand back into her lap. "Your own department cleared you. If there had been the slightest hint of culpability, you wouldn't be carrying a badge. You wouldn't be on this plane with me right now."

He had to admit she was right; still, it didn't ease the yawning ache in his chest.

"I've never wished you were dead. *Never.*" She eased back into her seat and gave a mock scowl. "If I had, you'd know it."

A reluctant grin tugged at his lips.

"It's time to forgive yourself. Let go."

"Have *you?*"

Pain etched her features, making her appear delicate, vulnerable—something he'd never seen before. "I'm trying."

She picked up her magazine again. "Thanks for your help with Valeria, Sam. I wouldn't be able to do anything on this case without you."

He sighed, laid his head back against the seat and closed

his eyes, trying to ignore the woman beside him and the awareness that hummed through him like a low-level vibrator.

She was using him. Just like he suspected that she had a year and a half ago. He'd almost been drawn in by her again—this time by her professionalism, by a side of her he'd never seen firsthand. It fascinated him, intrigued him, made him…want her. All over again.

He didn't like wanting her. And he wasn't going to do anything about it—he had no intention of making another useless trip down a dead-end road. But he could no longer deny it. He still felt the same gut-twisting, sweaty-palmed desire he'd always felt for her. That was dangerous. And the realization raised his guard the way nothing else could have.

He ignored the warmth of her arm against his, concentrated on breathing in and out, slowly, steadily. He might want her, but he didn't trust her. At least, not with his heart. Not after what she'd done. That one night together had ruined everything between them. This new and different level of trust—professional only—was enough. It had to be.

He and Dallas had hit every country-western bar in the city. The last one was The Rodeo, where he again flashed pictures of the victims. And as he'd hoped, the bartender, a woman named Sandy, recognized Mindy Rush, Lightsey's case. Sam stuck a fresh piece of gum in his mouth, nodding as the bartender told him Mindy had been a regular here.

Being inside the smoky bar gave Sam some relief. Since Dallas had agreed that driving two cars from bar to bar was silly, she'd volunteered to drive her rental. Sitting so close to her in the small two-seater had lashed his nerves taut. Their shoulders touched. When she shifted gears, her knuckles brushed his thigh. When she exhaled, he took it in.

He'd wanted to drive his truck, but she'd insisted. They should have driven his truck. They would have had more room and he would have had something to do with his hands. Inhaling the flesh-warmed scent of her sultry perfume had him flexing his hands endlessly on his thighs. Inside every bar, he welcomed the old ashtray-and-sweat smell.

As they drove from bar to bar, they kept their conversation restricted to the case. Sam had no intention of changing that. In most places, she stayed behind him and asked questions only when they met with resistance. No matter how close she stood, Sam was uneasily aware of her. More than once he noticed the sleek-fitting jeans she'd changed into after the flight. He wanted her, but he could get around that; he wasn't giving her the chance to hurt him again.

They were working together, period. Once this case was solved, Dallas would go back to Colorado and leave him in peace. Then he could move on.

The old anger welled up. He stuffed the victims' photos back into his shirt pocket and jerked his head back toward the entrance of The Rodeo. She nodded, trailing silently behind him through a weave of chairs, boot-scootin' cowboys and waitresses moving to the throbbing beat of a steel guitar.

They reached the door and Sam pushed it open just in time to see Tanna Catton slide out of a local news vehicle. Dallas stepped up behind him and he said over his shoulder, "We've got company. Go on to the car."

Her gaze immediately went to Tanna, then the cameraman behind her. Without hesitation, Dallas walked past Sam as if she didn't even know him and strode to her car. He knew she couldn't risk being connected to this case, especially by the media.

He stepped outside and let the door shut behind him, hoping Tanna hadn't seen him.

"Sam! Sam Garrett!"

Fatigue and his hangover wasted him, but seeing the investigative reporter at this bar with a cameraman tripped Sam's warning bells. As he waited for Tanna, a semitrailer roared by on the highway. A truck stop butted against the east end of The Rodeo's parking lot and Sam scanned the area. Lights blazed from the convenience store and restaurant. People milled about inside. Several cabs were parked in the lot and two were pulling in to fuel up.

Settling a smile on his face, he watched the leggy reporter approach, her platinum hair swinging over her shoulder. Her long camel-colored cashmere coat was unbuttoned, revealing a skintight sweater pulled taut over large breasts. She might look like a bimbo, but she was sharp. She knew something or she wouldn't be here.

She swooped down on him, halting only inches away and squeezing his arm. A thin, mustached guy in his early twenties trailed behind her, lugging a camera.

"How's it going, Tanna?" Sam's gaze skipped over her again. Yep, she was one fine-looking woman, but for some reason, that didn't stir his blood the way it usually did.

"Things are going well." Her blue eyes flashed with frank interest. "Have you seen me filling in for the ten-o'clock anchor?"

He nodded. "Yeah. Good job."

She eased closer, swathing him in a bold scent that reminded him of sex and cherries. Her gaze trailed slowly down his length, then back up again. Invitation gleamed in her eyes and she touched her tongue to her dark cranberry-slicked lips. "You're lookin' good."

He chuckled, flicking a glance to his left toward Dallas's car. The black 240SX sat in a pool of floodlight and Sam could see her outline, the gleam of her blond hair.

Tanna flipped her hair over one shoulder and said in a husky voice, "You haven't called me lately, Sam."

"I've been busy."

"Yeah, you've got dead bodies piling up everywhere."

"I do work Homicide, Tanna," he chided lightly.

"You know what I'm talking about." She slipped an arm through his, pressing her breast against him. "I know something's going on. Tell me."

Sam could feel Dallas's intense regard as if she were sight-

ing him through a scope. He lowered his voice to match
Tanna's. "Got nothing to tell."

The cameraman shifted from one foot to the other, wearing
a bored expression. Tanna smiled up at Sam with perfectly
capped teeth and lightly rubbed against him. Once upon a time
he would've felt that little buzz of desire, but this time he felt
nothing.

"Now, Sam," she purred. "How's it going to look if it gets
out the police knew they had a serial killer and didn't warn
the women of Oklahoma City?"

"A serial killer?" Sam deliberately kept his tone mild, his
gaze roving over her face. "How'd you get a hold of that?"
He grinned. "Or maybe I should say, who'd you get a hold
of?"

She dimpled. "You know me. Always looking for an angle."

He knew all about her angles. He'd had a hard and hot time
finding out, but that was over. She knew something or she
wouldn't be here. Leaning in close, Sam asked in a low voice,
"What angles you got going on?"

He could feel Dallas's gaze on him, melting the skin off his
neck.

Dallas gripped the steering wheel, stretching her gloves taut
over her knuckles. From her parking spot at the end of the
row, she could easily see Sam and Blondie. If that woman got
any closer to Sam, she'd be wearing his coat! Was there a
woman in this town whom Sam hadn't been with?

Why was she surprised? There was always another woman.
Just like a year and a half ago. She told herself she didn't care,
but she couldn't stop watching the two of them.

Scowling, she used the sleeve of her leather duster to clear
a spot on the windshield. Body language screamed the fact
that Tanna whoever-she-was wanted to get naked with Sam.
In fact, the longer Dallas watched, the more certain she was
that Sam and Miss News Chick had already gotten naked. A
sudden spark of fury left her stunned and a little shaken.

Dallas narrowed her eyes at the bombshell's expensive cashmere coat, the perfectly coiffed platinum hair that made Dallas shove a hand through her own hair and wish she hadn't changed into her worn jeans. But she'd needed to blend into the bar crowd. Tanna what's-her-name wouldn't blend anywhere.

That sharp heat stabbed again beneath Dallas's breastbone and she chalked it up to indigestion.

The woman was coiling around Sam like a cobra and he was eating it up. Dallas recognized the masculine play-with-me smile that kicked up the corners of his mouth. She didn't have to be any closer to know that a sultry fire was burning in his eyes, as it always did when he liked what he was looking at. Dallas was sorely tempted to let him walk home. This frigid air would cool him down.

Her hand dropped to the gun at her hip and she absently stroked it, scowling. The woman motioned the cameraman forward, but Sam shook his head, laughing.

He bent low to say something in the woman's ear and she leaned into him, waving the camera guy off. After a few seconds, Sam shrugged noncommittally and stepped around her. Blondie turned and quickly stuck something in his coat pocket. He kept walking as the woman called out after him.

He lifted a hand in acknowledgement. In the hazy light, Dallas saw the white flash of teeth as he grinned.

Blondie's gaze stroked over him as he walked away. Dallas fumed. Sam glanced back and the reporter turned away and disappeared inside the bar with her companion.

Dallas started the car, aware now of how cold her hands and nose were. Sam angled toward her, his grin gone now.

Finally the burning in her gut eased. She told herself she didn't care who Sam flirted with, and if it got the press off their trail, so much the better. Still, she couldn't squelch her irritation.

Her teeth chattered and she flipped on the heater. She liked the way Sam walked, easy and loose-hipped, not too fast, not slow, just sure. Like a man who knew where he was going and how he was going to get there.

She felt a sharp stab of regret for what they'd lost. Two years ago, she would have been able to tell if he'd enjoyed flirting with that woman or if he'd only done it to throw her off the case. Now Dallas could read nothing in his handsome features.

When he reached the car, she leaned over and popped the lock. He slid inside, closing the door and holding his hands in front of the blowing heater. "Ah."

His shoulder brushed hers and a potent cloud of expensive, cloying perfume hit her in the face. She wrinkled up her nose, fighting a sneeze as she pulled out of the parking spot and drove away from the bar. "What's up?"

"The story's about to break."

"So, Barbie really is a reporter?"

He slid a glance at her, a grin tugging at the corners of his mouth. "Tanna Catton, Channel Nine. She's been digging around."

Dallas drove past the truck stop and turned onto the highway, the car picking up speed smoothly. "Does she know anything?"

"She knows one of the victims was here the night she died."

"Shoot."

"And she knows there's a serial killer."

"Great." Dallas couldn't shake the image of that woman's fingers curled around Sam's arm, her breasts pressing against him. He smelled like he'd been hosed down in Chanel No. 5 and Dallas's nose twitched again. "You didn't tell her anything?"

He gave her a look. "No, but she'll find out anyway. She always gets what she goes after."

"Did she go after *you*, Detective Charm?" The words were out before Dallas could stop them.

He chuckled and that dimple flashed at the corner of his mouth. "She didn't catch me. For long."

Something dark and hot zinged Dallas and she told herself he was only taunting her. *Just ignore him.*

He blew on his hands, then stuck them in front of the vent again. "We've been able to place the victims on the nights of their murders, but all in different bars. There's no common location, no tie in the victims' looks at all. There's a link here somewhere. We just have to keep digging."

The scent of Blondie's perfume suffocated Dallas and she fanned a hand under her nose. "I didn't know you liked women with fake boobs and hair color out of a bottle."

He gave her a sideways look. "We've hit every bar tonight. Tomorrow, we'll go to each victim's neighborhood, see if we can find any other connections between the women."

She sneezed.

"Getting a cold?"

"It's that perfume. You smell like someone rubbed it all over you," she said pointedly.

"Smells good, huh?"

"If you like drowning in the stuff."

His gaze sharpened on her, peeled through layers of anger and guilt until she felt completely vulnerable. He gave a short, surprised laugh. "You're jealous."

Only Sam had ever made her feel emotionally raw, exposed. Infuriatingly transparent. She slid him a cool look. "How do you walk around with such a big head?"

"Admit it, Dallas," he said softly, leaning toward her. One big hand gripped the top of her seat at her shoulder. "Come on, admit it."

Something inside her squirmed. Their trip to Atlanta had proved they could work together, but that was all. She wanted—*needed*—to get away from him. "Oh, I thought I hid it so well," she mocked in a falsetto drawl.

He chuckled. "You know I can see right through you."

That truth hit a nerve. Sam did break down all her barriers, made her lose control and she didn't like it. She concentrated on speeding down the highway. They didn't speak again in the fifteen minutes it took to reach Sam's house.

They pulled into his driveway and he reached for the door handle. "See you in the morning?"

"Yes."

"Meet me at my house."

"Got it."

He studied her for another minute, then quietly got out of the car. "See ya."

"See ya." Her chest tight, she watched him walk across the grass and onto the porch. Her hands clutched the steering wheel so hard she thought she might break it off the column.

Hell! She slammed a palm against the steering wheel, then grabbed her gearshift in a chokehold. Dammit, she had not come back here to pick up with Sam Garrett.

So why did she care that Tanna Catton had plastered herself all over him like Saran Wrap? And why couldn't she forget that macho prove-you-don't-want-me kiss from last night?

Sam paused on his porch, looked over his shoulder at her. Disgusted with herself, she reversed into the street and drove away. She didn't look in the rearview mirror; didn't want to see if he still stood there, watching her.

Her, jealous? Ha!

It was only when she pulled into Carrie's driveway that Dallas realized her teeth were clamped together as though cemented. She relaxed her jaw, pulled into the garage and killed the engine. Damn. She wasn't jealous. She *couldn't* be.

She missed her friendship with Sam, that was all. A year and a half ago, she'd turned to him out of grief, nothing more. Still, that didn't explain the possessiveness she'd felt while watching him with the reporter. Or with Carrie, for that matter.

For the first time, Dallas wondered what might have happened between her and Sam if she'd stayed in Oklahoma. Would they still be friends? Something more? Or distant and awkward, as they were now?

Sam made no secret of the fact that he was only helping her with Valeria's case so he could close the door to his and Dallas's past. That was what she wanted, too. *Liar.* She ignored the irritating whisper of her conscience and went inside.

Chapter 7

Egotistical, self-centered, smug...*man.* Dallas was not jealous of any bimbo—any*one*—Sam associated with. And she spent the next four days proving it to him.

They canvassed the neighborhood of each victim and turned up nothing. They reinterviewed the neighbors in each neighborhood and turned up nothing.

She played along with his lighthearted banter, ignored his clean scent, refused to acknowledge the little flip her heart did every time he flashed those dimples.

Just as Sam had predicted, the story had been front burner on the six- and ten-o'clock news, front page in the paper. And Tanna Catton did have almost as much information as Sam and Dallas. The reporter didn't know about the victim from Edmond or that Valeria had been a protected witness, but she didn't need to.

Sam had already been called in by his lieutenant and they'd been joined by their captain, Maggie Price, and the governor's office. After that meeting, Sam had looked haggard and fiercely determined. And as the days passed, he and Dallas found no answers. The tension was sharp and showed in the hard glitter of his bloodshot eyes. His lips grew tighter.

Dallas felt it, too. The muscles in her right shoulder had settled into one long, aching knot. And there was a new tautness in her belly that had nothing to do with the case and everything to do with the detective—a sly insidious awareness of Sam that she tried to ignore by keeping her focus strictly trained on the investigation.

They'd had no hits from VICAP, nothing off the Internet. They'd combed every neighborhood with no new leads. According to the crime analysts in Sam's office, serial killers usually chose victims of the same race, so their killer was most likely a white male. If the killer stayed true to form, they only had five to seven days before he struck again.

She and Sam worked together every day—long, grueling hours. Her nerves were strained. She was still shaken and uncomfortably aware of the sting of jealousy she'd felt, which Sam had witnessed. Anger shimmered inside her every time she thought about it, and working so closely with Sam, she thought about it more than she liked.

Still, they worked well together. An unconscious rhythm developed between them. They could decide without speaking when Dallas would do better with a particular interview, and Sam would step back, let her handle it.

Still, she was very unsettled by that flush of jealousy she'd exhibited. It really couldn't be called anything else. The sooner Valeria's murder was solved, the sooner Dallas could go home. And she knew that she needed to leave.

The problem was, Oklahoma City was starting to feel more like home than Denver. And there was something about Sam—about *her and Sam*—that stoked her curiosity. Made her ask too many what-ifs. Stirred a restlessness inside her that she'd never experienced. Yes, she had to get out of Oklahoma City ASAP.

Sam made scrupulous notes at every interview, and each night when Dallas returned to Carrie's, she did the same—

scrounging, hoping for a connection besides the suspect's MO and the victims' music preference that connected all the murders.

That first night, she'd fallen asleep on top of her notebook and dreamed of her and Sam making love. Since then, she had worked. Or watched the myriad Christmas movies on television. Or read. Still, she couldn't shake her awareness of him, couldn't get rid of the frustration surging through her. She hated that, too.

She told herself it was the holidays. Last Christmas had been a blur. She'd been wrapped in a stinging kind of grief that had left her numb, apathetic about having a tree or even wrapping gifts.

She told herself she was just missing Brad. But it wasn't Brad's face in her mind in the wee hours of the morning as she lay staring at the ceiling, aching for sleep. It wasn't Brad's lips she remembered as she waited for daylight and more, tedious legwork. It wasn't Brad's voice in her mind as she struggled to kill the spark of need that now burned in her belly.

She and Sam tiptoed around each other, spoke only when necessary, compared notes by exchanging their notebooks. Everything they said centered around the case. And yet Dallas couldn't help wondering where Sam went when he left each night, wondering if he was with anyone.

She wondered what a real kiss between them would be like. Not one given to comfort, like what they'd shared a year and a half ago. Or one born of anger, like the one last week.

Randomly, like a surprise attack, an image from the night they'd spent together would flash into her mind. The curve of his smooth, bare shoulder. The taste of clean skin. The intense glitter of his eyes as he'd buried himself inside her.

Once it hit her when they were interviewing a clerk in a busy convenience store. It brought her up short. Appalled and infuriated by the mental flash of well-defined pectorals and knuckled abs, she lost her train of thought right in the middle of a question. Sam had looked at her oddly, as had the clerk.

She'd recovered, continued asking questions, but there had been a strange flutter in her stomach, an unsteadiness in her hands as she scribbled notes.

The next time, they'd been questioning an older woman with poor hearing. A stark image of Sam's body pushing into hers sliced through Dallas's memory.

She didn't react as obviously as she had before, but the picture left her just as shaken. The urge to get on the next plane to Denver had swamped her, but she'd remembered Valeria. And had redoubled her efforts to keep some space between her and Sam. It had worked until the fourth day of their interviews.

It was already dark and they were leaving the neighborhood where Valeria had lived. Sam scrubbed hard at his face, then plowed a hand through his thick hair. "Let's go get something to eat."

Massaging her right shoulder, she squeezed the tangled knot under her skin. "I don't think—"

"I don't want to talk about Brad, if that's what you're worried about. I just want some food."

"I could go on—"

"I'm too tired to argue with you, Kittridge. Or do anything else," he said pointedly. "I just want to eat. You've got to be hungry."

"What about going over what we got today?"

"We can do it after."

"I can't be seen in your office."

"I've got everything at my house."

She ignored the little trip of her pulse, yet she hesitated.

Impatience flared on his features. "Do what you want. I'm going to eat."

"Sure, that's fine." It was the smugness in his eyes that made her decision, the certainty that said he knew she didn't want to be alone with him. "Lead the way, Detective Charm."

She had the pleasure of seeing his mouth tighten, then he gave her the name of a restaurant close to his house in Edmond. She followed him up Broadway Extension and as she walked behind him into the bustling place, she wondered if she'd just made a big mistake.

She'd been here six days. The tension between them was palpable. She knew something had to give. But it wasn't going to be her. Besides, what could possibly happen? If Sam was anywhere near as tired as she was, the only thing he'd be up for was eating. She slid into the booth seat across from him. It was only dinner.

And it was. They ordered, ate their meal quietly. A couple of times, Sam's eyes went distant and intense and Dallas knew he was thinking about the case. They each paid for their own dinner and when Sam asked if she was coming to his house to look over the files, she nodded with only slight reluctance.

She ignored the hollow ache in her chest—the one that reminded her that she and Sam used to have more than this. She pushed aside the need that curled into a little pocket in her belly and followed Sam inside his house.

He'd been trying to ignore the fact that Dallas had been jealous of Tanna, but every time he thought about it, a smug, satisfied smile eased across his face. Served her right.

While Sam liked the way he'd made Dallas squirm, he didn't like the way his thoughts kept dwelling on her. Didn't like how his gaze kept sliding to her as they retraced every shred of evidence—recanvassed the neighborhoods of the victims, reinterviewed the neighbors.

Yes. Seeing that fire light her eyes had gone to his head like good Scotch, but his instincts screamed for him to back way off; to focus on solving this case so that Dallas could leave.

And the truth was, he needed her help. Rock was still out sick and the department dwindled daily due to the flu. Sam hoped he wouldn't come down with it. So, he'd spent the next four days dodging this frustrating, annoying, gut-twisting awareness of her.

His eyes grainy with fatigue, he got his second wind after they'd eaten dinner. Back at his house, Dallas put on a fresh pot of coffee while he stuck in a Tschaikovsky CD. He returned to the kitchen and took a chair at the end of the table. Dallas sat on his right, but closer to the other end, so they weren't touching.

Files scattered across the table. Sam flipped back and forth in his notebook as time scraped by. Between sips of coffee, Dallas muttered to herself as she compared files and scribbled notes. The graceful, mellow sounds of *The Nutcracker Suite* played softly in the background.

Sam thought his mind was fully focused on his work, yet he was still aware of every time Dallas moved her hand. When she shifted in her chair, his muscles tightened involuntarily. Beneath the smoky aroma of coffee, he could smell the tantalizing spice of her scent.

He had to read the same note in the file four times before he comprehended it. The sound of shuffling paper merged with the music in the living room. His skin grew tight, hot. He wished he could ignore her. Or better yet, tell her he didn't need her help on this case. An unfamiliar impatience churned inside him.

He didn't know how long they sat there, but the room seemed to shrink. Irritated, he rose. "I'm going to call Rock, see how he's doing."

"All right." She didn't even look up.

"All right," he muttered, going into the living room and grabbing up the cordless phone. Rock's wife, Patsy, answered and when Sam hung up a few minutes later, he knew there was no way he could tell Dallas to go back to Denver.

His partner had been admitted to the hospital with dehydration and would be in there for at least twenty-four hours.

The flu was sweeping through the department. Even Lieutenant Roberts had looked a little green around the gills when Sam had been in his office the other day.

So, it seemed all Sam could do was suck it up and work

with Dallas. Get back in there and find a connection so they could nail the sicko who'd killed at least four women.

Replacing the phone, Sam walked back to the kitchen but halted in the doorway. Dallas had laid her head down on her arms, her profile facing him. She slept peacefully, her brow smooth, her lashes dark against the cream of her skin. She looked as tired as he felt and as he stood there, something tugged at his heart.

Tenderness welled inside him; for a moment, he allowed it. He was reluctant to wake her, but the longer he watched her, the more he wanted to touch her cheek, stroke her hair away from her face, run his fingers through the tawny silkiness.

His body grew hard, annoying the hell out of him. "Dallas," he said softly.

She didn't stir.

His gaze riveted on her nape, pale marble above the collar of her denim vest. He fought the urge to press his lips to that patch of soft skin, taste the body-warmed spice of her—

"Dallas," he said, louder this time, with an edge, trying to dodge the need that throbbed through him.

She still didn't move and he realized how exhausted she must be. Still, if he tried to reach across her for her gun, which sat in its holster at her right elbow, she'd probably come straight out of that chair, her weapon cocked and ready. He squatted beside her and said her name again.

Her dark lashes fluttered, her eyes opened and she smiled at him—a smoky, unguarded smile. Sensation rippled up Sam's spine, igniting the old hunger. And the old wariness.

She blinked, looking confused for a moment. Then pleasure spread across her face and, despite the warning screaming through his mind, Sam couldn't tear his gaze from the soft flush on her cheeks, the way her tongue came out to wet her lips.

Slowly she pushed herself out of the chair. He straightened at the same time.

"I dozed off?" Her voice was low and raspy.

Desire kicked Sam in the gut. All he could manage was a nod.

Her eyes were soft gray, drowsy. Her gaze dropped to his lips and his heart turned over. As if she'd suddenly realized where she was looking, she jerked and turned away.

He shifted, putting some distance between him and her chair, thinking she would move in the opposite direction. When she leaned forward to pull her gun and holster toward her, her jeans stretched tight across her rear. Sam swallowed hard.

Then Dallas turned. Her shoulder bumped his chest and she jerked reflexively toward him, her eyes wide and uncertain. She looked away.

But not before he caught the raw hunger in her eyes.

The feel of her shoulder against his chest branded through his shirt. He caught the faint whiff of her after-dinner mint, the fresh scent of her shampoo. His gaze dropped to her breasts. They rose and fell rapidly beneath her long-sleeved black T-shirt. *She wanted him.* He tried to push away the thought even as his gaze slid upward to her lips, now parted and moist.

She didn't move. Her arm burned down his torso and belly. Teasing, torturing. Primitive, savage hunger roared through him. He took a step back. She leaned into him.

His mind blanked. Breasts pressed against him. Strong, slender thighs brushed his. Her hips... He could feel her hips nudging his arousal.

Her gaze locked on his—pleading, uncertain, hungry.

If he'd ever had any control, it unraveled on the spot. Her lips touched his and heat spiked his veins. This... *This* was what he'd missed, what he wanted. This was Dallas, the woman who'd turned him inside out. The only woman who could.

She moaned low in her throat and every thought in his head disintegrated like ash in water. She pressed against him, her breasts full, round, unleashing a fierceness in him he'd never known.

He hooked one finger into the belt loop of her jeans and tugged her to him. She made a begging sound that ripped right through his caution, his common sense. Her tongue traced the seam of his lips, and impatient, aching to taste her, he plunged his tongue inside her mouth. She was hot and sleek and tasted of her peppermint and coffee.

He kissed her slowly, awed, disbelieving, savoring the feel of her against his body, the heat of her soaking through his clothes, the sweet lushness of her mouth. Her hands curled around his neck. Her short nails scraped lightly over his skin and a shudder ripped through him.

He released her belt loop, curved his hand over her high, tight butt. He widened his stance, urging her into his arousal. She shifted, straddling his thigh. Heat pulsed from the core of her and burned through his jeans, branding his leg, making him fevered and desperate.

Some voice, barely audible in the back of his head, shouted that he was an idiot, but the desire, the *need* drowned the sound.

His chest ached. He needed to breathe, but didn't want to stop kissing her. She made an impatient noise in the back of her throat, which fired something dark and savage inside him. He tore his lips from hers and she clutched at his shoulders, pulling him back hard, greedily, more tightly against her.

He nibbled along her jawline and down her neck.

She arched into him. "Yes, yes."

Her nipples were hard, drilling his chest now. He cupped her rear with both hands, anchoring her to him. His arousal strained against the fly of his jeans. Her thighs tightened around his leg and he felt a moist heat. Knowing she was as excited as he was nearly sent him over the edge.

"Sam," she gasped, her voice strained.

He heard the raw hunger, *he felt it*. He wanted to peel off her clothes and take her right here on the kitchen table. And even while his blood heated to boiling, some part of his brain registered what he was doing. And with whom. *Dallas.*

The memories razored in. Her sweet lips moved from his neck to his ear and all he could remember was how she'd hurt him a year and a half ago. He couldn't open that wound again. A tremor racked his body. His hands shook, but somehow he found the strength to grip her wrists, try to draw a full breath. His heart pounded as if he'd just sprinted up a hill.

Wanting to sink into her, knowing that would be the biggest mistake of all, he tightened his grip on her wrists. Finally, she drew back, her eyes opening, cloudy with a naked desire that nearly made his knees buckle. She swayed toward him.

"Stop." His voice sounded harsh, broken. He tried to breathe.

"What—" Realization bloomed in her eyes, then horror.

That pissed him off royally. He shoved his face into hers. "I'm not Brad. Do you hear me? And I'm not getting sucked in by you again."

"I don't know what I was thinking." She yanked away from him. "Obviously I wasn't."

"I was." His chest burned. He couldn't stop the words. He didn't want to. "I was thinking about how you planned to leave without telling me. How you used me."

She looked away.

"How you looked right through me after we made love."

She winced.

"We—made—love," he said slowly, precisely. Daring her to deny it. Daring her to walk out. Hoping she would. Hoping she wouldn't. He wanted her to look at him.

She lifted her chin, her gaze slicing to his. "Stop."

"We did it. We can't change it."

"Don't act like you're proud of it. I know you're not."

Had he imagined that crack in her voice? "I'm not! It's just another scar, another mistake I made, another hurt against Brad."

She flinched, even though she didn't disagree with one thing he said. "Then stop talking about it—"

"We made love, but we're not going to do it again."

"I wasn't trying—I didn't think we should." She folded her arms across her chest, wishing she had on her gun, her coat, something to protect her from his searing gaze. She took a deep breath. "I kissed you and I'm not sorry."

"Was it what you wanted, what you thought? What you *remembered?* What were you trying to prove this time?"

"Nothing." Tears burned her throat, but she glared, anger and hurt merging inside her. "Not one thing."

"Think that's going to keep you warm at night? Do you ever lie in bed and remember that time? Snuggle up with that godforsaken memory? Memories, that's all we have. And damn sorry ones at that."

For one brief instant, he thought he saw the glimmer of a tear. He'd hurt her and he suddenly wanted to pull her to him, swear he hadn't meant anything he'd said. But he had to mean it. She was killing him, slowly chiseling away at his defenses, making him forget what she'd done. What they'd done.

And suddenly he was wasted, hollowed out by fatigue and sadness. He scrubbed at his face. "We've done all there is to do on this case. Go back to Denver. When I get something, I'll let you know."

"I'm not leaving until this killer is caught."

"You're only in the way here."

Hurt brightened her eyes, but she quickly masked it. "Forget it, Garrett. You're stuck with me until we get a killer."

"Kittridge!" he roared, his patience snapping. "I'm not kidding! I don't need you. We've gone over everything a million times. There's nothing else there!"

"Then we'll keep looking until we find something."

"I can do it myself."

"You need me and you know it, at least until your partner is back at work." As his eyes narrowed, she nodded. "I heard part of your conversation with his wife. He's in the hospital and you need help.''

A muscle ticced in his jaw. He did need her and he hated it. And suddenly she knew. She wanted him to want *her,* not her help. But he didn't want her. A bubble of sadness bloomed deep in her chest. She sighed. ''I'm staying.''

She snatched up her holster and stalked around him, grabbed her coat from his couch and walked to the door. Then she paused, looking over her shoulder as she struggled to keep her voice even. ''By the way, I know exactly who you are. And I know who I was kissing.''

And she walked out.

Sam stood there, assaulted by anger and hunger and a sweeping urge to call her back. But he let her go, just as he had a year and a half ago. Just as he had to do now—for the rest of their lives. He wasn't giving her another chance to filet him like a fish and stomp all over his guts. Been there, done that.

He wasn't who she wanted. He didn't know if she would ever be ready to move past Brad.

But even as he told himself that, he knew she already had. *He* was the one who hadn't.

He couldn't forgive himself for that night they'd spent together. And couldn't forgive *her* for the way she'd hurt him.

Part of him wanted to; wanted to try and regain the friendship they'd had. But the scarred, cynical, bleeding part of him knew that was impossible.

So why did he want to go after her, apologize for hurting her the way he had? Why couldn't he forget the pain he'd deliberately put in those gray eyes? How was he ever going to forget her, move on?

That kiss had sparked something new. Something shared by the two of them this time, with no thoughts or memories of Brad during that too-brief kiss. If Dallas was to be believed, they'd shared it even without Brad's memory. For one moment, she had belonged to him. Only him. No Brad. No past. No anger.

Sam didn't know how he could ever forget *that,* but he was damn sure going to try.

Chapter 8

What was the matter with him, anyway? Throwing Brad in her face like that. Dallas wanted to throttle Sam and at the same time, she…didn't. Desire snaked through her, touching nerves she'd thought numbed long ago. *Sam. Sam* had done that to her with a kiss.

She pressed her lips together, trying to erase the feel of him, douse the energy humming through her body. As she walked inside Carrie's, her cell phone rang. It was her boss.

He tersely asked what she was doing and when she was coming back. When she asked for another week, she thought he might explode. He agreed—finally—and fired a series of questions at her that she answered generically. She told him she was still in Oklahoma and that yes, she'd actually been hunting. Her time was running out.

She and Sam had to get a break in the case soon. She didn't know if she could put her boss off again. She was glad to finish the wearisome conversation, but even that didn't take her mind off Sam. And that kiss. Or what he'd said.

"I'm not Brad."

She touched her lips, still feeling the brand of his mouth. No, he most certainly was not Brad.

As she went to the guest bedroom, Dallas noticed Carrie's small travel bag in the doorway of her own bedroom. Good. Dallas didn't want to be alone tonight. Nor did she want to keep rehashing that kiss with Sam.

She changed into her dark blue satin pajamas and washed her face. After pulling on a pair of thick socks, she picked up her notes and walked back into the living room. Someone pounded on the front door and, after looking through the peephole, Dallas opened it to admit Carrie, who tromped in dragging a Christmas tree.

The chill of winter followed her, and Dallas quickly shut the door. Together she and Carrie got the tree into a stand and placed it in a corner near the front window. The fresh scent of pine filled the air and Dallas felt the first anticipation of the holiday that she'd experienced since Brad's death.

But as she strung lights on the tree and opened boxes of ornaments, it wasn't Brad she thought of, but Sam. That kiss had been more than the ones she remembered; not tainted by guilt or regret or the past, but simply his lips on hers, sure, tender, coaxing the strength right out of her legs. She had wanted to surrender to him. Had wanted more. *Still wanted.* Her face burned and sensation fluttered low in her belly as she opened another box of tissue-wrapped decorations.

She'd felt no guilt about Brad, she realized with awe and disbelief. That was new. She didn't know if Sam had or not. She did know that he had looked like he wanted to murder her there for a minute, but before that…

Just thinking about the way his lips had seduced hers sent heat prickling under her skin again. Shaken by the hunger sliding through her, Dallas didn't hear Carrie until she whistled sharply.

Her friend waved a hand in front of her face. "Hello?"

Dallas grinned self-consciously. "Sorry."

Carrie reached over for the ceramic Santa ornament Dallas held. "What are you thinking about? The case?"

"Yes." Dallas pulled a carefully wrapped wooden reindeer from the box.

"How's it going?"

"We're getting nowhere. We've spent the last four days going back over everything, but we can't seem to find any connections besides the fact that all these women like country-western dancing." She remembered Sam's bald suggestion that she leave. That shouldn't have hurt, but it did.

Frustrated, Dallas ripped open another box. Plucking up the ornament on top, she unwrapped it and handed a ceramic snowman to her friend.

The other woman nodded in sympathy, eyeing the tree critically before hanging the ornament. "And you and Sam? How are things going there?"

She peered carefully into the box as she lifted out another mass of tissue. "Fine."

Carrie laughed. "Real convincing, Dal."

Dallas made a face, handed her the pewter bell she'd unwrapped. "We haven't killed each other, if that's what you mean."

"It's a start, I suppose." Carrie moved around to the other side of the tree, readjusted a strand of lights that had drooped to the next branch. "Does that mean things have settled down between the two of you?"

"Settled down?"

Carrie moved a wooden reindeer to another branch, then held out her hand for the next decoration. "There's always some sort of friction there."

Friction? The word brought a startling image of two bodies straining together—bare, hot, sweaty. Dallas frowned and pushed the image away.

She stared at her friend for a moment, thinking again how beautiful Carrie was. Firelight burnished her dark hair with gold, etched her perfect profile in soft light. Dallas recalled how Sam had flirted with Carrie last week and something tight twisted in her gut. She tried to sound casual, but the words seared her throat. "Any chance you and Sam might pick up where you left off? He acted interested the other night."

Carrie laughed, hanging a scarlet glass ball. "Are you kidding?"

"Well, no—"

"Dallas." Carrie tilted her head and stared at Dallas as if she didn't have the sense to come in out of a storm. "How *dense* are you? It's not me he's interested in."

Dallas blinked, then laughed. "Get real. Not me."

"Of course, *you*." Carrie took another glass ball from Dallas and hung it on the tree. "Have you really never noticed?"

"Noticed what? That he can't stand to be in the same room with me?" she muttered, moving to the opposite side of the tree to hang a gold ornament.

Carrie peered around the tree. "For as long as you've known him, you don't know him very well."

"Sam loves women, but he doesn't love all of them," Dallas replied dryly.

"Well, he's only got eyes for one." Carrie stood back and admired her efforts, then started for the kitchen. "How about some hot chocolate? Or I can fix coffee if you'd like."

"Hot chocolate would be nice." Her fingers tightened around the smooth gold ornament as Carrie disappeared into the kitchen.

Dallas kept remembering that kiss and she kept remembering what Sam had said to her. She hadn't realized until tonight just exactly how much resentment he harbored toward her. How had they worked together this long? Could he ever forgive her?

A tightness squeezed her chest and panic swamped her. She needed space from him. She wanted to get on the next plane out of here.

She'd never thought of herself as a quitter or a coward, but maybe she'd been both. She saw now that she'd failed Brad. And when she'd left Oklahoma City, she'd failed Valeria.

At the time, she'd believed she was leaving to get away from the memories of Brad, the anger she felt over his dying and leaving her, the guilt she felt over what she hadn't been for him.

Now she knew the truth. She'd run from Sam; from what had happened between them. He thought she'd been thinking of Brad tonight when they'd kissed. He thought she'd imagined him as Brad during their lovemaking that one time. She hadn't. Not at all.

And she was tired of failing—Valeria, Sam, Brad, all of them. She couldn't leave. Not yet.

Taking a deep breath, she hung the gold ball on the tree. Something had happened tonight with Sam; something powerful and unexpected that had left her feeling… *Feeling what?*

Dallas stared blankly at the brilliant white lights on the Christmas tree. That kiss had brought her smack up against the truth. She wanted Sam.

She wanted to make love with him. She wanted to get rid of this piercing hollowness in the pit of her stomach. She wanted…his forgiveness. A desperate laugh bubbled up inside her. He'd made it perfectly clear that he resented the hell out of her.

She and Sam couldn't go back. But she wanted—*needed*— his forgiveness if she was ever going to be able to move on.

Just the thought of putting him behind her left a sharp pain in her chest, an emptiness that mirrored the one she'd felt when Brad had died—a loneliness that bored through her soul. She didn't know how she could put Sam in the past; he wasn't exactly forgettable.

Frustrated, she joined Carrie at the kitchen table for a steaming cup of cocoa. The warm drink made her drowsy and finally Dallas said good-night. The tension and pressure of the past several days weighed on her and she wanted only to go to bed.

For the first time since she'd arrived, she fell into a deep sleep.

It seemed only minutes later when she was jarred awake by the shrill ringing of the phone.

Groggy, groping for her cell phone on the night table beside the bed, she glanced at the clock—3:00 a.m. Dread curled in her belly as Sam's voice rasped in her ear.

"There's been another murder. I'm at the scene."

"Oh, no." She swung her legs off the bed and sat up, shoving her hair out of her face. "What can I do? I can meet you—"

"No," he said quickly. Too quickly. "I'll swing by Carrie's when I'm finished at the scene. The lab guys are here so I'll catch you then."

"All right." Dallas hung up, slipping out of bed to pull on her baggy gray sweats. She made her way quietly into the kitchen to make coffee.

If this was the same guy, the killer was picking up speed. He'd killed five women now. She and Sam had to find the connection, some kind of lead.

With a fresh cup of coffee in her hand, she opened her notes and began to go over them again. They had to get this creep before he killed again. And now they had no idea when that would be.

If nothing else, *this* would keep her mind off Sam.

Sam narrowed his focus and did his job. But the whole time he made notes and studied the latest victim's body and spoke to the medical examiner, thoughts of Dallas nagged at him. He wanted to regret that kiss. At the very least, he wanted to resent it. The memory of her lips on his, soft and willing and drawing his body into one long ache made him want more, made him feel weak. But for the first time, it hadn't made him feel guilty.

He needed that guilt, needed it to keep from reaching for Dallas when he wanted to shove her up against the wall and blank his mind to everything except the feel of his body inside hers. Usually, the memory of how she'd ripped out his heart served to keep him away from her. Last night it almost hadn't.

He could have had her. She'd been all liquid heat in his arms, her thighs squeezing his leg, her hips grinding against his. And Brad was gone.

He kept expecting that old familiar pang in his chest, the crush of shame, but it didn't come. Sam shook his head in amazement. Dallas belonged only to herself now and he was swept with a savage longing to have her on those terms. To start fresh, even though he knew it would lead him straight back to hell.

Dallas Kittridge was poison to his soul, but knowing that didn't stop the wanting. He'd suggested meeting her at Carrie's because he couldn't handle seeing her in his house again.

It was dawn when he arrived and as Dallas let him inside, his pulse quickened. Maybe he couldn't handle seeing her anywhere so soon after that little incident at home. Hell, even working with her every day for the past seven days hadn't diminished his body's reaction to her.

Her face was scrubbed free of the minimal makeup she usually wore; her thick lashes were dark against her pale cheeks. Her baggy sweats didn't disguise her lithe curves. Or the fact that she wasn't wearing a bra. Now, why did he have to notice that?

Luminous gray eyes met his warily. "There's fresh coffee."

"Thanks." He pulled off his gloves and stuffed them into the pocket of his sheepskin coat before shrugging out of it and hanging it on the coatrack behind the door.

She moved to stand in the doorway to the kitchen and he tried not to notice the lean muscle of her beneath the sweats, the sexy certainty of her walk. She gestured toward the couch. "Have a seat. I'll be right back."

He tossed his file onto the coffee table. Sinking down into one corner of the sofa, he leaned forward and braced his elbows on his knees. A fire burned cozily in the fireplace and warmth slowly edged toward him. He wasn't going to think about how appealingly sleepy she'd looked. Or let himself remember how her bare skin would feel against his, how her full breasts would fill his hands. An ache started down low and he squinted into the fire. No, he wasn't going to remember any of that.

"Here you go." A steaming cup of coffee appeared and he took it, warming his hands on the ceramic.

She passed in front of him and stopped at the corner of the coffee table. "Well?"

"It was our guy. The same ligature marks on her neck. No weapon at the scene." He pulled out the Polaroid he'd taken at the victim's home.

Dallas stared at the woman's young, pretty face and shook her head. "All the other murders were twelve to thirteen days apart. This time, it's only been seven."

Sam sipped at his coffee, trying to ignore the scent of her, trying not to wonder if she had on *anything* under those sweats. *The case, Garrett. The case.*

The frustration that had been seething through him since he'd gotten the call snapped. "Dammit, this shouldn't have happened."

"Sam, it's not your fault. We've been working double time trying to find some connection. How could you know this guy would strike so soon after the last one?"

"We should've anticipated him. Serial killers usually accelerate a little with each murder. The rush doesn't last as long. We should've thought of this."

"Even if we had, we couldn't have stopped it. His pattern has held until now. Besides, we can't predict how often he'll need that rush. And we don't even know if this one tonight ties in with the other victims."

"I saw some CDs at her place—George Strait, Alan Jackson, Reba McEntire. I think we've got a link."

"Shoot. I was hoping…"

"Yeah." Sam thought she looked as sick as he felt. He

tapped the photo he held. "Leslie Finch. She's only twenty-two. This sucks."

Dallas shifted, her lean, curvy shadow merging with the firelight on the floor. Sam glanced up, his gaze roaming across her breasts. He wanted to slide his hand under that shirt and feel the velvet of her flesh against his palm. He nearly groaned and with effort, forced his gaze to the steaming liquid he held.

"That gives us a place to start," she said softly, staring into the fire. "Later today, we can start hitting the bars, see if anyone recognizes her."

"Yeah." He glanced at his watch. "I'll need to go in and make a report on this latest one."

"I can make phone calls while you do that."

Sam nodded, wondering why he noticed every little thing about her. Faint crease lines ran along one cheek, attesting to the fact that she'd been asleep, but her eyes were bright, alert. A vitality flowed from her, even this early in the morning. She was saying something about nailing the guy, her voice fierce, teasing his nerve endings like flame.

"Let's see what we have." She eased down on the sofa beside him, placing her notebook beside his on the table and sitting an arm's length away.

He reached for his file as Carrie walked into the room dressed in jeans and a formfitting black sweater. Her hair, shiny and fresh looking, hung in a dark cloud around her shoulders. She smelled of delicate soap. "Morning."

"Hi, Carrie." Sam waved, then looked back at his file. He found it odd that he didn't experience the stirring in his blood or the interest he usually felt when he saw a beautiful woman, especially one as beautiful as Carrie. Of course, he did have a serial killer on the loose. He pulled out the pictures of all the victims, the bars, their homes.

He felt Dallas watching him, and when he looked up, she smiled curiously. His muscles tightened.

She took another sip of coffee. "So, we need to look at what kind of people hang around the bars?"

"We've checked employees. Nothing there."

"How about delivery people?"

"Yes." Sam pulled out his pen. "Beer, chips—"

"Ice."

He nodded, scribbling.

"These people would be on a regular schedule, right?"

"But would it be every two weeks?"

"He's changed that now," Dallas reminded.

"Maybe I shouldn't interrupt," Carrie said softly from the doorway where she stood putting on her coat. "But what about someone who has a job like mine?"

"You mean a flight attendant?" Dallas turned.

Her friend shrugged. "Or someone who's out of town at regular intervals."

"You mean like salesmen." Sam straightened, his gaze sharpening on Carrie.

"Or truck drivers," Dallas added.

Sam nodded, anticipation pumping through him as he made more notes. "Excellent idea, Carrie."

She smiled. "I hope it helps." She glanced at Dallas. "I'm going to the grocery store, then to do some other errands. I'll be back later. Good luck."

Dallas nodded.

Carrie walked out, leaving them alone. Suddenly Sam was aware of the solitude, the fresh pine aroma of the tree, the body-warmed scent of Dallas. He shifted on the couch, searching for a more comfortable position, forcing his attention to the file.

Dallas shifted beside him, reaching over to study the crime-scene photos spread out on the table. "What do they have in common? They all liked country-western music. They were all seen in a bar the night they died. Everything goes back to the bars," she mused. "But none of them have been at the same one."

"Maybe we'll get lucky with this one," Sam said grimly.

She glanced at him, firelight brushing one side of her face. "Is it the bar or the music?"

He shook his head, watching her carefully. She had beautiful skin, creamy and smooth and soft. Perfect lips—not too full, not too thin; determined, tempting.

"Did every bar have a live band? Maybe the same band played at these bars. Maybe that's the link."

"You're right." Mentally shaking himself, he turned his attention back to the case. "It all comes back to these bars, but what's the connection? Is it that the killer likes certain bars? The women who frequent certain bars? The music? Hell, it could be the peanuts, for all we know." Frustrated, Sam raked a hand through his hair, wishing he weren't so conscious of the woman beside him.

Again his gaze shifted to her long lean legs in the gray sweatpants, the white socks she wore, her rumpled hair. The whole picture made her look endearing. Deception if he'd ever seen it. She was danger with a capital *D*.

They tossed around ideas as to what might stimulate the killer—hair color, body type, age. But none of the victims shared any of those traits. Dallas explored theories related to the calendar, to the holidays. He heard everything she said. He even nodded a couple of times or pointed out a problem. And he continued to stare at her as if he'd never seen a woman before.

Annoyed with himself, he forced his attention back to the file, thumbing through the photographs until he came to a particular photo. "We need to look at the first homicide again. That's the key to the killer. Why her? What made him start?"

"Also, back to the kinds of people who might visit bars regularly..." She paused, then snapped her fingers. "What about repairmen?"

"They would work during the day unless it was an emergency."

"They could come back at night."

He shrugged. ''We can check and see if any of these bars needed repairs.''

''They'll open around eleven or twelve today for the lunch crowd. I can start making calls. Maybe some of them also use the same distributor or the same driver. I'll check that when I check out the delivery schedules.''

''Good.'' He slid a picture across to her. ''We've got outdoor pictures of all the bars. Let's try to find something they have in common.''

For long moments, there was only the pop of the fire, the slide of papers across the table. The scent of coffee hung rich in the air, mingled with the tree's outdoorsy smell. Dallas sat only inches away; he could feel her heat, the energy radiating from her. He stayed focused. Together they pored over the photos, searching, scrutinizing.

''We're missing something,'' Sam said. ''We've got to go back to square one.'' He pulled out the picture of the bar where the first victim, Hilary Poole, had been seen the night she died.

In the daylight, the building that housed Calhoun's looked weathered, its red sign chipped and peeling. Part of the parking lot showed in the frame. To the left of the building lay a piece of the interstate and in the background a truck stop. Neither Sam nor Dallas found anything on the building's facade that showed on any of the others. None of the parking lots were similar.

''Wait a minute.'' Dallas sounded breathless, excitement trembling in her voice.

Involuntarily Sam's groin tightened and he cursed silently.

''Truck drivers.'' She fanned through the photographs, snatching up one, then another. ''Look, look.''

She picked them all up, her hand brushing his knee. He saw her jerk, saw her hand tremble, but she continued. She looked at one picture, then passed it to him as she looked at the next. ''There's a truck stop near all these bars.''

Sam took the picture from her, ignoring the flash of heat as

It's fun, and we're giving away **FREE GIFTS** to all players!

PLAY ROULETTE!

Scratch the silver to see where the ball has landed—7 RED or 11 BLACK makes you eligible for TWO FREE romance novels!

PLAY TWENTY-ONE!

Scratch the silver to reveal a winning hand! Congratulations, you have Twenty-One. Return this card promptly and you'll receive a fabulous free mystery gift, along with your free books!

YES!

Please send me all the free Silhouette Intimate Moments® books and the gift for which I qualify! I understand that I am under no obligation to purchase any books, as explained on the back of this card.

Name (please print clearly)

Address   Apt.#

City   State   Zip

Offer limited to one per household and not valid to current Silhouette Intimate Moments® subscribers. All orders subject to approval.   PRINTED IN U.S.A.

(U-SIL-IM-12/98)   **245 SDL CKFM**

The Silhouette Reader Service™ — Here's how it works:

Accepting free books places you under no obligation to buy anything. You may keep the books and gift and return the shipping statement marked "cancel." If you do not cancel, about a month later we'll send you 6 additional novels and bill you just $3.57 each, plus 25¢ delivery per book and applicable sales tax, if any.* That's the complete price — and compared to cover prices of $4.25 each — quite a bargain! You may cancel at any time, but if you choose to continue, every month we'll send you 6 more books, which you may either purchase at the discount price...or return to us and cancel your subscription.

*Terms and prices subject to change without notice. Sales tax applicable in N.Y.

If offer card is missing write to: Silhouette Reader Service, 3010 Walden Ave., P.O. Box 1867, Buffalo, NY 14240-9952

BUSINESS REPLY MAIL
FIRST-CLASS MAIL PERMIT NO 717 BUFFALO NY

POSTAGE WILL BE PAID BY ADDRESSEE

SILHOUETTE READER SERVICE
3010 WALDEN AVE
PO BOX 1867
BUFFALO NY 14240-9952

NO POSTAGE
NECESSARY
IF MAILED
IN THE
UNITED STATES

their fingers touched. "You're right." Anticipation hummed through him. "We might have something here."

"A truck driver might have a schedule that would fit with the pattern."

"Except for last night."

Dallas shrugged. "Maybe he's gotten some time off. For Christmas or something."

"Could be." He grinned at her discovery, excited that they finally might have found something. "That was good, Dallas. Damn good."

"Don't act so surprised." She smiled and wrinkled her nose at him, in that old, teasing way she used to.

And it sent a knife-edged pain through his chest. "I wish Rock and I worked this well together. You and I make a good team."

He wished he could stop thinking about what else they'd do great together. "I'll be back this afternoon and we can hit the bars, see if anyone can ID last night's victim."

She nodded, her eyes bright with excitement. "We're getting somewhere, Sam."

"Yeah." He gathered up the photos and his notes, shoved them all back into his file.

She looked…eager. He understood the anticipation she felt, the exhilaration of maybe finally getting a break. He knew what it meant to her to find this killer. And yet he couldn't help wishing that she were here for a totally different reason.

Feeling a tightness in his chest, he rose. So did she. His gaze scooted over her and this time she followed it to her breasts.

She sucked in a quick breath. One arm went around her waist protectively, flattening her shirt against her. Through the fabric, he could see the faint outline of her nipples—rigid, pushing against the knit. He swallowed hard.

His gaze moved to hers and for a moment, she stared at him. Hunger flickered in her eyes, then uncertainty. She looked away.

So did he, staring blankly into his coffee cup, quashing the need that hooked into him with razor-sharp talons. "I'll get going."

Dallas turned quickly and walked into the kitchen. But he saw the flush on her neck and knew from experience that her breasts were turning that same delicate rose. Hell! He walked into the kitchen behind her.

She stood at the counter, pouring another cup of coffee, and he leaned toward the sink, careful to set his mug inside without touching her.

She twitched nervously, her hands gripping the edge of the sink. "I'll make those calls."

"I'll file my report." He stood there, ordering himself to move, but was entranced by the rapid flutter of her pulse in her throat, the dark sweep of her lashes, the softly sculptured jaw.

He had to get out of here or he was going to ignore every ounce of common sense he had and shove her against the wall, pump into her with all the frustration and knife-edged desire crashing through him.

He'd fantasized for months about her trying to seduce him and him rejecting her. Now he didn't want to reject her. He just wanted. Being with Dallas would solve nothing. In fact, it would screw up a whole lot. His mind knew it without a doubt, but that didn't stop his body from going hard at the memory of last night's kiss; didn't stop him from wanting another one. And more.

He cleared his throat and pivoted, walking out of the kitchen and grabbing up his coat from the chair in the living room.

She followed slowly, halting a safe distance away in the doorway of the other room, watching him with that old guardedness in her eyes.

He hated that. He was tired of the walls between them; of the past, the regrets. She was getting to him, no doubt about it. He wanted some peace; he just wasn't sure how to get it.

Lifting a hand in farewell, he moved to the door, then

paused. He looked over his shoulder and his gaze met hers. "I'm glad you stayed."

Surprise chased across her face and her mouth curved in a pleased smile.

"See ya later." He grinned and felt a warmth spread through him even as he stepped into the winter air.

Chapter 9

"We've got a suspect." Later that night, Sam's excitement mirrored her own as they walked out of Bubba's, the last bar of their sweep. Not only had the bartender remembered last night's victim, Leslie Finch, but he'd also given them their first real lead on the killer. "We've *finally* got a suspect. We're gonna nail this SOB, Dallas."

Unexpectedly, he grabbed her hand and twirled her.

She laughed, anticipation speeding through her. "White male, five foot eleven, about one hundred sixty pounds, brown hair. No beard, no mustache—at least last night."

"Tattoo on his right hand. Paying with a hundred will make any bartender remember you. That's gonna help." As Sam lightly hooked an arm around her waist, his other hand grasped hers and he shuffled her in a backward two-step. "And a small-link chain holding his wallet to his belt loop. Yee-haw!"

He was laughing in earnest now, when Dallas's hip gently bumped his as he boot-scooted toward her. Immediately his smile faded. So did hers. Need quivered through her.

His hands fell away from her. Sidestepping her neatly, he

walked across the parking lot toward his truck, shoving his hands into the pockets of his coat. Swallowing her inexplicable disappointment, Dallas picked up her pace to match his.

Clouds obscured the moon and flood lamps shot a ghostly yellow light into the darkness. The chill night air was dense and still. Their footsteps clicked on the pavement.

"It's too late now," Sam said, "but first thing in the morning, I'll run this guy through Crime Analysis. See if we can find any Field Interview cards on him."

Dallas nodded. "Several people in the bar knew this girl, Leslie. Someone saw him. We just have to find out who."

He opened the passenger-side door and stepped away, with no hint of the earlier sparkle in his eyes. "You did a great job in there interviewing people while I spoke to the bartender. Dinky Malone. What a name, huh?"

She climbed inside, closed her door and leaned across to unlock his as he walked around. "I talked to one woman who knew Leslie Finch was a regular here," she said as Sam slid inside. "She confirmed that Leslie was with a brown-haired guy at the bar, but she never saw his face, only his back."

"The bartender said she picked up guys every once in a while—not on a regular basis." Sam started the truck, then pulled off his gloves and dropped them onto the seat between him and Dallas. "Too bad she couldn't have picked someone different."

Dallas's sadness over the woman's murder was equaled by the growing anger she had at the psycho who'd killed her. None of their earlier hunches about distributors, drivers or repairmen had panned out. She flipped open her notebook and leaned closer to the window, using light from the parking lot to read. "I think we spoke to all the regulars."

"Yeah, and tomorrow we'll canvas the victim's neighborhood. I'll take one side of the street, you take the other."

She nodded, snapping her notebook shut and scanning the parking lot. Her nerves were on fire with anticipation. She felt more alive than she had since...well, since that kiss with Sam.

She ducked the memory, her gaze coming to rest on a sign across the highway. Her eyes widened. "Look, Sam! There's a truck stop, just like by the other bars."

He followed the direction of her gaze, then opened his door, stepped out and snapped a Polaroid. Cold air swirled in his wake and he quickly got back inside. "These truck stops keep turning up. What do they mean?"

Dallas shook her head. "But we'll find out."

"Yeah, and we've got to do it before this slimeball kills again." Sam's voice was tense and fatigued, but underscored with steely determination. And there was a new buoyancy there, a hope. "Oh!" He snapped his fingers, picking up his cell phone. "I'd better call Lieutenant Roberts." He punched in the number, then settled back against the seat. "Hey, boss."

As Sam told his lieutenant what they'd found, Dallas looked out the window, a nervous excitement riding her. Finally they were making progress. It wouldn't be long now before they found Valeria's killer. Before Dallas would have to leave.

Sam spoke quietly to his superior. A gradual heat spread through the truck as it idled. Out of the corner of her eye, she caught the flicker of lights and looked over to see a Christmas wreath on the bar's door come alive with a multicolored twinkle. Rubbing the knot in her right shoulder, she smiled as more lights came on, outlining the building's roof, where a miniature Santa appeared.

She studied the night. The whoosh of passing cars sounded around the deep timbre of Sam's voice. There was still no sign of the moon, and clouds splotched the sky like great ink blots.

He hung up. "The lieutenant says our secretary's got the flu now. I guess it's only a matter of time before I do."

"Maybe not. You've been away from most of the ones who've come down sick," Dallas murmured, her gaze riveted on the Christmas lights. They pulsed with blurry cheer. Welcoming, homey, reminding her of the times when she used to decorate for the holidays. She hadn't done it since Brad's death.

''Holidays are hard.'' Sam spoke quietly beside her, startling her.

She glanced over, saw him staring pensively over her shoulder. They had to be hard on him, too. She nodded as an ache bloomed in her chest. ''Last year was worse.''

''Yeah.'' He rubbed his face. ''Seems like I miss him more on holidays. Do you?''

Did she? It sometimes seemed she missed Brad so deep inside that she couldn't tell one day from another. When she spoke, her voice was rusty, hoarse. ''It's usually the little things, like not talking to him across our morning coffee or not having to hunt down the toothpaste cap.'' She gave a short laugh. ''Stupid, huh?''

For a long time he didn't speak, just stared hard out the window as if he hadn't even heard her. Then his gaze swerved to hers, agonized, compassionate, understanding. ''I don't think it's stupid at all. Sometimes, just reaching into my locker at work makes me think of him. Sometimes when I hear the click of a gun, I think of him. And sometimes—'' He broke off, his jaw suddenly clenching. ''Sometimes, just the empty space at my back makes me think of him.''

Tears burned Dallas's eyes. ''Yeah,'' she whispered, looking quickly out the window.

''Do you ever regret not having children?''

She winced. As usual, Sam could pierce straight to the heart of her. It didn't matter if it was guilt over the night they'd spent together or something she'd never even talked about like this.

''Sorry. I'm an idiot—''

''It's all right.'' She smiled, though she felt like crying. ''He wanted kids. He probably told you that.''

''He mentioned it.''

''I didn't want them. I wasn't ready. I told him we'd talk about it in another year. Then another. But we didn't.'' Her voice faded to a whisper. ''We won't.''

Sam's hand fisted on his thigh. She wished he would touch

her. "It wasn't that I thought he might be killed on duty or anything like that. I simply didn't want children. Why wouldn't—" Her voice cracked. "Why wouldn't I want his children?"

"Hey," Sam said softly, his hand covering hers. "He didn't blame you."

Dallas stared down at Sam's big hand over hers. His fingers were cold, but she could feel the warming of his palm through her glove. "I know what it feels like to fail him, Sam," she said fiercely. "You never did. Not when he was alive. And not when he died."

Sam stiffened, but she tightened her hand in his, her gaze searching his blue eyes. "*You* didn't. It was me. I failed him. I failed Valeria. I ran when I'd never run from anything in my life. I think he was always disappointed in me because we never had children."

"He never told me he was anxious about kids. And he never said anything about being disappointed in you. How could he be?"

Sam looked genuinely puzzled. She searched his face, aching to believe him; reading the sincerity, the surprised compassion in his eyes. "I've felt guilty about that ever since he died. I could've given him a part of us. I could've had a part of him now."

"Yeah, well, maybe that's why you have me. I'm like your psychic link." As soon as he breezily said the words, an awkward tension filled the air.

He added quickly, hoarsely, "You were right. Not to have kids, I mean. Things happen for a reason. It's best the two of you didn't have children. You spared a child the horrible grief of losing a parent. You have to look at it that way."

"I didn't do it out of any noble motive," she said with self-derision.

"It doesn't matter. What matters is that he didn't blame you, Dallas. He never once said anything about you not wanting kids, just that it wasn't time yet."

"Really?"

Hope lit her eyes and Sam's chest constricted. How easy it had been to give her this. He nodded, gently disengaging his hand from hers. "Really." He gave a short laugh. "Brad would shoot both of us if he heard this conversation. You know his motto, 'Say you're sorry and—'"

"'Move on,'" Dallas quoted, her hand itching to retake Sam's.

For one brief instant, she wondered if in some weird cosmic way, Brad had left Sam to her. If so, she'd ruined things. Once upon a time, she might have believed that Brad was the only source of the connection she felt with Sam. But things were different now.

There was something else there; something independent of her husband, his partner. "Sam, I want you to know…" She faltered, trying to gather the courage to say what it was time to say; to build a bridge. "What I feel for you has nothing to do with Brad. It's true we became friends because of him, but we have our own history now."

"Yeah. For good or bad." The pain in his voice tore at her.

She wondered if she'd regret this later, but for now she was compelled to reach out and curl her hand around his forearm. He looked at her, surprised and wary. "It's not all bad, is it?"

His gaze held hers for a long moment. Indecision, regret and pain flashed across his face.

Her chest tightened and she started to withdraw.

"No, Dallas." His other hand moved to cover hers and squeezed tightly. "It's not all bad."

She looked at him, reading the same questions in his eyes that she felt. Could it be more? Could they build past the guilt, the grief? Suddenly she wanted him to kiss her. Wanted his hands on her, his body against hers.

Startled by the rush of desire she felt, she dragged her gaze from his and looked out the window. She had a lot of regrets about the past year and a half, but Sam was the worst. She rubbed at a new knot in her shoulder. "I know now how badly I hurt you."

"Okay, let's don't go there." He reached for the gearshift, ready to pull out.

She grabbed his wrist. "Just hear me out. Please," she entreated softly when he looked about to refuse.

He looked mutinous, his jaw rock-hard, his eyes glittering in the darkness like obsidian. Finally she felt him relax a little, and she pulled her hand away.

She wanted to stare out the window, study her hands, look anywhere but at him. However, she forced herself to meet his gaze. Dubious, resentful, rigid, he studied her. She licked her lips. "I didn't realize until last night how very deeply I did hurt you. I never meant to. And I want to apologize."

The truck hummed. Sam stared, his expression inscrutable and hard. Their breath fogged the windows and a chill wrapped around Dallas's ankles. Still she watched him, her chest tight, waiting, hoping for something. Even a rejection.

His voice was harsh and choppy when he spoke, as if he couldn't quite breathe. "You didn't *mean* to hurt me?" he asked, incredulous.

She barely kept from flinching at the ruthlessness in his voice, the rage.

"I'd say you did," he accused. "You had plenty of opportunity to tell me something—anything—about that transfer."

"I told you, both you and Brad, months before that I'd been offered the transfer. But I didn't think about taking it until after...Brad died."

"Was it then, Dallas?" Sam braced one arm along the back of the seat, his fingers digging into the upholstery as he leaned toward her, intense, compelling. "Or was it after the night you and I were together? Weren't you running from that? If you're going to apologize, at least tell the truth."

"I am!"

"Really?" He gave her a skeptical look. "I'm not just talking about your plans to leave. I'm talking about when I asked you—when we— You know what I'm talking about.'' He glanced away.

"That was wrong of me, too, Sam. That's what I'm saying. I'm apologizing for that, for all of it. Can't you forgive me? Can't we be friends again?''

He stared at her for a long moment, his breath ragged, his eyes shooting fire. His arm fell to his lap and he exhaled loudly, his head dropping back. "I don't know.''

"Can't you try?''

His gaze, fierce and hot, shot to hers and his voice dropped to a low crispness. "You ripped my heart out. I thought we were at least friends. Despite what happened between us, I never would've believed you could treat me like a... Leave without telling me.''

She was certain he'd been ready to say something else, something about the night they'd spent together. "I handled everything wrong. You, Brad, Valeria. But I need to know that you're my friend, Sam. These past eighteen months have been hell. Something would happen to remind me of Brad and I couldn't call you. I've never felt so alone. I need to know that you're there.''

For a long moment, there was only the sound of their breathing, the near-silent vibration of the engine. "I guess I need to know that about you, too,'' he said gruffly.

Her eyes widened in surprise. "I want that,'' she said a little breathlessly. "I'm willing to give it a try.''

He studied the windshield, his profile hard, carved in lamp-light and shadow. "It's Christmas. I should say it's all for-given, shouldn't I?''

The hurt gouged deep at that. "Only when you're ready,'' she said stiffly. "If you ever are.''

"I don't know if I can ever trust you again.''

Her breath whooshed out.

"And I'm not talking about working together on this in-vestigation. Things aren't the same between us and I don't know if they ever will be." He shoved a hand through his hair, his voice thick with frustration.

"Do you think you can accept my apology? Can we start with that? Can you…forgive me?"

"I don't know." He wanted to, wanted to forget it had ever happened, but he would never forget the way she'd looked through him, the way she hadn't been able to answer him when he'd asked her whom she'd been making love with. "I won't let you walk all over me again. I won't let you use me again."

"I'm not using you, Sam. And I wasn't then, either."

"I think we both agree that we turned to each other for comfort," he said dryly, passing a hand over his chin.

She'd told herself that for the past year and a half, but now she wondered if it might have been more. She cared for Sam and she had then, or she wouldn't have made love with him, no matter how desperately she'd wanted to be held or comforted. "I don't want to use you. I want to be friends again. That's all."

He turned his head, staring at her for a long moment, his gaze probing and sharp. "Is it that simple?"

"Maybe," she whispered, desperately needing to believe it was. "Well?"

Sam studied her, swamped by conflicting emotions. This tangled mess between them intrigued him, aroused him, but he didn't know if he could risk getting involved with her again. He didn't want to give her another chance to hurt him. And he didn't want to give her a chance to prove she wouldn't.

Yes, they could have great sex, but for the first time in his life Sam wanted something more, something *else*. What, he didn't know. He just knew he was ready to fill up this emptiness inside him, ready to thaw out the cold hard place behind his heart that she'd left behind. Pure instinct guided him and he stuck out his hand. "All right. Friends."

"Friends." She smiled and put her gloved hand in his. Warmth fused their palms and Dallas ignored the sharp kick of desire in her belly, refused to look at his lips the way she wanted to. This was a start. They both needed this. And maybe they could build on it.

Friends. The next day, Sam was still mulling it over even though he knew it was the best thing. It was what he wanted, too. She'd talked about how hard the past eighteen months had been for her. Well, they'd been hell on him, too. He'd missed her as much as she'd missed him.

Even though he hadn't told her, he couldn't count the times something had happened and he'd wanted to call her. He wanted to forget all the nights he'd woken up, wishing she were in his bed. She hadn't been there—not for any of it. And now she *was* here, and that was a problem.

He knew he didn't want to get involved with her again. So, why couldn't he stop *thinking about* getting physically involved with her again?

Gritting his teeth, he thanked the older gentleman he'd been speaking with—the last of his interviewees—and walked down the man's front-porch steps. Just as planned, Dallas worked one side of Leslie Finch's neighborhood while he worked the other.

The sun was out for the first time in a few days and, though cold, the sky was a clear pale blue with white fluffy clouds. He waited for Dallas in his truck, where she joined him a few minutes later. He tried not to notice the way she strode purposefully toward him, her hips rolling slightly, enticingly. Or the way the sunlight turned her hair to polished gold. But his efforts, like they had been for the last eight days, were futile.

The information they'd gotten on Leslie from her neighbors was similar to what they'd gotten on the other victims. She liked country music, country-western dancing and the bars. As Sam and Dallas drove out of her neighborhood in the Village, a small annex of Oklahoma City, his cell phone shrilled. It was Crime Analysis telling him they'd pulled several FI cards matching his parameters of a Caucasian male with brown hair and a right-hand tattoo.

"I'll swing by and pick up what you have," he told the woman on the phone, then hung up and glanced at Dallas. "We've got somewhere to start."

"Good." She frowned down at her notebook, scribbled something and nodded.

As he drove south on Penn toward the highway, he mentally sorted through aspects of the case. The whole time, he was aware of the way Dallas chewed on the tip of her pen and tapped her thumb against her thigh, haunted by the spicy scent of her. Awareness coiled low in his belly, but he forced his mind to stay focused on the investigation.

Maybe he and Dallas were both kidding themselves. Maybe nothing could be saved from their old friendship. Maybe he'd be better off just to tell her to stay the hell away from him, shove this friendship thing.

But he couldn't do it—not only because of the glimmer of peace he'd gotten—the sense that he was finally moving on with his life—but also because she'd surprised him last night. He'd known that she had postponed having kids with Brad but Sam had never known about her unwillingness to have kids with her husband. It was only after her confession that Sam had realized for the first time why he felt so tied to her. Why he always would.

They shared a past. They shared a secret both of them would like to forget. And they both felt they'd failed Brad.

Sam still couldn't get over it. He hated that she was beating herself up over not having had children with Brad. His efforts to convince her otherwise had been useless. He'd wanted to do more than hold her hand, but he hadn't. At least he'd done that right. Still, he hadn't felt this helpless since the day she'd walked out of his life.

He shot a look at her, studying the clean profile, the little furrow in her brow, the intense concentration on her face. He didn't view her desire not to have children as a failure. He wished she could see it that way. Of course, she didn't see his part in Brad's death as a failure, either.

He was starting to think there might be a lot of things about her he didn't know. Oh, he knew she loved coffee, especially French vanilla. He knew both she and her brother had been named for cities in her mother's native Texas. He knew running had been her passion for years and she'd finished in good time in the Boston marathon the year before Brad had died. Judging from the lean muscle of her legs, she still ran. He knew she collected pictures of city skylines. But he didn't know the deepest part of her—the secrets, the wishes, the disappointments she hid, just as he did.

She shifted slightly, drawing his attention again. She alternately looked out the window and scribbled in her notebook.

Her guilt over not giving Brad a child had hit Sam like a blow. He'd never thought of Dallas as anything other than driven and focused; sentimental only about Brad and her family. But he'd been wrong. Beneath the guilt, there was a soft core in her, a vulnerability that intrigued him, roused all his protective instincts.

It had taken a long time, but he was starting to see cracks in her cool, unflinching facade. Now he could recognize the flicker in her eyes as anger or exasperation or arousal. He knew the way she clenched her jaw when she was annoyed. Knew she carried her tension in her shoulders, especially her right one. And her face could be a smooth mask, but those gray eyes would smolder. "Still waters," his mom would say.

Unease scooted through him at this nagging awareness of her. But hey, friends noticed things, right? They just didn't act on them. If he had a simmering tension inside him, that was his problem. He knew the score. He still felt the hunger, probably always would, but it was time to move on. He wasn't going back.

No matter how badly he wanted to peel those clothes away and feel the weight of her velvety breasts in his hands, taste the silky heat of her, stroke the lush curves of her body.

Murder, he told himself as he thumbed a bead of sweat from his upper lip. Think murder.

Sam was going south on Broadway Extension, headed for the station, when his phone rang again.

Lieutenant Roberts barked into his ear, "Got a call from Bubba's Bar. One of the regulars remembered something they wanted to tell you."

"Great. What's up?"

"Get your butt in here and bring your partner with you."

"Rock's in the hospital," Sam reminded without thinking, taking his exit.

"Not him," Roberts said. "Dallas."

Sam bumped against the curb, earning a sharp look from Dallas. He quickly straightened the vehicle and slowed to a stop at the light. "Uh."

"Seems your caller wanted to speak to the nice lady detective with the 'cool' name."

"Yes, sir. We'll be right there." Sam turned off the phone, shooting a wary look at Dallas.

She stiffened, concern flashing across her features. "What?"

"We're busted."

"Just what is going on here?"

Fifteen minutes later, Sam and Dallas stood side by side in the lieutenant's small second-floor office. Filing cabinets crowded one wall of the boxy room. A single window behind Roberts's desk overlooked the street below. The door was closed. The double rows of desks in the squad room sat empty, as did the secretary's chair, which explained why the lieutenant had taken the phone call from Bubba's Bar in the first place.

Roberts gave Sam a long, measuring look, then did the same to Dallas. Sam fought the urge to squirm. Finally his lieutenant spoke. "Are the feds involved in this?"

"No, sir."

"Did the marshals come to us for information?"

"No, sir." Sam swallowed, clenching his fists.

"Since when do we open up our cases?"

"We don't, sir—"

"Well?" the lieutenant roared. Hard, dark eyes snapped in his florid face. "Is this your way of keeping the marshals informed, as I asked you?"

Sam couldn't remember ever seeing his boss so agitated.

"Sir, it's not Detective Garrett's fault," Dallas interjected.

"Oh?" Roberts eased down on one corner of his desk, crossed his ankles and folded his arms. "And why not? It's his case."

She glanced at Sam, who frowned. *Let me handle this.* He knew she got the message. He just hoped she would back off.

She offered a weak smile and Sam took over. "Kittridge has been helping me."

"On the whole case?"

"Well...yes, sir."

Roberts gestured impatiently. "Get to it, Garrett."

"The third victim, Audrey Hayes, was actually a protected witness by the name of Valeria Luciano."

"Yes, I saw that in the file. I do know how to read." His gaze sliced to Dallas. "Why are you down here, Kittridge? I'd heard you moved."

"Yes, sir, I did, but—"

"But this is *your* protected witness."

She nodded.

"Marshals have no jurisdiction in murder cases."

"No, sir."

"Well?"

She shifted imperceptibly, looking uneasy, but meeting the older man's gaze. "Long story, sir, but I feel responsible."

He leveled a measuring look at her. "That sounds like one for a shrink. I'll take your word for it." He turned to Sam. "Tell me none of these other victims are protected witnesses."

"They're not."

"And we're sure there's no Mob connection here?"

"Yes, sir," Dallas said. "It's a serial killer. Not a hit."

The lieutenant cleared his throat, looked pointedly at Sam. "Where do you stand?"

"We've just canvassed the neighborhood of last night's victim. Nothing new or surprising there. Crime Analysis ran our suspect through and I was on my way upstairs to pick up the hits. And maybe you've got something?"

"Someone saw the victim and the suspect walking toward a truck stop—"

"Across the highway," Dallas interrupted excitedly.

Sam and his lieutenant both raised an eyebrow. Immediately she fell silent, smiling apologetically.

"That's right," Lieutenant Roberts growled.

Sam continued, "Now that we have this lead on the truck stop, we'll take some pictures by there. Find out if they recognize any of the hits we've pulled off the FI cards."

Roberts pinched the bridge of his nose. "There's no reason you can't cover that ground alone."

"It's a lot of ground, sir." Sam slid a sideways glance at Dallas, saw the anxiety pinching her features. He might not want to cuddle up with her—okay, he did, which was why he wouldn't—but he didn't want her to get kicked off the case, either. "I need Kittridge to help me, sir. Besides the extra brainpower, it's good to have a female perspective on this case. We've got to get this guy before he kills someone else. He caught us with our pants down again."

The older man scowled. "Don't try to sell me, Garrett. I know where our pants were."

"Yes, sir."

Dallas interjected. "I really can help, sir. It's possible this guy might be a truck driver. We're getting somewhere, we just don't have anything solid."

The lieutenant gave them both a hard-eyed look. "If I didn't have three fourths of my people out with the flu, this wouldn't be happening."

"Yes, sir," Dallas and Sam murmured in unison.

Sam itched to say something else in her defense, but he knew not to push his boss. It surprised even him how much he'd come to need her help on this case.

Roberts looked at Dallas. "I'm not going to call your chief, Dallas, as long as you stay low and play by *my* book."

"Yes, sir." Her voice was husky with pleasure.

Sam's body tightened in response. He told himself it was just the sense of victory, of closing in on the killer, of winning this particular battle with his boss.

"And I don't want to be getting a call from him, either."

"No, sir."

Roberts considered them both for another minute, then pinched the bridge of his nose again. "All right, you're a go. Keep it to yourselves. Now get out there and find me a killer."

"Thank you, sir." Sam opened the door and followed Dallas out.

She laughed softly as she passed him, looking pleased with herself. He couldn't stop an answering grin or the heat that sizzled through him. They made it about ten feet from the door.

"Kittridge!" the lieutenant bellowed.

She froze, exchanging a wary look with Sam. He shook his head.

She half turned to find Sam's boss standing in the doorway of his office. "Sir?"

"It's good to see you again," Roberts said gruffly and slammed the door.

She stared for a moment, a smile breaking over her face. She glanced at Sam and he chuckled.

She waited at the top of the stairs as he stopped off at Crime Analysis. A few minutes later, he returned, carrying a printout and the mug shots of several suspects that he'd pulled from Records. Excitement shone in her eyes, making them smoky and pulling at that ever-present awareness in his belly.

He tried to ignore it as they walked out, together. Adrenaline pumped through him. And he suddenly felt an ease with Dallas he hadn't experienced since before Brad's death. He chuckled. "That reminds me of the time Brad and I were called in. We'd just started Vice and we were so green. Our assignment was to observe these girls at the Red Dog Saloon. 'Blend in,' we were told, which meant order drinks, but don't drink them.''

"What happened?" Dallas's eyes sparkled and a smile tugged at the corners of her mouth.

Sam laughed. "Our lieutenant got a call from the bar owner, complaining that his potted plants were dying. We were—''

"Pouring your drinks into the plants.'' She chuckled softly. "Brad never told me that one.''

"Really? He probably didn't want you to think he was anything but perfect.''

"That was it.''

Was she hurt by the fact that Brad hadn't shared the story with her? Sam couldn't tell.

She nudged him with her shoulder, laughter warming her voice. "'A female perspective'?''

He grinned, relieved that she seemed fine. "Hey, I was working it back there.''

She threw back her head and laughed, a full-throated sound that made him join in, feeling as self-satisfied as if they'd gotten away with making out under the bleachers.

Bad analogy, he immediately thought, ambushed by vivid memories of the long, hot kiss they'd shared the other night. He shoved the memory away and slid into his truck.

Something had shifted—something he couldn't define even though he felt they were poised on the edge of something momentous. She'd tried to cover for him in there. They'd fought together *and* for each other. That fact had not escaped Sam. They were partners now; real partners. It felt good, better than it probably should. He liked Rock and got along great with the older man, but with Dallas, Sam felt his strengths as a detective were complemented by hers.

There were boundary lines between male and female partners, he reminded himself sternly. Lines he didn't cross. He had to know he could trust her at his back, no matter what. Sex between partners was not a good idea, no matter how good the cop. Or the sex, he added wryly.

It blurred the lines, confused the rules. It was the reason Sam had never gotten involved with female cops, and he wasn't about to change now. Besides, he and Dallas had a lot of history. It would be stupid to get all that stirred up. Very stupid.

Sam let the truck idle as he opened the file he'd gotten from Crime Analysis. "I didn't know Roberts knew you."

"Just a little. He came to Brad's funeral."

Sam nodded, feeling a keen empathy with her, connected by more than Brad this time, and noticing he didn't feel the sharp stab that his partner's name usually brought.

"What did Crime Analysis find?"

He dumped the photos out on the seat and discarded two from the top. "Both these guys are still in the pen at McAlester. This one—" he plucked a picture from the bottom "—is dead."

"That leaves us four." She picked up the printout, then a photo. "It doesn't say on here which hand his tattoo is on."

Sam leaned close, inhaling the crisp scent of winter on her, aware that she suddenly went stone still. "Hmm, he was stopped for a busted taillight in the winter. Sometimes the officers at the scene don't note specifics."

She nodded. A delicate flush pinkened her cheeks and her tongue darted out to moisten her lips as she pointed to another name. "It's the same with this one, too."

Desire punched through his gut. He dragged his gaze from her and stared, unseeing, at the card she held in her hand. "Yeah."

"What's next?" She gathered the pictures and cards, put them back into his file.

"Let's show these pictures at the truck stops." He cleared his throat, which felt scratchy. "See if that gets us anywhere."

"Okay. We can also see what kind of logs, if any, truckers keep. Maybe these stops keep a record of the cabs that stay overnight in their parking lot or stop there. Maybe credit-card receipts for gas or food?"

"Good ideas." He glanced at the clock on his dash. "I've got to be somewhere in a few hours. We can start with these truck stops, then I can meet up with you afterward."

"I'd hate for a murder investigation to interfere with your social life." Her voice was caustic. Immediately, regret flashed across her features and she shoved a hand through her hair. "I can make some calls while you're gone."

He laughed, irritated by the pleasure he'd felt at her obvious jealousy when she thought he had a date. He'd hoped to have moved past that. "My big date is with my folks."

"Oh, you still have dinner with them every Friday night?" Fondness laced her words.

"Yep, the whole family." He glanced over at the pleasure on Dallas's face, the wistfulness. "Mom's a stickler for it."

"That's nice. I've always liked your parents. How are they?"

"Doing great. Dad's getting in plenty of hunting now that he's retired. And Mom has been taking some classes at the university. She's into photography." He added, "Yeah, they like you, too."

"Brad and I always enjoyed it when we were included in your family's summer cookouts."

He glanced over at her and suddenly realized she had no one. Brad was dead. Her parents were in Texas, as was her law-enforcement brother, the ranger.

"How are those crazy brothers of yours? I heard Linc got married again."

"Mace and Devon got married, too. They have a baby girl now."

She started. "I thought they'd called off their engagement."

''They did.'' He grinned and explained how Devon had walked away from Mace out of fear for his job, only to wind up needing his protection a year later when her father's murderers came after her.

''And now?''

''She testified against the scum who masterminded the whole deal and sent him to prison. She and Mace are together and I've got my first niece, hopefully not the last.''

''They're happy.'' She looked genuinely pleased.

''More than anyone has a right to be. Both Mace and Linc married way better than they deserve. You'd like Jenna, too. She's Linc's wife—a veterinarian.''

''You always said your brothers were animals.''

He chuckled. ''Linc saved her from a stalker. Actually, Mom and Dad say that Jenna saved Linc from himself.''

''Oh?''

''After Michelle left him, he wasn't much good to anyone. At least until Jenna came along.'' Sam went on to explain how his middle brother had sheltered the veterinarian from a stalker who was intent on killing her for her role in getting him convicted of rape.

''Wow,'' Dallas said quietly. ''Doesn't anyone in your family just meet someone, date them and get married?''

''Not so far.''

''Jenna sounds very special.''

''My brothers know how lucky they are and I think they've gotten the last good women. So does Dad.'' A swell of warmth moved through him as he spoke.

Devon and Mace had overcome their past mistakes and the hurt between them, and were now building a life together. For one blinding instant, he wished fiercely that he and Dallas could do the same, but he didn't see how that could happen. Besides the pain they'd caused each other, Dallas had another life in another state. Partners and friends were all they could be. All they *should* be.

They pulled into a truck stop and she opened the door to step out. "Tell them I said hello."

Something hit him hard in the chest. It was the holidays. She was all alone. An impulse swept through him. For the first time since she'd arrived, he didn't analyze his actions. "Tell them yourself."

She looked startled. "Oh. No, I didn't mean—"

"They'd love to see you. All of them have asked about you. Several times." She didn't need to know that he'd told his family to mind their own business.

"Really?"

He nodded. "We can play pool."

Her eyes lit up. "I haven't played since last summer."

"And—" he waggled his eyebrows "—Mom's making coconut cake."

Dallas groaned. "No fair. You know I can't turn that down."

"Then don't." He shrugged, as if it were simple. And for the moment, it was.

"What should I bring?"

"Nothing. You know how she is."

"She won't be expecting me."

"You know there'll be enough food for thirty people."

She smiled in agreement. "All right."

"We'll head there around five-thirty."

"Okay." Pleasure warmed her eyes.

As they walked up to the doors of the first truck stop on their list, Sam wondered what he had just done.

"Thanks." A beautiful soft smile curved her lips. "See, Sam, this is going to work. We can do this friends thing."

"Sure. Yeah." Despite the slow burn of desire through his blood, he felt for the first time that there was a chance they might salvage something from their past. "Now, let's get busy."

Friends. Yeah. He could do this.

Chapter 10

"Number nine, corner pocket." Dallas measured her shot, leaned over the pool table, slid the cue stick lightly between her index and third fingers and shot. The cue ball cracked its target and number nine disappeared into the corner pocket.

"Oh, man," Sam groaned. "Not again."

"You sank the last three shots." Mace chuckled.

"And won three games," Sam reminded dryly.

"How long did you say it had been since you played, Dallas?" Mace asked.

"A few months." She grinned, holding out one hand. "Pay up, boys."

Sam's oldest brother shook his head. "How about double or nothing?"

"You're going to owe me fifty bucks." She eyed him critically. "Are you good for it?"

He laughed. "Hey, I'm a cop. You can trust me."

"Ha!"

"Sam, what about you?" Dallas turned to where he stood at the back corner of the table. "You up for another game?"

''Sure,'' he answered easily, but she didn't miss the tightening of his mouth.

Mace racked up the balls for their fifth ''ring game'' or Nine Ball. Dallas had played well today, surprising even herself. In the second and third games she'd sunk the nine ball early. Sam and Mace had both protested, but they knew she'd followed the rules by using the lowest-numbered ball to knock in number nine.

She was trying not to analyze Sam's every move. They were getting somewhere, finally, and she wanted things to stay good between them. This case was still about Valeria, but it had also become about a second chance with Sam. A chance to try and repair the damage they'd done a year and a half ago. He'd defended her to Lieutenant Roberts. He wanted her help. She didn't want to blow that.

Because she and Brad had occasionally been guests of the Garretts, a part of Dallas dreaded the evening. But her unease had disappeared once she'd walked through the door. Sam's parents had greeted her warmly, making her feel as welcome as they always had. In his late fifties, Clif Garrett was still a very handsome man. Mace and Sam had both gotten their thick black hair from him. And those killer blue eyes. Linc favored Bonnie, with his sandy hair and quiet gray eyes.

She enjoyed the warm greeting both Sam's brothers had given her. It was great renewing her acquaintance with Mace's wife, Devon, and meeting Linc's wife, Jenna, for the first time. Judging from the total openness of their smiles, Dallas decided none of them were aware of what had happened between her and Sam before she'd left Oklahoma City.

Devon had hugged Dallas and whispered how good it was to see her. Mace and Devon's daughter, Ashley, was at Devon's mother's house, but Devon had pictures of the tiny dark-haired baby. Jenna Garrett, a pretty auburn-haired woman, seemed quieter—like Linc—but very warm.

When Sam's dad and Linc pulled on their coats to run an errand, Dallas had offered to help in the kitchen. But Sam's mother and the other two women had shooed her off into the game room with Sam and Mace to play pool, insisting she was their guest. She and Sam had stopped at a bakery on the way over where Dallas had chosen an apple pie. Of course, it couldn't hold a candle to anything Mrs. Garrett made, but Dallas felt better for making the effort.

Since she and Sam had moved into the game room with Mace, she'd felt the ease between them slowly evaporate. They'd worked at truck stops all afternoon, coming up with nothing yet from the pictures of the suspects. But she knew that wasn't the problem.

She wanted them to be friends. This was going to work. She would make it work.

The game room, converted from Linc's bedroom after all the boys had left home, was warm and comfortable. The oak wainscoting and billiard-patterned curtains gave it a cozy, casual feel, as did the oblong light fixture shaded with green glass that hung over the center of the pool table.

As Mace broke for the next game, Dallas slid a look at Sam. He stood in the back corner, where he'd been for the other four games, leaning on his cue stick as he carefully watched his brother's shot.

Both his large hands were wrapped around the sleek polished wood. Light shone on his thick dark hair, casting his chiseled features in a ruddy light. He wore the same tight faded jeans he'd worn all day, the same red corduroy shirt. The soft fabric hugged his broad shoulders, molded the hard edges of his biceps. He'd worn his coat all day, so she hadn't noticed before, but she noticed now. He looked good. Way too good.

"You with us here, Dallas?" Mace's voice pulled her back to the game. "I just missed the two ball."

The rules of Nine Ball stated the balls had to be sunk in numerical order. The nine ball could be sunk at any time in the game as long as the lowest-numbered ball hit and sank the nine. Since Mace had missed his shot, it was now hers.

She balanced her stick lightly in one hand and eyed the placement of balls on the table. The two ball was far right and the cue ball rested in the back corner by Sam. To make the shot she'd have to chip the edge of the ball, not take it straight.

Moving to the back corner, she smiled slightly at Sam. He smiled back, even if it did look forced, and he shifted, giving her room.

"You think you can make that?"

At the low rumble of his voice, a shiver chased up her spine, but she grinned at him over her shoulder. "Wanna lay some money on it?"

"I already owe you twenty."

His eyes sparkled and Dallas realized just how much she'd missed him in the past eighteen months.

"Show me what you got, Kittridge."

He meant absolutely nothing suggestive by that, Dallas told herself. Still, the huskiness in his voice released a flurry in her stomach and she had a difficult time tearing her gaze from his.

Feeling suddenly breathless, she turned her attention to the table and tried to ignore the musky hint of his body heat, the lingering whiff of his early-morning shower. She leaned forward, gauging her stroke. She could feel him behind her, not touching, but his warmth silhouetted her entire body. She could feel his strength, the power emanating from him.

For a moment, she stared unseeingly at the green felt tabletop. Her hands trembled slightly and sweat dampened her palms.

Friends, she reminded herself, focusing again on the ball. She took the shot, but her hands shook and she jerked back at the last minute. The force of her shot had been weak and she held her breath as the ball rolled slowly toward its target.

The cue ball wobbled into the two ball and nudged it into the pocket.

"Aaargh!" Mace groaned. "That shouldn't even have gone in. What kind of puny stroke was that?"

"The kind that works," Dallas said sweetly, moving around

the table to take her next shot. Her back felt cold without Sam's heat there, but she could concentrate better away from him.

The three shot was a tricky hook and she missed it just barely.

"Your turn, Ever Ready," Mace prodded.

Dallas glanced at Sam, her insides knotting. She'd forgotten about the nickname his brothers had given him. Brad had also called Sam that on occasion, telling her it was because Sam always traveled with at least two condoms in his wallet.

As Sam studied the lay of the balls, she studied him, annoyed that her knees felt weak and wobbly. Intent and focused, he quickly sized up the shot. Dallas's attempt had left the three ball wide-open and perched on the edge of a side pocket.

Sam made the shot easily, then frowned at the four, which was surrounded by a circle of balls.

"Think you could make that, Dallas?" Mace glanced over at her.

"It's a tough one," she conceded, mentally calculating how she would do it.

Sam looked up, challenge gleaming in his blue eyes. A thrill shot through her. She'd seen him pick shots like this out of a group before and it was beautiful to watch.

He walked toward her, smiling cockily, and her stomach fluttered. He edged between her and the table, his thighs brushing hers. Her smile slipped. He looked away, rubbed the chalk on the tip of his stick and tapped the butt on the floor while he considered his shot.

Only inches separated them and Dallas backed up as far as she could, unable to touch the wall because of the stick rack hanging behind her. If Sam had straightened, his arm would have brushed her breast.

A low throb drummed through her and she shifted, suddenly very aware of the thin camisole and panties she wore, the silky slide of her cranberry shirt over her chest and arms. She gripped her pool cue tighter and forced her attention to the table.

Sam leaned forward, his hip nudging hers. "Sorry," he muttered.

She didn't move. She couldn't. His hip was situated right at her leg and she knew how it would feel against her—warm, hard, heavy.

Liquid silk unfurled between her legs. She closed her eyes briefly, chanting to herself, *Friends…friends….* When she opened her eyes, Mace was staring at her, his eyes twinkling. She smiled, though it cost her, and tried to get a grip on her exploding hormones.

Sam didn't seem bothered by their closeness. Dallas wrapped her fingers tighter around her stick and released a shuddery breath.

He smiled at her over his shoulder and she smiled back, her throat dry, her heart racing. His gaze dropped to her lips and for an instant, she saw heat, response. Then he shifted, still close, and yet not close enough. "I always said this room was too small for a pool table."

Was his voice shaking? Or did she imagine that because she was?

He made the shot cleanly, sharply, betraying not one iota of the turmoil she'd glimpsed in his eyes. He punched a fist in the air. "Yes!"

Dallas smiled, knowing he'd have to move to the opposite end to sink the six ball. And she was glad of it. As he walked around the table, she rubbed her shoulder, which was suddenly one big aching knot.

Sam studied the table from the other side, his gaze hooded and avoiding hers.

Mace glanced at his watch. "We've just got enough time for this game before the food's ready. Finish Kittridge off, Sam."

Sam's gaze locked with hers. In the span of a heartbeat, she read frank hot interest before reserve slid in. "Hmm."

A slow heat suffused her veins. She shifted, clenching her fist tighter around her cue stick.

Mace's gaze skipped from her to Sam, turned speculative. Dallas licked her lips and fought to keep her features schooled.

Sam missed the next shot and Mace stepped up for his turn. She kept her gaze on Sam's brother and away from him. Mace sank the six ball with a fairly difficult shot and leaned forward to line up for his next one. He was going to try and bounce the seven off one corner and into the diagonal pocket.

Dallas felt Sam's gaze, but didn't look at him. Restless and unsettled, she absently stroked the long shaft of her stick. Sam made a choked sound beside her and she looked at him quickly.

"You all right?" Mace asked his brother, staring as if Sam had suddenly appeared in a dress.

A flush colored Sam's neck, but he nodded. "Sure."

He glanced at her, then at the stick. For a moment, their gazes met. She felt electricity arc between them. Despite the wariness in his eyes, she knew what he was thinking and her face heated.

He tore his gaze away and a muscle worked in his jaw.

Pursing her lips, she forced her attention back to Mace, though she couldn't ignore Sam. Anticipation fired her nerve endings, set off a flutter in her stomach. She quashed the feeling. Sam had made it perfectly clear there would only be friendship between them. And even that had been hard to come by.

They were good as friends, she told herself. They *should* be friends. Just friends.

Something about that chafed at her. More and more often, she found her gaze wandering to him. Memorizing the way faded denim gloved his strong legs, cupped him the way she longed to do. And he looked just as good from the back; tight butt, long legs, broad shoulders. She wanted to feel him against her, inside her.

Struggling to keep her mind on the game, she tried to snuff

out the desire flaring to life inside her. Mace missed the eight ball so it was up to her.

Sam laughed at something his brother said and Dallas's stomach curled. Hot, edgy need spiked her frustration higher.

This was ridiculous! Just looking at him made her all soft and trembly. She needed some distance from him or she was going to do something stupid. She set her jaw, lined up her next shot and took it. The cue ball cracked against the eight and it torpedoed cleanly into the pocket.

For the last shot, she had to move over next to Sam again. This time, she stopped about six inches away. She leaned forward and he stepped pointedly back. Far away from her.

Heat burned her cheeks and she sternly ordered herself to concentrate. She easily picked off the nine ball.

Sam and Mace groaned.

Dusting off her hands, she walked over to put her cue stick back in the rack. She swallowed the hunger carving a hole in her gut and grinned. "Fifty bucks ought to cover it, guys."

Mace turned to Sam. "Can I borrow—"

"You still owe me for that poker game at Greg's bachelor party." Sam whipped out several bills and laid them on the table for Dallas. "I knew I should've stopped while I was ahead."

She instinctively knew that he wasn't talking about pool. She'd felt the need humming between them. She'd tried to ignore it, because he was.

"I'll owe you, Dallas." Mace replaced his stick and headed for the door. "Whew, it's steamy in here," he said, and chuckled.

Sam followed his brother out, scowling. Dallas stuffed her winnings into her jeans pocket, her cheeks flushed.

As the three of them went to join the family for dinner, she knew with a sinking heart that this "friends" thing wasn't going to work. At least not for her.

She'd agreed to be friends. Heck, she'd proposed it. And it had lasted less than a day.

While she liked the new ease between them and the new unity, something deep inside—something she'd tried to deny—wanted more. She wanted him as a lover. She knew he wasn't unaffected by her. But she also knew he didn't trust her not to hurt him. At this point, she didn't know if he would ever trust her again.

She wanted to patch up their friendship, but she shouldn't allow him to get closer. She didn't really belong here anymore. When this case was over, she planned to head back to Denver. Trouble was, she didn't feel she belonged there, either.

Sam had never played a game of pool like that in his life. What they'd just done amounted to foreplay, pure and simple. At least for him.

His skin burned as if she'd had her hands all over him. She'd teased and tormented him and he wasn't sure if she'd done it on purpose or not.

If she'd dragged her hand down that stick one more time, or touched the tip while wetting her lips, or stroked that cue ball with her thumb again, he would have had to excuse himself. As it was, he hadn't been able to control the immediate and fierce hardening of his body. And even now, his arousal throbbed painfully, but at least they were sitting at the table and he could corral his raging hormones while his family distracted her.

A fine sweat peppered his neck and his chest. Hell! He hadn't been able to keep his eyes off her. Mace knew it. *She* knew it.

Maybe he was sick in the head. Maybe he'd finally gone over the edge. What else could explain him wanting her like this after the way she'd hurt him?

Friends? What the hell had he been thinking, to agree to that?

During that pool game, mild panic had set in. Now, with the width of the dining table between them, he was calming down. He still felt the buzz of need, but he could control it. It would fade.

Every so often, Mace would look at him with that knowing smirk in his eyes. Even Linc's gray eyes would settle contemplatively on him, but Sam ignored both his brothers. He focused on his roast beef and homemade bread with gravy, listening as Devon and Jenna peppered Dallas with questions.

"How long have you been a marshal? What kind of training do you need for that?"

"You carry a gun, don't you?"

"How's your family? Are they still in Texas?"

"Do you like Colorado? I think it would be too cold for my liking."

His father dished more food onto her plate. "We miss you, girl. Ever think about coming back here? This is where you belong. Come down this summer and I'll take you to Broken Bow. We'll catch a fine mess of largemouth bass."

As Sam let the conversation flow around him, his blood pressure receded. His groin still ached, but it was nothing he couldn't handle. He took a big gulp of iced tea, urging it to cool the sizzle in his veins.

His mind taunted him, flashing pictures of her in those tight jeans, leaning over the pool table. The overhead light in the dining room shimmered off her blouse, drawing his eye. Dark cranberry silk flowed over her breasts, caressing and curving, making him want to rip off those buttons and see what, if anything, she wore underneath.

He'd invited her to dinner on sheer impulse. *Swift, Garrett. Real swift.* It had been an increasing agony for him, but it had been good for her. She enjoyed his family and it was mutual, he thought irritably.

He told himself that it was Christmas, her family was in another state, and she needed this. She really did. And he wanted that to be what he cared about, instead of this selfish, aching need in his body. But he couldn't dismiss what she was doing to him.

Watching her smile and laugh with his family, he realized how rarely she did either of those things with him. It hit him how well she fit in with his family, how right and natural it felt that she was here. Which frustrated the hell out of him.

He *did* want to be friends with her, but he wasn't sure he could pull it off. He was thinking distinctly un-friendlike thoughts. And he was determined not to. After all, when they wrapped up the case, she'd head back to Colorado. She had a house there, a life there. He wanted to move on with his life. That meant he had to start thinking of Dallas Kittridge differently. As a friend. As a cop, a partner.

All he wanted to do was stroke that velvet skin, taste the warm sultry surrender of her kiss as he had the other night, so he made sure not to get within three feet of her.

After the meal, everyone cleared their plates from the table. The women offered to clean up so the guys could go into the living room. Sam suspected his mother and sisters-in-law wanted to engage Dallas in a little ''girl talk.''

As he followed his father out of the kitchen, he could already feel his blood pressure returning to normal. His dad and Linc sat down to play checkers at a card table in the corner. Mace picked up today's newspaper.

Sam was digging through some Christmas CDs to put on the stereo when the women entered the room about thirty minutes later. Dallas laughed at something Jenna said and his gut knotted up all over again.

The smooth sounds of Bing Crosby's ''White Christmas'' filled the room and Sam turned, catching Dallas's solemn gaze on him. She gave him a funny little half smile and went back to her conversation with the other women, but Sam wondered what she'd been thinking.

He moved to the couch and sat beside Mace, talking to his brother about the state's college football teams and their chances for a bowl win. The women settled diagonally across the coffee table from Mace and him.

From the corner of his eye, Sam could see Dallas sitting

cross-legged on the floor beside Jenna. Dallas asked questions about the veterinarian's family, how she'd met Linc, how long they'd been married. Devon and his mom sat in chairs close by, his mom holding a bowl of pecans to shell. Bonnie never ''just sat'' anywhere; her hands were always moving.

''I knew Linc was a goner the first time I heard about Jenna,'' Devon teased, throwing a glance at Sam's middle brother.

Linc looked up from his checkers and grinned at his wife. Her beautiful blue-green eyes twinkled as she smiled serenely.

Sam glanced over and saw a look of intense longing flash across Dallas's features, then disappear quickly. Her voice was steady as she asked Sam's mom how she'd met his father, but that one instant of pure need on her face shook Sam.

Was she missing Brad? Her family? Or was she hurting as much as he was, wanting him like he was wanting her? *Don't go there, Garrett.*

He and Mace engaged in a spirited discussion about the football teams of Oklahoma University and Oklahoma State University, but he never could shake the awareness of Dallas that stalked him like a shadow. He could hear the rise and fall of her voice as she chatted with the other women, the husky sound of her laughter. And he swore he could catch an occasional hint of her spicy scent, despite the cinnamon smell of potpourri bubbling from the kitchen.

His mom rose, taking the shelled pecans and walking toward the kitchen. ''Let's break out the cards, boys. I'll get the snacks. Sam, could you help me?''

While Mace and Linc moved to set up two card tables behind the sofa, Clif carried the checkerboard over to the bookcase, leaving the pieces intact and ready to pick up the next time.

As Sam disappeared into the kitchen, Dallas walked behind him, helping Mace carry folding chairs. Mace said something and she laughed. Sam's muscles tightened.

In the kitchen, he opened packages of snack mix and

dumped them into two large bowls while Bonnie filled glasses with ice and soft drinks. He caught her as she tilted the bottle over the last glass.

"Dallas will probably want water. She's not much for pop."

Bonnie set the bottle on the countertop and filled the glass with water. Her soft gray gaze honed in on him. "She looks wonderful. How's she doing?"

"Pretty well. She's very strong."

"Yes." His mother patted his arm. "And she has you."

"Not really—"

"Together, y'all could probably be quite a team, and I don't mean as cops." She gave him a sassy smile, her eyes twinkling, and carried a tray of drinks into the living room, leaving him there with a protest dying on his lips.

Didn't his family even care about the way she'd betrayed him? Of course, his rational mind pointed out, they didn't know about that, but he didn't care at the moment. He just wanted to get rid of this sly, insidious awareness of her that was eroding his resolve to stay clear of her.

Of course, no one else felt that way. They all acted as if she were a member of the family. In all fairness, he shouldn't feel this bubbling resentment. She and Brad had been friends with his family and they all still cared about her.

"Hey, Sam, come on!" Mace yelled from the other room.

"Coming." Seething, he reached for the bowls of snack mix.

Mace and Linc appeared in the doorway.

"Hey, Ever Ready, why're you hiding in here?" Linc asked. "Where's the food?"

"The cards are set up," Mace added. "Of course, Dad wants one of the women, so he's with Devon. Dallas and Jenna are a team. You're with Mom and I'm with Linc. Winners switch tables."

"Yeah, yeah," Sam grumbled, covering his relief over not being paired with Dallas.

His brothers exchanged looks and both stepped inside. Linc lowered his voice. "So, how's it going?"

"Are you two—"

Mace wiggled his eyebrows suggestively.

"Give me a break." Sam pushed past them and went into the living room, ignoring their laughter behind him.

He took his place beside his mother and across the table from Devon and his dad. At the next table, Dallas smiled tentatively—a benign, friendly smile—and he forced himself to return it.

He was damned if he was going to give in to this need. It was lust. It was trouble. He wasn't having it. Even though his muscles bunched beneath his shirt, he tried to appear relaxed. He joked and laughed with his parents and Devon, but every second he was aware of Dallas's movements, her laughter when she bested one of his brothers. The tension slashed tight across his shoulders, deep in his belly.

His gaze never left his cards, yet he could hardly concentrate on his hand. Twice, he almost blew the set because of the husky sound of her laughter.

Frustration chewed through his control. He wanted to get her alone and tell her to stay away from him, tell her they weren't picking up where they left off. They played for over two hours and twice Dallas and Jenna moved to their table. He managed to laugh and joke and annihilate their hand, but he was about to lose it.

Christmas music from Harry Connick, Jr., played in the background. In the near corner, the tree sparkled with multicolored lights and silver icicles. A sense of peace and cheer permeated the air. Yet Sam felt as if he were being held hostage. Nerves twisted tighter. His concentration fragmented.

He'd been so proud of himself for inviting her; so smug, telling himself he'd done the "friendly" thing. It had felt good when they'd first arrived. Now he was in agony.

He and his mom won another hand.

Clif tossed his cards on the table. "Devon, why are you letting them do this to me?"

His petite daughter-in-law laughed. "Maybe we should play something else, like charades."

Everyone groaned.

Bonnie chuckled. "You boys are hopeless. Every time Devon looks at Mace, he grins like an idiot and tosses out any old card without even looking. And I think Linc and Jenna are talking in some kind of secret code. Sam and Dallas are the only ones trying."

For some reason, Mace and Linc thought that was hilarious, and they both laughed—too long and hard for Sam's liking. Jenna and Devon exchanged small smiles and his dad hooted, slapping his thigh.

Sam didn't see what was so funny, but he'd had about all he could stand of watching the flush of joy on Dallas's face, watching her push those slinky cranberry sleeves up her pale, strong forearms. He wanted to get her alone in a dark room and—

"We've got to get an early start tomorrow." He stood abruptly, looking at his watch and glancing at Dallas. "Ready?"

"Oh, not yet!" his family cried.

"It's only nine o'clock," Linc protested.

"Sorry." He shrugged, stepping away from the table and going after his and Dallas's coats. If he didn't get some air soon, he was going to suffocate. All he could smell was Dallas. Her tantalizing scent invaded his senses, wrapped around his gut like velvet tentacles. He needed some space.

When he returned to the living room, she rose, as well. Her eyes glowed and a faint blush of pleasure suffused her cheeks as she took her coat, careful not to touch him. "We really do have to go. Thanks so much for having me."

After a round of hugs and "Come backs," they were finally on their way. Just stepping into the expanse of the outdoors gave Sam some relief. But it only lasted until they climbed into his truck.

As they pulled out of the gravel drive, Dallas thanked him and said she'd had a great time.

His tongue felt thick and clumsy in his mouth, making him sound harsh. "You're welcome."

She grew quiet then, saying nothing more. She simply stared out the window and a sense of isolation pierced the silence.

Sam didn't know what to say. He didn't want to talk about the case. He felt caged, his nerves shot like he was about to shatter.

One minute, he wished the case were over so she would leave. The next minute, he found himself wanting her to stay forever. It was no wonder his head was pounding. He scrubbed a hand across his eyes and stepped on the gas.

Dallas, stay here? Right. She'd left him once without a word. He couldn't trust that she wouldn't do it again. And besides, even if he could convince her to stay, what would be the point? They'd both moved on. He didn't want to get involved with her again, did he?

He slid a glance at her, his gaze fixing on the pale alabaster of her face in the darkness of the truck, the compelling strength of her profile, that little shadowed hollow in her throat where he wanted to press his lips. He jerked his gaze away. No, he didn't want to get involved with her again.

He clenched his jaw and drove in focused silence. As soon as they reached Carrie's, he was going to tell Dallas that this wasn't going to work. They needed to keep things strictly professional between them.

Twenty minutes later, he pulled into her friend's driveway, then stepped out of the truck to walk her to the door.

"You don't have to do this," she protested as he came around to open her door. "I have my gun."

"It's the cop code, you know. I need to check things out, especially since it looks as if Carrie isn't home right now," he said grimly, telling himself he'd take a quick look around, then get out. "I won't sleep unless I know you're okay in there."

Her gaze met his, probed. She looked as if she might say something, then she shrugged. They walked together, silent and strained, to the door.

As soon as they stepped inside, he could tell the place hadn't been disturbed. Still, he walked through, checking closets, under the beds, in the kitchen. "All clear," he announced a few minutes later when he returned to the front.

"Thanks." She'd taken off her coat and now placed her holster and gun on the table behind the sofa. "Thanks for inviting me tonight. I loved it."

"They enjoyed seeing you, too." He waited for a moment, feeling awkward.

She stared at him uncertainly. He'd wanted to get away from her all evening. So what was the problem? Why didn't he just go?

He turned for the door. "See ya tomorrow."

"Do you have to leave so soon?"

He tensed, agony stretching across his chest. He should tell her, but he couldn't get the words out. Turning to face her, he said, "There's no point in me staying, is there?"

She paused, then suggested eagerly, "How about a cup of coffee?"

"Dallas—"

"I needed tonight, Sam. I... Thank you, again."

"I'm glad it was good for you." He felt wasted and tired. Tired of fighting what was between them, but knowing he couldn't *stop* fighting.

"Well, I guess I'll say good-night, then."

A disappointment he didn't understand stabbed sharply through him. "I think we need to keep things professional between us."

Silence boomed.

His shoulders stiffened. "So, you agree."

Her voice came, shaking but determined. "A year and a half ago, when we slept together, it scared me to death."

His head came up. He froze, caught completely off guard.

"The reason I left was not because I used you and couldn't face it." Naked emotion glittered in her eyes. "I left because I felt something for you and it scared me to death."

He couldn't move. His heart slammed into his ribs even as his mind tried to push away her words.

Panic sharpened her voice, but she went on. "It— You, what we did, was too soon after Brad. I couldn't face what that made me feel. I wasn't ready to let him go."

"You made that pretty clear," Sam retorted, telling himself not to look into those deep eyes.

"You're wrong, you know," she whispered. "I didn't use you as a substitute for him."

"Don't insult me." Anger flared and he advanced on her, getting right in her face. "I was there, remember? I know the way you looked right through me. I know the way you turned away afterward and reached for Brad's picture. You couldn't even look at me when I asked you straight-out!"

"I know." She didn't flinch, but met his gaze squarely, hers pleading, desperate. "And it was because I felt something for you so soon after Brad died. It made me feel—"

"Dirty?" he snarled. "Thanks."

"No! Confused. Afraid. Shallow." She took a shaky breath. "You idiot, I didn't leave because I couldn't forget Brad. I left because…being with you wiped him completely out of my mind!"

Stunned, Sam could only stare. His pulse pounded in his head, and lower down. Had he understood her correctly?

"What kind of wife did that make me?" she cried. "What kind of person? I'd been married to him for eight years. He'd only been dead two months! I *should* have been thinking of him while I was with you, but I wasn't. *I wasn't.*" Her chest heaved.

His wounded heart screamed not to believe her. But his

instincts hammered out a completely different signal. He'd never seen such agony, such vulnerability in her features. His throat tightened. "Are you saying—"

"Yes."

"It was just me?"

She looked him square in the face, raw hunger plain in her gray eyes. "Yes."

He didn't know what to think, but his body responded with swift, certain speed. In an instant, he was hard and throbbing. Reflexively, before his mind could even catch up, he hauled her to him.

"I'll probably regret the hell out of this." Then his mouth covered hers.

Chapter 11

Her gasp of surprise was smothered by his mouth and he gripped her butt in his hands. She felt good, so damn good.

She stiffened and Sam expected her to push him away. Then her initial resistance disappeared. Her hands slid up his back, clutching wildly, hungrily.

He'd seen women since she'd left, but for the life of him, he couldn't remember who or when or why. Dallas seemed the only one worth having. It occurred to him that he'd lasted only eight days before giving in to this knife-edged need she unleashed in him. His reason shattered. All that existed was the spicy tang of her scent, the softness of her skin, the way her tongue stroked his.

His groin was painfully tight and hard. She murmured hot greedy words in his ear and against his neck as her hands pushed away his coat, yanked the hem of his shirt out of his jeans.

He wanted her naked and spread before him. Fire and greed and desperation spurred him on. He couldn't form a rational thought. He couldn't get a full breath. All he could do was hang on and try to answer the savage craving boiling in his blood.

He unbuttoned her satiny shirt, eased it off her shoulders and to the floor. Beneath it she wore a skimpy black camisole. Her hands fisted in his hair and she panted against his mouth, "Touch me."

At last he got his hands on her bare skin. His palms slid under her little cotton camisole, up the silky warmth of her back. "Here?"

"Everywhere. Anywhere," she moaned, kissing him hard on the mouth.

She wrapped her arms around his neck and the thin-strapped shirt rode up her torso. The soft skin of her belly nudged his hairy one, the snap on his jeans. Then her hand closed over him through his jeans, and she stroked, igniting a fury of need that made him clench his teeth.

He had to have her. Fumbling with her jeans, he pushed them down her hips, then shoved away the tiny scrap of fabric that passed for panties. He wasn't gentle or slow. In some distant corner of his mind, he told himself to be both, to look at her, to save some part of this for later.

She arched her neck and he took in the flush pinkening her delicious skin, the flimsy undergarment that covered her breasts. She was magnificent, touching something deep inside him, something raw and naked and vulnerable. He couldn't define it, didn't want to. He felt clumsy and rough, yet some fierce primal need drove him on.

He somehow managed to open his jeans and then he picked her up. Those long, lean, beautiful legs wrapped around his hips. Her mouth found his again and fused to his with fire and desperate heat, her tongue urging him on. Her breasts pressed full and soft against his chest.

He backed her against the wall, skimmed one hand up her side to cup her breast. The weight of her nestled in his palm and sweat broke over his nape. His skin burned. She cried out and arched into him. Hunger blazed in her eyes, incinerating the small piece of control he had left.

He bunched her camisole into one hand, pulled it over her head. His gaze riveted on her breasts, flushed and full and quivering. Just for him. He lowered his head, urgent now, shaking all over. Before, he'd wanted her surrender, wanted to hurt her the way she'd hurt him; but now he wanted something entirely different. He wanted only the essence of her, the softness, the steel.

He wanted to take the time to taste her, prime her, but the blood throbbed mercilessly in his arousal. Teetering on the razor-edge between reason and ecstasy, he groped for his wallet. An instant later, one of her trembling hands covered his and they rolled on the condom. His lips closed over one nipple and her fingers dug into his back.

She moaned his name and he knew he couldn't wait any longer. He lifted her, his mouth still on her breast, then plunged into her. She came down on him hard and clamped her legs around his hips like a vise.

Gloved in the sleek, tight heat of her, Sam went dizzy for a moment. Then he began to move—long, hard strokes. She met him every time. His mouth shifted to hers and their tongues mated with the same fierce intent as their bodies.

She rode with him, forcing him closer, deeper. His arms corded from the strain of holding back. Their gazes locked. He stared into her eyes; cool gray, so controlled. He wanted to see the same desperation that he felt, the same helplessness.

He shifted slightly, tilting her hips and bringing the core of her even tighter against him. Her eyes widened as his body found the small nub at her center. His body stroked hers deeper, mercilessly, demanding all, taking everything she had. Then he saw it—a streak of panic as her control slipped.

"Come on, doll," he rasped. "Give it to me."

Protest flared in her eyes; then wild, naked surrender. Her gaze, smoky gray and piercing, stayed on his. A fine sweat misted her face. She gripped his shoulders and her dark lashes swept over her eyes. He felt her inner muscles clench around him and she gripped him tightly. His name—a ragged plea—spilled from her throat.

He let himself go, his fingers digging into her hips as he thrust into her repeatedly. Harder, faster, deeper. She clutched at him with that fierce stubbornness she showed in everything.

She screamed in release and he nearly did, too. Breathing harshly, sweating, he collapsed against her, bracing them both against the wall. She sagged into him, her legs still tight around his hips, her breasts soft and sleek against his chest.

His legs felt like string. His chest hurt. His arms shook. It was like walking out of a dream. He knew what had happened. Yet he didn't understand *how* it had happened. He rested his forehead against hers for a second, inhaling the mingled scents of their bodies, soaking in the warmth of her body.

She'd been wonderful, better than he'd remembered, but he couldn't bear to look into her eyes and see if she was with *him,* or somewhere in the distance with Brad.

On some distant plane, he recognized that the desperation driving him had been for Dallas, not a way to escape pain over Brad. The realization ignited a fleeting panic, but the sensations sizzling through him burned it away.

Slowly he navigated into the kitchen, aiming for one of the dining-room chairs. She lay limp against him, her arms loosely around his neck, but when he moved, her body shifted, gripping him tight again. His thighs quivered as he stepped to the nearest chair. He wanted to ease down onto the seat, feel her take him even farther inside.

But as he reached the chair, Dallas untangled her legs from around his hips and slid down his body. Hurt stabbed through him. He straightened his jeans, feeling a brush of cool air against his bare chest.

He saw panic flash in her eyes, and that same panic sped through him. He didn't know what to say or do.

She stood naked before him, proud and unashamed, her body flushed from his. Beautiful. So beautiful that his chest ached. His arousal still throbbed. He waited for her to ask him to leave, to stare through him.

Instead she held out her hand to him. *Stay.*

The silent request blazed in her gray eyes. His heart thudded painfully.

"You weren't planning on going anywhere, were you?" Fear and a hint of loneliness threaded through her soft words.

He read the uncertainty in her face and knew she was remembering how he'd stupidly gone to another woman last year. As if he could walk away from her tonight. "No," he said hoarsely, taking her hand.

He followed her into the bedroom and closed the door, shedding the rest of his clothes as they climbed into her bed.

Dallas awoke the next morning, her body pleasantly tired and aching. She'd wanted him to slow down last night, but was afraid that if he did, he'd back away and she'd lose the small door of accessibility he'd offered. So she hadn't thought anymore, she'd simply felt.

A slow smile curved her lips and she reached behind her, only to find empty space.

It wasn't panic that squeezed her heart, but pain. "Sam?"

She turned over, pushing herself up on her elbows. The sheet slid to the tops of her breasts.

He stood at the foot of the bed, buttoning his jeans, watching her with sultry, intensely blue eyes.

Pleased and relieved that he'd stayed, Dallas smiled slightly. His gaze seared her and made her aware all over again that beneath the sheet, she was completely naked. A flush heated her bare breasts, crawled up her chest to her neck. She caught the sheet a little closer to her.

He shrugged into his shirt as he walked toward her. Just the sight of his broad, hard chest tripped her pulse.

A boyish smile tugged at the corners of his mouth and he sat down beside her, leaning in for a slow, soft kiss. "Morning."

''Morning.'' She stroked a finger along his eyebrow. Her stomach curled as she searched his eyes for regret or goodbye, but she found neither. Still, there was...*something*. A wariness that she felt rather than saw. A tentativeness.

He adjusted the sheet, his fingers grazing her breasts and setting off a flurry in her belly. ''I'm going to go home, take a shower and change. I'll pick you up in about an hour or so and we'll get back to work.''

She nodded, still trying to absorb what they'd done last night. What had happened had been special, explosive and wonderful. But Sam's subtle reserve this morning unleashed a flood of uncertainty. Unwilling to spoil what they'd shared, she tried to push away the doubts.

It crossed her mind that he might be punishing her for what had happened eighteen months ago, but she quickly dismissed that idea. He wouldn't do that. He hadn't said he'd forgiven her, but she sensed it.

He started to rise, but she stopped him by placing a hand on his chest, inside his open shirt. She loved the feel of the warm, hair-roughened skin and smooth, hard muscle. ''I'm not sorry,'' she whispered, holding his gaze. ''I don't think it was a mistake.''

Indecision flickered in his eyes—so quickly she might have imagined it. Then he covered her hand with his, pressing both to his chest. ''Neither do I. I really don't. But...Brad wanted me to take care of you. Somehow I don't think he meant for that to include what we just did.''

She stared at him for a long minute, her eyes bright with pain and understanding. ''Maybe,'' she said slowly, ''you're telling yourself that if you don't feel something, you haven't committed the ultimate betrayal.''

''Yes.'' That was exactly how he felt. Stunned, he leaned toward her. ''Yes.''

''But that doesn't change what we did. Or the fact that he's gone.''

''Or the part I played in his death,'' Sam said grimly.

She started to protest, then she cupped his jaw with her other hand. "You have to work through this. I know that. But please don't shut me out. I want to be here for you, if you'll let me. To talk, to listen, whatever you need."

"Thanks." He stroked her cheek, then pressed a soft kiss to her lips. "I'll be back."

He was still troubled and she wished there were something more she could do. As he walked out, she could feel his uncertainty, his unease over what had happened, and she frowned. Swinging her legs over the side of the bed, she gripped the edge of the mattress and heard the front door open and shut. A hollow silence spread through the house.

Maybe they *had* made a mistake. Maybe it had been too soon. As she walked to the bathroom, she cautioned herself not to get jumpy or anticipate trouble. *Don't ruin a wonderful memory, Dallas.*

She liked the way Sam made her feel—as if she were the only woman who could touch the deepest part of his soul. Had she felt like this the night they'd first made love? She'd told herself no for months. Now she wasn't sure.

During her shower, she blanked her mind and allowed herself to remember only the glorious feel of his body against her, inside her. There had been a huge shift in their relationship. Last night was about only her and Sam. She liked knowing that.

After she blow-dried her hair, she slipped into a fresh bra and pair of panties. She'd just pulled on her black jeans when Carrie knocked and came into the room.

Her friend dropped onto the corner of the bed, a broad grin spreading across her face. "Well, well. I see Sam spent the whole night proving how uninterested in you he is."

Dallas laughed softly, blushing in a way she hadn't since her first junior-high crush. She'd been so wrapped up in Sam that she'd never heard Carrie come home last night.

"So? Was it fabulous?"

''Yes,'' Dallas answered huskily, then cleared her throat when she heard herself. ''It was.''

The first time had been fast and hard and had sent her straight over the edge, but the second time... At the memory, her breath caught. He'd been slow and gentle and thorough, taking her to the brink three times before she'd climaxed, before he'd let himself go. Her bones had melted. *She* had melted.

''So?'' her friend prodded. ''What's going on?''

She pulled a thick black angora sweater over her head. ''I don't know.''

''Dallas, it's all right to have feelings. It's okay to want to be with Sam. Brad's been gone a long time.''

''That's not it. I do want to be with him.''

''What, then?''

She adjusted her mock turtleneck and sank down on the bed beside Carrie. The distance she'd sensed in Sam haunted her. The unease she'd read just below the surface of his words— had she imagined that? ''I'm not sure.''

''Are you sorry?''

''No.''

''Think it will interfere with the case?''

''Neither one of us can allow that.'' She paused. ''Maybe he doesn't completely trust me.''

''And what about you? Do you trust him?''

Dallas considered her friend solemnly. She trusted Sam not to turn away from her now. She trusted him to be her friend again, no matter what. ''Yes.''

''So, what you're saying is you're not sure where it will go?''

''Maybe that's it.''

''Welcome to the dating world, hon.''

Dallas smiled, pulling on socks, then her left boot. She never would have guessed Sam could be so giving. A year and a half ago he'd been a generous and tender lover, but early this morning, he'd been focused only on learning her body, giving her pleasure. She'd always enjoyed sex with Brad, but in their eight years of marriage, he'd never lavished that kind of intense attention on her. A shiver chased down her spine at the memory and she smiled.

Carrie chuckled. "It must've been *really* good."

Dallas ducked her head, pulled on her other boot. What she'd always thought of as affection for Sam had turned into attraction. Actually, no-holds-barred lust. Maybe it had been that even a year and a half ago—something she didn't like to admit.

"So, you guys obviously kissed and made up."

"We did do the kissing part." She grinned like an idiot as she went over to the dresser and buckled on her holster.

"I think it's wonderful. It's been a long time coming."

"Has it?" Dallas shook her head.

"What does Sam say?"

She paused, torn up inside over the torture she'd seen in his eyes. "I don't think he's any more sure than I am."

"Hey." Carrie rose and enveloped her in a hug. "It will work out. You'll see. I bet you'll be surprised."

Dallas nodded, her throat tight as she released her friend. Last night had been wonderful, but it had been reckless and out of control. The truth was, she hadn't had one thought past that initial searing kiss. Making love with Sam didn't feel wrong, but *something* did.

The day was beautifully clear and the temperature a comfortable fifty degrees. Translucent blue painted the sky. The sun shone, chasing away the gloom of the last couple of weeks and encouraging a false hopefulness, an aura that the day would be easy and slow and simple. Sam knew nothing would be easy or slow or simple. Not the case. And not what had happened last night.

He and Dallas had come together strictly out of physical need and an emotional connection he wasn't sure he could define. They had not made love for comfort or in grief or deception.

Sam believed what she'd said. About thinking only of him while they'd made love eighteen months ago. About being confused. About her guilt over the whole issue. He'd wanted to call her a liar, but she wasn't lying. The battle she'd fought to come to terms with it on her own, and to admit it to him, had been all too clear. And he could understand that guilt.

It was eating him up. He'd thought that he'd come to terms with it. She didn't hold him responsible for Brad's death. That should have let him off the hook, right? But it didn't.

He'd wanted her while she was married to his partner. And now she'd admitted that while she should have been grieving for her husband a year and a half ago, she'd wanted him. Yes, Sam understood her guilt all too well.

He kept telling himself that he and Dallas were free agents and over twenty-one. Still, he couldn't deny the shame, the sense that he'd cheated on his best friend, that things had worked out a little too conveniently for him.

His head knew he hadn't taken another man's wife—his *best friend's wife.* But his conscience condemned him for it.

He picked Dallas up at Carrie's. And as they checked the remaining truck stops on their list and spoke to the managers, Sam couldn't quiet the insistent scorn in his mind. Nor could he block the images of last night that reeled through his mind like a film.

The first time they'd made love, he hadn't been able to help himself. Some elemental instinct had taken over and he had focused only on satisfying the raging hunger he'd felt. But that second time, he'd been slow, deliberate. He had no excuse for that and couldn't shake the sense that he'd trespassed into a forbidden place.

As she rode beside him in the truck, Dallas's distance mirrored Sam's own. She didn't try to breach the wall he'd erected. Once, he saw pain in her eyes but she looked away;

and when she directed him to the next truck stop, her voice was steady.

Just recalling her responsiveness last night tripped his pulse. He didn't remember from eighteen months ago how a certain touch could make her melt all over him. And he hadn't remembered the way her eyes glittered like smoky crystal when she climaxed, or the wickedness of her nimble fingers. A new rush of guilt flooded him.

As they moved from truck stop to truck stop, Sam forced his mind to the case. He couldn't allow himself to think about her or dwell on the bleak sense of failure pricking at him.

He'd done it. He'd finally crossed the line, betrayed his best friend. He couldn't take it back. He'd spent a year and a half telling himself he didn't want Dallas, but he did. He wanted to explore things between them, but he couldn't shake the sense of disloyalty he felt toward Brad. He didn't know what the hell to do. He did know he needed to figure it out, because he didn't want to give her up again.

Tension filled the space between them like water gushing from a reservoir, rapid and forceful and drowning the little progress they'd made. Their silence emitted a sharp static that charged the air with unease, discomfort. Sam knew he was pushing Dallas away, putting distance where they'd finally managed to build a bridge, but he did it anyhow. It seemed the only way to deal with the festering wound of responsibility Sam felt over Brad's death, all the self-loathing he'd experienced when he realized his lust for Dallas.

They pulled into the last truck stop on their list—the third Love's Country Store they'd visited today. As they climbed out of his truck, she remained as she had for most of the day, professional and as distant from him as if they'd never glimpsed each other's souls last night.

She met him at the front of the truck. "If nobody recognizes any of these mug shots, what do we do?"

"Look harder."

She gave him a measuring stare, but said nothing.

Once inside, they bypassed the convenience-store area for car travelers and walked to the left, into a diner smelling of bacon grease and cigarettes. A low roar of voices hummed through the boxy room. Plates and glasses clanged in the back, accompanied by the hiss of food on the grill.

A burly man with only a fringe of hair around his bald head looked up from his booth near the entrance. Small eyes, like raisins pressed into his doughy face, leered at Dallas.

Sam gave him a hard-eyed look, trying to shrug off the protective instincts that suddenly roared to life.

Dallas met the man's gaze calmly, and casually pushed back one side of her black duster—just enough so the guy could see her .9mm Taurus in all its glory.

The man's slimy smile disappeared and he looked down at his plate, his jowls working furiously as he ate.

Sam scanned the room full of men and two waitresses, wondering why he'd even been worried. Dallas could take care of herself. He started for the cash register to his left and she followed.

A tall, large-boned woman with flaming-red hair stood at the register. She wore a Hawaiian-print shirt in turquoise, orange and yellow, with lumpy turquoise stretch pants. Beefy fists settled on her ample hips. Powder-blue eye shadow covered her lids up to her thinly plucked eyebrows.

As Sam walked up, flashing his badge, her hazel eyes turned hungry and she licked her lips. He fought to cover his distaste.

"You handle this, Detective Charm," Dallas murmured. "I think she's waiting for you."

"I'm Detective Garrett." He smiled at the woman and tapped the mug shots he held. "I'd like to show you some pictures, if I could."

"Hello, sweetness," the woman purred. "I'm Charmaine." Her gaze honed in on Dallas. "*You* can ask me anything you want. I'm not much for talking in a crowd."

He glanced over his shoulder, catching the twinkle in Dallas's eyes.

She said in a strangled voice, "I'll talk to the customers."

Sam nodded as she walked off. Charmaine shifted so that her huge breasts pointed straight at him. He bit off a smile and had no trouble keeping his eyes on her face.

Fifteen minutes later, he walked out, breathing deeply of the fresh, cold air and shrugging off the way his skin crawled. That woman had been a piece of work, touching and stroking and salivating all over him as if he were a candy cane. Gold flashed from his windshield and he saw Dallas waiting in the truck, sunlight playing on her tawny hair.

He climbed in, relieved to be away from the distasteful woman inside the truck stop. "Get anything?"

"No. What about you, *sweetness?*"

At her playful tone, he shot her a look, pulling out one of the mug shots. "She recognized him."

"Bernie Dwyer?"

"Yeah. Prior rape conviction. This could be our guy."

"Let's check the bar over there and see if they know him."

Sam nodded, reversing out of his parking space.

"Someone's missing you already." Laughter warmed her voice.

He glanced up to see Charmaine just beyond the window, waving. He waggled a small piece of yellow paper in the air. She pursed her lips in a pouty kiss and Dallas choked, quickly turning away from the window.

As they drove off, she burst into laughter. "Oh, this is something else, Garrett."

He glared, shoving the paper into his ashtray.

"Her phone number?"

He grunted.

She laughed harder, clutching her side, and Sam grudgingly smiled. He tuned out the refreshing sound of Dallas's laughter. They were on to this SOB. They were going to nail him.

But inside the bar, the bartender said he'd never seen the guy.

"You're sure?" Sam pushed the mug shot across the bar again.

The bartender studied it carefully again. "Yeah."

The two women cleaning the bar didn't recognize Bernie Dwyer, either. Beside Sam, Dallas sighed. "Are we ever going to get a break?"

He felt that same hopelessness as he thanked the bartender and stuffed the photo back in his coat pocket, frustrated that they had hit another wall.

Dallas stepped around him and said to the bartender, "Maybe you remember a customer with a tattoo of a cross on his right hand?"

The bartender frowned. "I don't think so."

"Hey, I might!" One of the women, a washed-out blonde, walked over, balancing a round drink tray on her bony hip. "Well, I don't know if it was a cross, but I do remember a guy with a tattoo on his right hand. It was weird because it went all the way up his hand."

Hopeful, Sam asked, "Could you identify this guy?"

She shrugged. "He looked like every other customer I see."

"If you remember anything else, will you give us a call?" Sam fished a card out of his pocket and handed it to her.

"Sure."

"Maybe you can remember his hair color?" Dallas asked. "If he was young? Or old?"

"Sorry, the tattoo's about all I remember."

Sam nodded. "Thanks, then."

He and Dallas walked out, exchanging grim looks.

"Well, that was a dead end." She opened her door and slid inside.

Sam joined her. "We'll go ahead and show Bernie's picture to the other bar owners on our list. Maybe he's a regular at one of those."

They spent the afternoon retracing their steps to the previous bars, but no one recognized Bernie Dwyer.

''Maybe he doesn't drink.'' Dallas massaged her shoulder, her forehead puckered in concentration.

''Or do anything else.'' Sam rubbed a hand over his face. ''At least we jogged the memories of a couple of those bartenders and they remembered the tattoo.''

She looked over and gave him a tired smile. ''We'll find him, Sam.''

''Yeah. I'm just ready, is all.'' It was dark. He was tired and hungry. Dallas had to be, too. He didn't remember seeing her eat the sandwich he'd gotten them for lunch. ''Let's go grab some dinner.''

''Sounds good.''

A couple of hours later, after they'd eaten, they pulled into Carrie's driveway, satisfied, and with some of their flagging energy renewed.

''Looks like Carrie's home,'' Sam observed, relieved he wouldn't have to walk Dallas inside.

Her gaze followed the direction of his, took in the lights glowing from the front and kitchen windows. ''So, what next?''

She unbuckled her seat belt and shifted in the seat until she faced him. Moonlight played over her hair, silvering the short thickness. Her lips were shadowed and tempting in the half-light.

Sam picked up the mug shot of Bernie Dwyer. ''I'll make a call to this guy's probation officer. I don't think he's our man, but I'll check a little further. I'll ask about that tattoo, too.''

''And tomorrow?'' She rubbed her neck.

Sam sighed, dropping the photo he held. ''Back to square one. We must've missed something.''

''Sounds like a plan, *sweetness*.'' She chuckled.

For the first time, the friction that had been between them all day dissolved. He grinned, tossing the mug shot onto the dashboard. ''Hey, only large, redheaded women can call me that.''

''You were looking a little sick in there, Detective Charm.'' Her eyes sparkled with pleasure, kicking off a burst of heat low in Sam's belly. And that blistering edge of guilt.

Despite that, his heartbeat quickened. Heat lightning whipped between them.

Her smile faded. Dark smoky eyes met his, gauging, then her gaze dropped to his mouth. Desire exploded like a flare through his body. He went rigid. All over.

Silvery light streamed in through the back window and skimmed over her creamy skin, glittered in her eyes like stars.

''Sam?'' she whispered.

His hand came up to her shoulder, partly in defense. The spice of her scent threatened his resolve to keep a distance. If he leaned forward, he could kiss her. He recalled the dark honey taste of her and it coaxed him to ignore all the doubt roaring through him and surrender, give in to mindless, reckless desire the way he'd done last night.

He wanted her. No amount of guilt could disguise that. But all day he'd been haunted by images of that fateful day in the warehouse with Brad. The scene of Sam seeing the perp too late, feeling the brutal hit on the back of his head, waking up to find Brad dead by Sam's gun ground through his mind like a record stuck in the same groove, resurrecting agony and condemnation.

He hadn't thought about the specific events of that day in more than a year, but making love with Dallas had dredged up everything.

Her eyes were wide with questions. She skimmed a finger along his eyebrow, then touched his cheek, her palm soft and smooth against the whiskery roughness of his face. He knew her breasts would feel like velvet in his hand. He knew, painfully, how tightly she would grip him when he slid inside her.

The guilt took over then. He was probably out of his mind, but he couldn't do this.

With a shaking hand, he gently gripped her wrist, forcing himself to remain unresponsive when what he wanted was to haul her to him and answer the need building to white heat inside him.

She looked at him for a long time, confusion clouding her eyes. She wanted more, but he couldn't give it to her—at least not right now.

"I want you, Dallas. Don't doubt that." He closed his eyes briefly against the battle of his heart and mind. "But I'm having trouble sorting all this out. I can't let go of Brad. I can't let go of what happened."

Pain flashed across her features and she gave a small smile. "I understand. I really do. I'm here, Sam. When you're ready, I'm here."

"Thanks." He pressed his lips to her temple and murmured, "I'll see you in the morning."

She nodded, not moving, her lashes brushing softly against his jaw. For a moment, they sat like that, his lips on her warm skin, a poignant ache stretching between them.

Then she pulled back. She studied him, desire and frustration battling in her gaze.

He waited, his nerves raw, tempted to change his mind, knowing she could make him if she touched him one more time.

Finally accepting, she nodded, reached back to open the door and stepped out. Her voice had only a trace of huskiness. "Good night, then."

"Good night," he said.

Silhouetted in the pure white of moonlight, she looked pale and fragile. A lie, he knew. She was very strong. And very beautiful. His throat tightened.

It was possible Dallas might hurt him again, but as Sam watched her walk toward the house, he realized that wasn't what was holding him back. Maybe it never had been. It was Brad.

Sam shoved his fingers through his hair. He'd wanted Dallas since the day he'd met her, but she had been Brad's wife. That day in the warehouse, was there something he could have done to save Brad? Was there some dark, unthinkable, *unconscious* motive that had slowed his responses?

Dallas was now free to be with Sam because Brad had died. *Was that what Sam had wanted?* Had Sam wanted her so badly that he hadn't given every effort to stop Brad's death?

Everything in him vehemently wanted to deny it, but he could no longer ignore the questions.

Chapter 12

He drove around for an hour, impatient, muscles straining as if he were caged, feeling indicted and resenting it. If he was so certain in his mind that he hadn't wanted Brad out of the way, that he hadn't wanted Dallas at any price, then why couldn't he get past the guilt?

Dallas hadn't given him an ultimatum, but he felt they were at a crossroads. *He* was at a crossroads. Frustrated, desperate to escape the heavy darkness weighing on him, he considered getting good and drunk. That would solve nothing. Resigned to a long, agonizing night, he headed home. And that was when it came to him.

Mace. Mace had been through something similar with his old buddy and late father-in-law, Bill Landry.

Because of his and Dallas's work today, Sam had managed to ignore how awkward and miserable he felt, how strained things were between them. But he couldn't ignore it anymore.

He needed to talk to his brother.

"How's my favorite girl?" Sitting on Mace's couch, Sam cuddled his nine-month-old niece.

Her wide blue eyes crinkled as she grabbed at his nose. He chuckled, blowing air kisses on her bare belly. She gurgled and fisted two chubby hands in his hair.

"Yeow!" he yelped, then laughed. Mace's daughter was already a heartbreaker with her dark hair, the china-fair skin she'd inherited from her mother, and those blue Garrett eyes.

Sam had arrived just after bath time. Ashley, freshly diapered and smelling sweet, had crowed upon seeing him. She had him wrapped around her little finger and he loved it. He gave her a piggyback ride until she was breathless and bounced her on his knee until she bubbled with laughter.

Finally Devon came in with the baby's pajamas and Sam handed her over.

"Tell Uncle Sam 'Night-night.'" Devon held Ashley up and the baby planted a slobbery kiss on his cheek. His heart tilted.

Mace reached for his daughter. "Ready for Daddy to put you to bed?"

"Why don't you visit with your brother?" Devon said.

Mace glanced over. "All right." He kissed Ashley. "I'll be back to tuck you in later, sweetheart."

Resting her head on Devon's shoulder, she gave a toothy grin. The two of them disappeared down the hall.

"You're gonna have to beat the boys off with a stick," Sam said.

"I'm locking her in her room until she's thirty," Mace replied, taking a seat in the recliner near the end of the couch where Sam sat. "So, what's up? And don't tell me it's the case."

Now that he was here, Sam didn't know how to start. He rolled his shoulders against the tension knotting them. "It's Dallas. We've, uh— Something's happened."

Mace arched an eyebrow. "As in sex?"

Sam shoved a hand through his hair. "Yes, among other things."

"And you want to talk to *me* about this?" Laughter traced his brother's voice. "How about a beer?"

"No."

"What's the problem? If you've slept with her, I assume she was willing."

"It's not that."

Mace's smile faded and his blue gaze sharpened.

Sam scrubbed a hand across his face and took a deep breath. "I've always wanted her, you know. From the first time I met her. Brad and I had just partnered up and he kept going on and on about Dallas, telling me I had to meet her." He paused, recalling the instant connection he'd felt with her, the gut punch of awareness when he'd walked into Brad's house and come face-to-face with her for the first time. "I couldn't believe it. No woman had ever hit me so fast and hard. Certainly not another man's wife."

"She's nobody's wife now, Sam," Mace gently reminded.

"I know that. I do." He squeezed his eyes shut.

"It's Brad." Mace's quiet observation brought Sam's gaze up. "Your sense of responsibility for what happened in that warehouse is tied to Dallas."

He nodded, relieved that his brother understood, but shifting uneasily anyway. He considered telling his brother about that night a year and a half ago, and how they'd parted, but felt that should remain between him and Dallas.

Clenching a fist, he surged up from the couch and stalked across the room to the fireplace. "Despite her being the wife of my partner, my *best* friend, I never stopped wanting her. I tried not to let on, but—" He turned toward his brother, agony pinching his gut. "Brad never knew how I felt. I'm sure of that. But did I want her so badly that I let him down? Was there some part of me that might've been—*should've been*—alerted to those perps in the warehouse?"

"Hey." Mace rose from his chair and came toward Sam, hard-earned understanding glittering in his eyes. "You can't play this game. You're not to blame. It could just as easily have been *your* grave in that cemetery.''

"That's what Dallas says," he said grimly.

After a long pause, Mace fired a question at him. "Are you glad Brad's dead?''

"No!" Sam jumped as if someone had laid a whip to his bare back.

"Did you wish him dead?''

"No!" The questions rained down on him like arrows— sharp, pricking, opening like a wound his worst fears about himself. He paced, trying to dodge the pain, the ugliness.

"Have you once felt relieved that he was gone?''

"Hell, no! What's the matter with you?" Pushed to the edge, afraid he'd looked into the blackest part of his soul and succumbed to it, Sam shoved past his brother. "I didn't come here for this. I thought you could help me understand—"

"Did you ever make a move on her while Brad was alive?''

Fury rolled through him and a deep hurt that his brother would even ask. "No, dammit!''

"And you never would have." Mace's voice gentled suddenly. "I know that about you. Because you loved Brad, you respected his wife and you valued your friendship with both of them. Those things are still true, Sam. Still true.''

Feeling as if he'd been steamrollered, Sam stared blankly at Mace, then made his way to the couch and sank down onto the thick cushions. It *was* true. All those things were still true.

Mace resumed his seat in the chair. "If you'd wanted Dallas at any price, you wouldn't be struggling with this now.''

Realization unfolded and with it, the first sense of relief he'd felt since Brad's death. He believed what Mace said. He knew, deep in his gut, that he never would have crawled over Brad to get to Dallas. Never. Not unless Brad was out of the picture. And Sam had never wanted Brad out of the picture.

He rose and clasped his brother's hand hard. Gratitude tightened his chest. "You don't know how much this helps.''

"I'm glad." Mace grinned. "It'll be all right.''

"Because you say so, big brother?"

"Yeah."

Sam shrugged into his coat and slapped Mace on the back. He drove away, contemplative and solemn. For the first time, he thought he might be able to come to terms with what had happened that day in the warehouse—his inability to save Brad. The guilt and sense of disloyalty didn't just disappear, but now Sam actually believed they would someday. He needed to pay a visit to Brad.

The phone jarred Sam out of a deep sleep. He pushed aside the photo of him, Brad and Dallas and squinted at the neon green numbers on his clock—3:30 a.m. When he heard Lieutenant Roberts's voice on the other end, the fog of sleep cleared away. And when Sam hung up the phone, he knew this case was about to blow wide-open.

He immediately called Dallas. At the sleepy huskiness of her voice, desire tugged low in his belly. "It's me."

"Not another one?" she asked with a combination of dread and anger.

"We just got lucky. He tried again, but the woman escaped."

"We've got a live witness?" She was anxious now, her voice clear and alert.

"Yep."

"He's getting antsy. It's only been three days since the last murder."

"Yeah."

"Let's go talk to the witness."

"I'm on my way to pick you up."

"I'll be ready."

Sam hung up and threw on his clothes, then drove to Carrie's. Dallas was the best. There hadn't been a hint of hurt or feminine aloofness in her. After the way he'd left things tonight, he'd expected at least one of those. But she was just as much a professional as he was. And they both wanted to catch this killer.

The fact that Sam had stalled things between them smarted, but Dallas was glad he'd been honest about why. She hurt for him because she really did understand. Somehow she'd worked through the guilt, and she wanted that for him.

He wanted her. He'd admitted that. For now, it would have to be enough. Dallas struggled to push aside her wounded pride before Sam arrived, needing to put herself on autopilot. Christmas was two days away and they had a killer to catch.

Dallas was waiting on Carrie's front porch when Sam pulled into the drive, his headlights stabbing through the blackness of the night. Her breath puffed out ghostly white as she walked down the steps and climbed into his truck.

He handed her a cup of steaming coffee he'd picked up at a nearby convenience store and she took it with a grateful thank-you. As they drove to the station, light from the street-lamps flashed periodically into the truck, illuminating the strain on his handsome features. But there was also expectancy, intensity. She felt an increased energy in the air, and the hope that this time they were finally on the right track.

Thank goodness, they'd gotten the break they needed in this case. She didn't know where things between her and Sam would end up, but for now she was here with him and they were working together.

During the trip, both of them were silent. Dallas tapped her foot nervously. This had to be their guy.

Twenty minutes later, they stood in Interview Room One, where a young woman sat in a metal chair at the long center table. A small card table rested against the adjacent wall, holding cups, coffee, stir sticks and pink packets of sweetener.

The witness's name was Christine Liddell and she'd been picked up at Calhoun's just after midnight.

"These are the detectives who'll work your case, miss." Lieutenant Roberts motioned Dallas in behind Sam. "You'll need to go over your story with them and answer any questions they have.''

"I gotta tell it again?" the girl asked, glancing from Sam to Dallas.

"Just so we can make sure we've got everything straight." Sam smiled reassuringly as he slid into the chair across from her.

She flicked a wary glance at Roberts, then nodded, tucking a strand of lank dark hair behind her ear. Dark circles of fatigue ringed her brown eyes, which were also bloodshot.

Probably from liquor, Dallas thought. "Would you like something? Coffee or water?"

"I got coffee." She lifted a small foam cup and seemed to relax somewhat.

The lieutenant walked out, closing the door behind him. Dallas remained standing, letting Sam guide the investigation so everything would be aboveboard.

"According to what you told the officer at the scene, this guy's about five-eleven, a hundred and sixty pounds."

She nodded.

"Why don't you start by telling us how you hooked up with him?"

She gave a loud sigh. "I left the bar with him. I was gonna— You know."

"Sleep with him?" Sam prodded, flipping open his notebook.

"Yeah." Her gaze flicked to Dallas.

Dallas offered what she hoped was an encouraging smile. It was all she could do to control her impatience to hear the whole story.

"Then I changed my mind. There was something about him. I don't know. He just creeped me out. He pulled this chain off his wallet and put it by the bed."

Sam shot a look at Dallas and she smiled. *This is him. It's got to be.*

"I was drunk—real drunk—but that scared me," Christine

continued. "I couldn't get away at first. He held me down and I fought him."

"Did you scratch him? Bloody his nose, maybe?" Dallas asked quietly.

"I don't think so. I don't really remember." She raised a hand to her throat. "He tried to put that chain on my neck. That's when I got away."

"Did you notice a cross tattoo on his right hand?"

"Yes. I told that to the first man, too." She glanced at Dallas. "Do y'all think you know who it is?"

"We can't be sure of that yet," Sam said. "Did he drive to your house?"

The girl nodded. "One of those big cabs. Not like a taxi— like what semitrailer drivers drive."

Bingo. Dallas met Sam's gaze over the girl's head. Triumph gleamed in his blue eyes.

"Is there anything else?" he asked.

Dallas could sense the urgency beneath his gently worded question. She admired his restraint because she knew his hunting instincts were out in full force.

Christine shook her head. "Oh, wait! At the bar, he told me his name was Winston. That helps, doesn't it?"

Sam scribbled in his notebook. "Yes, that will help."

"You called from a neighbor's?" Dallas interjected.

"Yes. By the time the police got there, he'd left my house."

It all fit. Same MO, same description. The link to the truck stops. And now they had a name. Adrenaline buzzed through Dallas.

"Is that all? Can I go home now?" Christine asked plaintively. "This will help you catch him, right?"

Dallas exchanged a look with Sam and he nodded, pushing the mug shots across the table. "Could you look at these photos? See if you recognize any of these men?"

She studied the pictures, shook her head slowly. "No."

"Are you sure?"

"I was really drunk."

Sam pushed away from the table and rose. "Thank you, Miss Liddell. You did the right thing to report this. If we get him, will you want to press charges?"

"Yeah, I guess." She looked uncertainly at Dallas.

Dallas smiled broadly as she opened the door to the interview room. "Good decision."

Christine rose and walked past her, then halted. "This probably wouldn't have happened to you, would it?"

Dallas stared into the young woman's eyes, saw shame and embarrassment. She patted the girl's shoulder. "That man took advantage of you. It could happen to anyone. You got away and you did the smart thing by coming to us."

Christine's dark eyes measured Dallas, then she smiled. "Thanks."

"Thanks for coming in," Sam called as she walked toward the stairs.

He motioned to Dallas and together they went into the lieutenant's office. "We're going to check the truck stops for this guy," Sam told him.

"Okay," Lieutenant Roberts said. "Keep me informed."

Sam nodded. Dallas lifted a hand in farewell and followed Sam downstairs and out to his truck.

Though it was cold, there was no wind and the sky was clear. Stars winked on a velvety black canvas and a three-quarters moon hovered overhead.

She glanced over. "This girl was picked up in the same bar as the first victim."

"Yeah, I caught that. Think he's starting his pattern over?"

"Could be. Let's start with the truck stop across from there."

Nodding in agreement, Sam opened her door, then walked to the driver's side.

In the fifteen minutes it took to reach the truck stop near Calhoun's, Sam and Dallas talked about inconsequential things like how the weather had turned out nice and the slim possibility of a white Christmas. As they chatted about nothing,

Dallas was struck by how good Sam was at his job, how he never gave up or seemed to get discouraged. Most especially, she was conscious of how different things were between them now than when she had first arrived ten days ago.

There was still friction between them, but whereas before, Sam's distance had been about her and his inability to trust her, now it was tied to Brad and the guilt Sam carried.

When she'd come to Oklahoma City, she'd been clear and determined about what she wanted. She would catch Valeria's killer. She would go back to Denver. She wouldn't become involved with Sam.

She'd told herself she could work with him, that she was immune to his charm and the lure of their past friendship. She'd told herself that the yawning void in her heart—caused by missing him—would heal.

Now Sam had turned her emotionally inside out and she was sure of only one thing: she was going to get Valeria's killer.

When they reached the truck stop and started into the building, Sam turned to Dallas. "If we run into a Charmaine clone in here, I want you to draw your gun."

Dallas laughed. "Can't you handle her?"

"That's just it." He gave a mock shudder. "I don't want to 'handle' anything about her."

They laughed together and it was then that she realized what she hadn't admitted before. She'd been so sure of herself, so sure she could work with him, then walk away. Now she wasn't so sure. Sam reached a part of her no man ever had, and it scared her. Part of her liked being in control, and she knew a relationship with Sam would bring down all the barriers.

He wanted her, but she didn't think either of them was ready for anything else. At least not yet. Maybe never.

She reined in her impatience. This professional ease was better than stilted silence or awkward pauses, but it still left Dallas feeling unsatisfied.

Inside the truck stop, the odors of ammonia and stale cig-
arette smoke hung heavy. The clerk at the cash register called
the manager out from the back.

"Winston?" The painfully thin man with tobacco-stained
teeth frowned. "First or last name?"

"We're not sure," Sam said.

"You got a picture?"

"We were hoping you could give us a full name so we
could get one."

"Sorry." The other man clucked his tongue. "Can't help
ya."

Sam's jaw hardened, but he thanked the man. The manager
nodded, starting down an aisle as Sam and Dallas turned for
the door. Frustrated, Dallas shoved a hand through her hair.
Someone had to know this guy!

"Hey, I know a guy who works for *Winston* Trucking."
The manager halted next to a display of magazines. "Does
that help?"

Hope flared to life inside Dallas.

Sam shot her a grin. "Yeah, give me what you've got."

They couldn't get what they needed from Winston Trucking
until the morning shift reported at eight o'clock, so they
stopped at a diner on the south side of Oklahoma City and
had breakfast. The sun rose in a rainbow of pastel pinks and
yellows. The optimistic sense that the case had finally turned
their way was evident in their companionable silence.

At Winston Trucking, the day supervisor and the secretary
were very helpful, giving Sam and Dallas a list of their drivers,
along with the log of their runs for the past three months. Out
of the fifty-three drivers, four of them had been in Oklahoma
City on the dates of all murders.

The first, a woman, was eliminated right off. Sam called in
the names of the other three to Records, waiting on the line
as the secretary read the information to him over the phone.

One of the men showed up in OCPD records. He had served time for rape, but he was Hispanic and in his mid-fifties. Number two eliminated.

The other two men didn't show up in the computer, so Sam ran a check through NCIC—the National Crime Information Center. One of them turned up as having served time in Arizona for assault and burglary. But he was bald as a new egg and weighed almost three hundred pounds. The remaining driver, a Richie Lewis, fit the general description of their suspect, but had no priors.

Another check with the secretary at Winston Trucking revealed that Richie was on an overnight run to Fort Smith and should be back late tonight or in the morning. Dallas asked if Winston had an employee photo of Richie Lewis, but the company didn't use picture IDs.

Finally they hit pay dirt at the Department of Public Safety. It was Dallas who convinced the woman in charge to give them a copy of Richie Lewis's driver's-license photo.

It was late that afternoon, thirteen hours after they'd first spoken to her, when they knocked on Christine Liddell's door and showed her the picture of Richie Lewis. The sun had already set.

In the glare of her porch light, she shook her head. "It could be. I'm just not sure."

"Look again," Sam said impatiently.

The girl bristled.

"Please," Dallas urged quietly.

The girl glanced at Sam, then studied the photo again. Tears welled in her eyes. "I'm sorry. I was so drunk, I'm just not positive."

"It's all right," Sam soothed, though Dallas could feel the frustration seething inside him.

They assured Christine they'd get back to her when and if they had something else. As they walked across her lawn, Dallas glanced back. "Now what?"

Sam stopped and studied Christine Liddell's house. Then he started decisively for his truck. "We've got enough for surveillance. Same MO, same general description, the tattoo. And the fact that she said he was driving a truck cab."

Heady with the thrill of closing in on their suspect, Dallas followed him to the curb and opened her door. "You think Lieutenant Roberts will okay it?"

"Yes."

Inside his truck, Sam put in a call to his boss and after a few minutes, hung up. "We've got authorization for surveillance. Starting tonight."

"We're going to need about forty gallons of coffee."

"Good news. Lieutenant Roberts has put together three teams. He wants this guy before Christmas. Rock's back and the lieutenant's called in Mace and his partner. You and I will take the evening shift." He glanced at his watch. "We can head over there now. Rock's already at this guy's house."

They'd grabbed a sandwich on the way over to watch Richie Lewis's house. Dallas had met Virgil "Rock" Moody, Sam's partner, and she'd liked the gruff, big man instantly. Then he'd left, saying he'd be back at eight in the morning, unless something happened.

She and Sam had been sitting in his truck for almost four hours. They'd been working nonstop since three-thirty this morning. Fatigue and tension were taking their toll. Dallas rubbed the aching muscles in her shoulder and was surprised to feel Sam's big strong hand close over hers.

"Here, let me." There was nothing seductive in his tone, but a flurry of heat sparked in Dallas's belly anyway.

She dropped her hand to her lap, bowed her head and gave herself up to the deep massage of his fingers. Slowly he kneaded away the tension, the ache of her muscles, leaving behind a warm looseness.

"That feels wonderful," she groaned.

She thought she felt him stiffen, but then couldn't be sure.

"We should be at a movie or something." He chuckled. "How many guys would take you on a stakeout?"

She lifted her head slightly to look at him. "A movie? Like a date?"

He shrugged, his hand falling from her shoulder to fist against his thigh. "Yeah."

"Are we dating?" She couldn't help the surprised skepticism in her voice.

He hesitated long enough that her head came up. Her gaze locked with his and anticipation drummed along her nerves.

His Adam's apple bobbed. "We could be."

He sounded as uncertain as ever.

She'd so been hoping he would come to a decision about them, but perhaps it was too soon. Disappointment stabbed at her and she blinked back a sudden burn of tears. She laughed to cover the unexpected emotion. "I suppose so."

"Dallas?" Her name was almost a plea.

Unable to look at him, she stared out the window. And straightened. "Hey, here comes Lewis."

Whatever Sam had been about to say was lost as they followed their suspect to The Rodeo.

Dallas put her hurt aside and concentrated on Lewis. "This is the bar where the second victim was picked up. Looks like we were right about him starting the pattern over."

"Yeah." Sam's excitement was as palpable as hers.

They parked and followed him inside at a discreet distance, taking a table across from the bar so they could see him clearly. The hours ticked away, draining their enthusiasm and their certainty that something was about to happen.

When the bar closed in the early-morning hours, Richie Lewis went home. Alone. Sam checked in with Lieutenant Roberts, who ordered them to go home and get some sleep. Sam and Dallas were to report back this afternoon at four.

Mace and his partner, O'Kelly, were now in place at Richie Lewis's house.

When Sam pulled into Carrie's drive, Dallas knew another ten cups of coffee wouldn't have kept her eyes open. The emotions of the last two days with Sam and the middle-of-the-night call about Christine Liddell had combined to wear Dallas flat out. Sam had to be as exhausted as she was.

His eyes were as bloodshot as hers felt, his features haggard and worn. Exhaustion had worked its way through her, leaving her brain fuzzy and her muscles limp.

He scrubbed a hand across his face and said in a grainy voice, "See you this afternoon."

She nodded. "Around three?"

"Yeah." He glanced at his watch. "It's about three-thirty in the morning. That gives us about twelve hours. Try to get some sleep. I have a feeling we'll be out late again tonight."

"All right."

She opened her door, then Sam's hand closed over her arm. "Good work today, Dallas."

"You, too." She looked over at him, wanting to smooth away the fatigue and anxiety on his face.

To her surprise, he reached up and stroked her cheek. "This will all be over soon."

Was he trying to tell her they would then be able to sort out this thing between them? Or that it, too, would be over?

"Yeah." She smiled, even though she wanted to grind her teeth in frustration. But he'd reached out. She'd have to be content with that for now.

It was damn little comfort. Without the distraction of working the case to keep herself from thinking about him, Dallas didn't know if she'd be able to sleep. But exhaustion finally quieted her racing thoughts and she slept.

Sam had slept for eight hours straight, then gotten up at noon, showered and eaten lunch. On his way to pick up Dallas, he stopped at a toy store to buy one more gift for Ashley's Christmas. It was just before three when he arrived at Carrie's.

As Dallas opened the door, she was talking on her cell phone. She motioned Sam inside and shut the door. "Yes, Mom. Sure. Tell Austin I'll see him then. Love you, too."

Sam grinned as she hung up. "How is your family?"

"They're doing great. Austin's coming home for Christmas."

"Where's Carrie?"

"Finishing her Christmas shopping. I'll just be a minute." Dallas turned to go down the hall and it was then that Sam realized what she was wearing.

Black jeans hugged her tight, round butt and sleek legs as if they'd been glued on. They outlined every curve and then some. Sam's mouth went dry. A savage heat throbbed in his groin.

His awareness of her, latent yesterday because of their long hours and intense concentration, ratcheted up to vivid pulsing life. His gaze scooted over her, taking in the silver earrings dangling from her ears. She wore a red-and-white tailored shirt that veed in twin points below her waist and lay flat on her belly. The shirt wasn't snug, but he could see the full curves of her breasts.

The black ropers were hers, but he couldn't ever remember seeing her in a getup like this before. "Nice," he said, eyeing her appreciatively. "What are you wearing?"

"Do you like it?" She walked back into the room, looking down at herself, then smiling at him.

"What's not to like?" Hunger deepened his voice and he looked up, his gaze clashing with hers.

The moment arced between them, suspended and electric. A pulse fluttered in her throat and her eyes went silver with desire. She stepped toward him, her lips parting.

Desire gripped him down low. All he had to do was reach out. She would come to him. *Whoa, man,* he cautioned. They didn't have time for this. They were getting ready to sit for hours on end watching a suspect and they had to be focused solely on that.

He looked away, breaking the contact. Instantly Dallas pulled back, too, masking the invitation in her eyes. Her withdrawal hit him like a physical blow, but he knew it was the right thing.

He forced a smile. "About ready?"

With Dallas dressed like that and sitting only inches away from him in his truck, Sam realized it would take every ounce of willpower and discipline to maintain his focus during the coming hours. His palms itched to touch her. He couldn't take his eyes off her and he hoped he was the only one who would see her this way.

He wanted to get his hands on her right now, pull her into him, cup that shapely bottom in his hands and kiss her until they both lost all sense of time and reason again. Trying to dispel those thoughts, he shook his head.

"I thought I'd fit right in at the bar tonight."

Sam nodded slowly, sudden suspicion snaking up his spine.

She glanced down at herself, smoothed her shirt. "I noticed most of the women had on Rockies last night, but these jeans are all I brought. I borrowed the shirt from Carrie. And the earrings." She touched her ears and smiled. "Think I'll blend?"

He cocked his head, finally comprehending the detail she'd employed. "What's going on?"

She frowned at her holster, obviously trying to decide whether or not to wear it over this getup. "I had the greatest idea. I can pull him in, Sam."

"'Pull him in'?" Warning bells screeched through his mind. "As in solicit him? As in let him pick you up?"

"Well, not solicit, but yes, let him pick me up. It's brilliant, if I do say so myself."

"Brilliant!" For a moment, Sam couldn't speak. All he

could visualize was Dallas going off somewhere with this slime who strangled women, who had sex with them after he killed them.

"Yes." Dallas went on as if he were just as excited as she was. "We'll follow him tonight, then I'll let him pick me up in the bar."

No way was Sam letting her go anywhere alone with that scum. A fierce protectiveness surged through him and he roared, "The hell you will!"

Chapter 13

Her eyes widened. "Why not?"

"How about because this guy kills women, then has sex with them?" Sam realized he was shouting, but he didn't care.

Dallas looked at him oddly, as if he'd told her something she already knew. Which he had.

"Why wait for him to pick up another defenseless woman?" she asked reasonably. "I'm law enforcement. I'm trained. This way, we can control it."

"The guy's a maniac." Why was she being so damn practical about this? "I don't want you putting yourself in that kind of danger."

"That's sweet. Kind of," she said with strained patience. "But female police officers go undercover. Why not me? He'll try to kill me before he tries anything else and I won't let it get that far."

"*You* won't let it get that far? The guy's a total sicko. What if he knocks you out?"

"I'll wear a wire. You'll back me up." Irritation flashed in her gray eyes. "We can do this, Sam."

He clenched his jaw so hard he thought it would snap. "I see you've got this all worked out. Without talking to me first."

"I'm talking to you now," she said evenly.

"I don't like it."

"I'm getting that pretty clearly." She let out a slow breath. "We've been working this for eleven days and now we've got a huge break. Today's Christmas Eve. This is a good plan. We can wrap this up."

"So you can leave?" he said bitterly.

She stared at him for a long moment. Hurt and something indefinable passed across her face. "So no more women get killed."

He tried to rein in his emotions—a jumbled crush of frustration, protectiveness and downright opposition to her plan.

"Remember what Lieutenant Roberts said? He wants this finished—"

"He didn't say anything about you putting yourself on the line," Sam growled.

"I won't be walking in there blind. I'll have backup." She crossed her arms and lifted her chin. "What part doesn't work for you?"

She was blatantly challenging him to define what was going on in his head. And he didn't know if he could, even for himself. It didn't help that her plan *was* a good one. Or that she was trained. "No."

"Get over it, Garrett!" she exploded.

He shoved a hand through his hair, hating the fury that batted at him at just the thought of Richie Lewis getting anywhere near Dallas. "If he hits on you, then what?"

"I'll go with him—"

"Where? His MO is to take the victims to their own home."

She paused, then lit up. "Your house. That would be perfect."

Sam bit back a curse. It was smart. Sam knew the place inside out, as did Dallas. And if Dallas didn't come back here, it would keep Carrie out of things. Still, the idea rattled him. "This guy picks up women for sex, *after they're dead.*"

"I'm aware. I'm not planning on either dying *or* sleeping with him."

"Do you hear yourself?" he yelled. She sounded so...so damn reasonable, he thought he had to be hallucinating. "You're telling me you feel safe because this guy would have to kill you before having sex with you?"

"That's not exactly what I'm saying."

Was she biting back a smile? Sam was almost positive of it. "Dammit, Dallas! I won't let you do this."

She went rigid. "You don't have that say, Sam. Just because we slept together, doesn't mean you can tell me how to do my job."

"Last time I checked, marshals didn't do *this.*"

Her jaw firmed. "I know how to handle myself in dangerous situations, Sam. I baby-sit hit men and terrorists, drug dealers and bombers. *That's* my job. I can do this."

His mind raced for another alternative. "We can use a policewoman."

"I *am* a policewoman, and no one else has worked this case." Resentment sharpened her voice. "Valeria was my witness. This is *my* case. This guy's mine and I'm going to get him."

"It's not your jurisdiction—"

"Don't go there with me!" She stood toe to toe with him, chest heaving, eyes flashing dangerously. "I've been on the case this far. I'm staying."

Her gaze locked with his—no give, no surrender. Not Dallas.

She planted her hands on her hips. "Admit it. You're letting your personal feelings interfere with this."

"So sue me," he snarled.

"We can set it up any way you want, Sam. You can have the whole department waiting at your house."

"Don't make light of this."

She threw up her hands. "Why is it any different than if *you* went undercover?"

He ground his teeth. "It *is* different."

"Why? Because you think you can take better care of yourself?"

Her question hit home with the force of a missile. He and Brad had gone into that warehouse *knowing* they could take care of themselves, and look what had happened. There had been no guarantees for them and there wouldn't be any for Dallas.

"Well?"

"I don't like it."

"I doubt it's going to be the most fun I've ever had, either." When he didn't speak, she continued, "I don't want to do this without you, Sam, but it's a good plan. I'll talk to Lieutenant Roberts myself if I have to."

His jaw tightened. He understood her need to get the killer. He knew the thrill of closing in on a suspect. Her plan was as sound as any they could execute. How could he deny her what he would want himself—the chance to finish a case he'd started?

He blew out a breath. At least if they did it Dallas's way, he could back her up. And have a team in place in case the guy got hinky. She was right. They could end this with some control. He paced behind the sofa. "You'll wear a wire."

"Didn't I say that?"

"And I'll be there the whole time."

"Great idea," she said dryly. "Why didn't I think of it?"

Resigned, he snatched open the door. "All right. But if the lieutenant says no—"

"He won't."

"Dammit, Dallas!"

"If he says no," she finished, grabbing up her coat, "we'll come up with something else." Walking out in front of him, she smiled.

But he shook his head. He hated this. He hated everything about it.

Once in his truck, she reached over and offered him the cell phone. "So, do you call your lieutenant or do I?"

His lips flattened. He took the phone and punched his speed dial.

Roberts not only approved it, but liked the way Dallas thought. Sam kept his mouth shut about that.

On the way to relieve Mace and O'Kelly of their shift, Sam swung by the station and picked up a wire. After a few instructions, Dallas felt sure she could put it on herself before she went into the bar. If she needed help, Sam would be there.

Just thinking about it made him boil inside. Tension bowed tight across his shoulders. He was ready to catch the killer, too, but not at the expense of her life.

Conversation between them was sporadic and terse. He couldn't shake the dread eating at him, the edginess. It was caused by something besides the fact that Dallas would soon be walking into danger.

Sam refused to consider what might go wrong with her plan. Knowing they couldn't predict this guy's behavior, he would have to trust her to know when to get out. There would be a space of time during the operation—when she rode with Lewis to Sam's house—when she would be on her own. With no contact with him, no communication with the surveillance van. That twisted Sam's gut in knots.

Dallas was pale and quiet and he knew she was anxious, too. He also knew she wouldn't be swayed.

He felt compelled to make promises, make plans for the future, tell her they'd get things straightened out between them. But he didn't know that, did he? As much as he was trying to let go of Brad, guilt still chained him to his dead partner.

The silence between him and Dallas swelled with apprehension, stretching so thin that Sam was afraid any words, argument or not, would unleash the torrent of frustration and fear he fought to keep at bay.

Half of him hoped Richie Lewis wouldn't go anywhere tonight, but Sam knew that would only prolong the agony. Dallas wouldn't give up this idea. And she shouldn't, he acknowledged reluctantly. If anyone else had come up with it, he wouldn't have blinked.

She deserved the chance to nail this slime, not only for Valeria, but for all the other women who'd died. Sam would be listening the whole time. He would be with her in the bar, following her if she left with Lewis. Two teams would be waiting at his house.

The precautions reassured him, but they didn't assuage the one merciless fear that sawed at him. What if she needed him and he couldn't get to her in time, just like he hadn't been able to get to Brad? *That* was the fear hacking away at his self-confidence, but he didn't voice it.

Cold sweat slicked his palms and his belly quivered. He realized his hands were shaking, so he clenched his fists tight, willing away the terror, forcing himself to fall back on his training and his instincts. Doubts immediately surfaced. An insidious little voice reminded him that his training and instincts had supposedly been just as good that day in the warehouse with Brad.

No. He wouldn't freeze. Dallas was counting on him and he wouldn't let her down. She would be fine. Sam refused to believe anything else. He wouldn't let anything happen to her. And she would be on her guard.

But it was no use telling himself not to worry. Until this thing was over and she was safe, he would.

When Richie Lewis got into his car at eight-thirty and pulled out of his driveway, Sam followed at a discreet distance, focusing intently on the suspect's '82 Camaro. They couldn't risk losing Lewis—not tonight of all nights.

The steering wheel was slick in Sam's hands. Bile rose in his throat. He considered turning onto a side road and calling off the whole thing. The apprehension, the self-doubt threatened to overwhelm him, but he forced them back and drove on. He had to function for Dallas, steel his mind against anything other than success. And he would. Somehow.

As Sam swung his truck into a parking space two rows over from Lewis, he watched the guy walk across the lot toward Whiskey Joe's, the bar where Valeria's photo had been recognized. Sam's gaze narrowed as Lewis disappeared inside.

Beside Sam, Dallas shifted in the seat and he glanced over to see her unbutton her blouse and adjust the wire taped to her chest. Swallowing hard, he looked away, his fingers curling over the steering wheel. He felt her readjust her shirt.

"All set?" he asked hoarsely, pushing away the maverick image of his hands on her breasts.

She slid him a solemn look. "Ready." She sounded slightly breathless as she opened her door.

His hand closed over her wrist. "Wait."

She looked back, protest flaring in her eyes.

He reached down, dipped inside his boot and unbuckled his ankle holster. He held it, and his Walther PPK out to her. Floodlight gleamed on the blue steel of the .380 automatic. "Take this."

"What about you?" She patted her coat pocket. "I've got my Taurus."

"My .45's in my pocket. The .357 is behind the seat. Please take this."

"I guess I'm glad you're a gun nut." Searching his eyes, she took the weapon. She pulled up her jeans leg, buckled the holster in her boot on the inside of her calf. After sliding the Taurus into the holster, she slipped the Walther into her coat pocket. "Thanks."

"Dallas," he rasped. "Be careful."

She leaned in and squeezed his hand. "I will, Sam. It means everything to know you're there with me."

He scowled. "When this is over, we need to talk."

Wary now, her gaze snapped to his. "Are you going to tell me goodbye?"

"Hell, no! Not even close. We're going to get some things straightened out."

"All right." In the darkness, her gray eyes were curious and openly vulnerable. She took a deep breath. "I'm ready."

Her voice echoed with a thrill, a hint of fear. Energy poured from her. He wasn't ready at all. "I'll be with you the whole time."

She nodded, smiled and walked off. He gave her two minutes to get inside and get settled, clenching and unclenching his fists the whole time. Dread washed over him in a cold, suffocating wave. *Get a grip, Garrett. If Dallas can do this, so can you.*

Sam got out of his truck, stalking toward the bar. If Richie Lewis—or anyone else—harmed one hair on her head, Sam would beat him to a bloody pulp. There would be nothing of the man left to go to trial.

Giddy with a mix of anticipation and nerves, Dallas stepped into Whiskey Joe's and draped her coat over her arm to the crooning sound of The Judds on the jukebox. Squinting into the hazy light for Richie Lewis, she checked out the interior of the bar.

Smoke, turned to neon by the flashing lights of the jukebox, swirled around her. A huge wooden dance floor dominated the room. The jukebox sat at the near end. Across the dance floor was a small stage and on this side, nearest the bar, small round tables were staggered down its length.

The live band, billed as Nowhere Road, was setting up on-stage. Until they began to play, the jukebox would provide the music. Dallas raked a not-quite-steady hand through her hair. Sam was right—she'd never done anything like this before. But that didn't mean she couldn't. For luck, she dipped a hand in her back jeans pocket and touched the warmed metal of Brad's silver dollar.

Only a few couples moved in a shuffle around the scuffed dance floor, but customers streamed steadily through the door behind Dallas. A mound of dance wax, which customers rubbed on their boot soles for easier movement, waited at each corner.

Not seeing Richie Lewis on the dance floor, Dallas shifted her gaze and spotted him moving through a throng of people. Just like their description, he stood five-eleven and weighed about one hundred sixty pounds. He wore a colorful new-style Western shirt with a stand-up collar, like most of the other men here.

She wasn't close enough yet to see if he had a cross tattoo on his right hand, but she would be. He elbowed his way through a group of people and she got a glimpse of his tooled leather belt, which sported a design of galloping horses. He reached the bar and stopped, speaking to the bartender.

Dallas threaded her way through the crowd, maneuvering until she stood at Richie's right. She didn't recognize the woman behind the bar from her previous visit about Valeria. As she waited for the woman to take her order, Dallas glanced down.

Richie held a beer in his right hand. Because of the angle, she could see part of a tattoo on his wrist, but couldn't make out the design. She needed to see the whole thing. Tamping down her impatience, she ordered a vodka tonic from the bartender and squinted into the hazy light behind the bar, checking out the other employees.

A ponytailed man came out of the back, hoisting a keg of beer on one shoulder. Muscles bulged under his T-shirt, black with a neon outline of a cowboy hat. The woman returned with her drink and Dallas pulled some money out of her jeans pocket.

She picked up her drink and turned to the left, deliberately jostling Richie's arm.

He turned, balancing his beer mug so it wouldn't slosh and

Dallas got a full view of the cross tattoo that began at the knuckle of his middle finger. Bingo.

"Sorry." She flashed a smile.

"No problem." The irritation in his hazel eyes shifted to cool interest.

She turned away and chose a table where she had a clear view of him just at her shoulder. As she hung her coat on the back of her chair, she surreptitiously studied him.

Bile rose in her throat as she recalled the crime-scene photos she'd seen of Valeria's and the other women's bodies. He looked so harmless standing there, wearing a goofy grin as he turned, hitched one boot over the bar rail and surveyed the crowd milling around the dance floor.

What are you looking for, Richie boy?

Lifting her vodka tonic, she pretended to sip. Part of their suspect's MO was that he bought his victims a drink. She wanted to give Richie something to go for if he decided to buy her one. As she looked around, she noted the large number of women here, some with men already, but many alone or with other women. Waitresses, clad in denim miniskirts and ropers, weaved through the crowd, taking drink orders.

Up on the stage, a guitar twanged, drawing Dallas's attention. One of the band members, a man resembling a young Conway Twitty, exchanged a microphone for one in the back, then tapped on it. "Test, Test."

"Ya-hoo!" someone yelled in the audience. "Y'all are good!"

The guy onstage grinned, waving a dismissive hand.

Dallas glanced casually over her shoulder. Richie was in the same place. And she saw Sam, too. He'd slipped past her and now stood down the bar from Richie, at the end facing the door. He had a good view of the suspect. And her.

Sam caught her eye and raised a questioning brow. *Is this our guy? Are you okay?*

She gave a barely perceptible nod, turning away as the bartender approached him. Dallas lifted her glass, but didn't drink. Unless someone sat down with her, they wouldn't notice.

After strumming a few warm-up chords, the band announced they would start with a "bus stop." Dallas had figured out last night that a "bus stop" was a line dance. As the line dancers queued up in the middle of the floor, several other couples took to the outside. They would move counterclockwise and dance their own preference.

The band struck up "Reggae Cowboy" and the floor erupted into motion. Dallas tapped her foot, hoping Whiskey Joe's was similar to The Rodeo in that they only played two or three line dances in a night. She didn't know any line dances, but could fake her way through a shuffle or a waltz, possibly a two-step.

As soon as the song ended, the band launched into "My Maria." Couples paired up for a shuffle. A thickly muscled man with a dark mustache introduced himself as Jamie and asked Dallas to dance. She accepted readily, hoping Richie was watching. She'd observed that if a woman was asked to dance and refused, no one asked her for the rest of the night. She wanted Richie to ask her.

Jamie was a pretty good dancer, as he enjoyed telling her. "I dance all the clubs. Been dancing most of my life."

She nodded, moving to the six count, trying to loosen up and pretend she was enjoying herself. She found she needed to stay on her toes to keep up with Jamie, who should have been nicknamed Swifty.

"I haven't seen you around before."

"I'm new in town," Dallas lied. The occasional glance showed Richie still at the bar, scanning the couples on the floor. She hoped she was a passable dancer. Here, just as at The Rodeo, she'd noticed that people judged your ability by the first dance. If you were good, there was no shortage of partners.

By the time the song ended, she was starting to perspire. Jamie led her back to her table and thanked her. She smiled, dropping down in her chair and casually glancing around. Richie was looking her way so she smiled noncommittally and let her gaze sweep past his.

Despite the crush of bodies and the smoke, Dallas could feel Sam's eyes on her like a laser. She lifted her glass to her lips, pretended to sip, then casually lowered her drink and dribbled some of the liquor onto the floor.

"Ma'am?" a deep male voice said above her.

She was soon on the dance floor again for another shuffle. This man, Van, was taller and less bulky than her last partner, and more comfortable to dance with.

At the end of that dance, the band went straight into a song by Vince Gill and she danced a second time with Van—a waltz this time. Between dancing and trying to appear relaxed, Dallas felt her nerves were stretching thin.

"Maybe we can dance again later?" Van asked when he returned her to her table.

"I'd like that." She smiled encouragingly as he walked away.

"Can I buy you a drink, ma'am?" Sam's voice startled her and she schooled her features into friendly aloofness.

He held a tumbler of clear liquid out to her.

"Is that water?"

"Yes."

"Good." She accepted it and took a dainty sip, though she longed to down it.

"Dance with me."

That sultry no-one-ever-refuses-me tone sent a shiver through her. She hadn't heard it in a long time and it made her want to do more than dance with him. Hoping her reaction didn't show in her face, she let him lead her onto the floor as the band launched into "He's Got You."

At the slower rhythm of the lonesome ballad, couples scooted closer and she found herself hip to hip with Sam. Even though this reminded her of what they'd shared the other night, it felt so good to touch him, to have him hold her. She fought the impulse to lay her head on his shoulder.

He smiled into her eyes. "I've had worse jobs than this."

"Me, too."

They moved in a one-two-three beat around the floor, gliding in perfect rhythm. Sam's hard body silhouetted hers, his chest to her breasts, thigh to thigh. It would be so easy to forget why they were here.

"He's been watching you," Sam said close to her ear.

His warm breath tickled and she shuddered, fighting not to tighten her hold on him. Beneath her palm, his arm was solid and muscular. His other hand, broad and strong, curled around her free one. His woodsy scent wrapped around her, set off a flurry low in her belly.

Or maybe that was due to the hypnotic touch and retreat of their bodies, the brush of their thighs against each other, the heat of him. She forced herself to focus on the case. "Think he'll try to hit on me?"

"If he has any taste at all," Sam said tightly. "You look indecent in those jeans. I'd like to peel them off your body and I guarantee you I'm not the only man here who feels that way."

Her breasts grew heavy at the thought of Sam undressing her, but she couldn't ignore the risk she might be walking into. She looked up at him. "I'll be careful."

He nodded curtly and she felt his body harden. "This isn't helping my concentration worth a damn."

"Mine either," she offered with a nervous laugh.

Her leg dipped between his, teasing, fleeting. Their bodies strained together, then shifted automatically to the best fit. Her breast here. His hand there. Familiar, comfortable, disconcerting. If she and Sam danced like this much longer, it would be obvious they had been lovers.

They moved into a deep shadow in the corner and Sam groaned at her temple, "Are you trying to drive me crazy?"

"It's mutual." Her voice sounded foreign, labored. She

wanted to get Sam in a dark corner and kiss him until the world disappeared. He hadn't touched her since they'd made love, and her body craved his.

They danced back into the light. Lines of strain fanned out from his beautiful mouth. Blue eyes, telegraphing silent, sultry messages, seared her.

His focus shifted abruptly to their steps and the people around them. She knew he was trying to disguise what was between them.

"I'd like to take you home and make love to you for about ten hours."

Dallas shivered in his arms and his eyes darkened. Before she did something stupid like kiss him, she laughed. "Too bad I don't do that on the first date, sweetness."

Her light reply broke the sensual web enveloping them. He grinned and when the song ended, he led her across the wooden floor. "You're doing great. This will soon be over."

She nodded, growing more anxious. It wasn't easy pretending to be here only to have a good time. "Thanks for the dance," she said as other couples followed them off the floor, milling around.

He smiled and dropped her hand as they reached her table. "I've got your back," he said for her ears only.

She trusted that, but this waiting made her restless, edgy. Dancing with Sam had reaffirmed her purpose, bolstered her flagging optimism about Richie. She knew she had to be patient, but she was starting to wonder if she could get his attention.

She danced another waltz with an older gentleman named Buzzy, then the band took a break. During the fifteen minutes they were gone, the jukebox played. She kept close tabs on Richie and felt a moment of panic when he partnered a petite brunette for the last dance before the band returned.

Fearing he might leave with the woman, Dallas had a tense few minutes, but after the song's end, he handed the girl over to another man and returned to his spot at the bar.

"Another vodka tonic, miss." A waitress appeared at Dallas's elbow.

"Oh, I didn't order—"

"It's from the gentleman over there." The stocky redhead hitched a thumb over her shoulder.

Dallas glanced around and saw Richie touch the brim of his hat in recognition. *Finally.*

Her senses prickling, she took the drink and lifted it with a shy smile. He dipped his head in acknowledgement, then pulled out his wallet. Light flashed on silver and Dallas made out the chain that secured his wallet to his belt loop. This had to be their guy.

Come over here, you creep. A short two minutes later, her request was answered.

"Hello." He had a pleasant voice that, surprisingly, sounded a little tentative.

She looked up and summoned a smile, feeling Sam's antenna go up as if it were hers. Her sense of triumph was mixed with caution and an insistent, drumming dread.

Richie pulled up, his knee bumping hers in the crowded space. "I haven't seen you here before."

"I'm new in town."

"Where're you from?"

"Denver." She toyed with her napkin. "Are you from here?"

"Yeah," he said. "You're a good dancer."

"Thanks."

"Would you dance with me?"

"Sure," she said brightly. Why had she believed she could do this? she wondered, on the wings of a sudden panic. She thought of Valeria and the other dead women. She recalled Sam's resistance to the idea—and her own determination to nail this guy.

Richie rose and held out his hand to her. She accepted, amazed that her own hands were dry and cool while her insides felt hot and jumbly.

They danced a couple of shuffles in which she asked his name and he told her it was Winston, the same name he'd given Christine Liddell.

When she told him hers, his eyebrows arched. "Dallas? That's kinda weird."

"My mom's from Texas."

At the end of the second song, the band announced another line dance to "Achy Breaky Heart" and Richie looked disgusted.

"Would you like to sit this one out?" she asked quickly, not wanting to lose him.

"Yeah." He guided her back to her table, but when she prepared to sit down, he leaned close.

"Hey, would you like to get out of here? Go someplace quiet where we can talk?"

Man, this guy didn't waste a second. She hesitated, not wanting to appear too eager, her stomach winding into a knot.

Something flickered in his eyes. Irritation? She could practically hear him wondering if he'd misjudged his instincts about her.

"Yes, I'd like that. It's pretty noisy in here." She smiled, mentally crossing her fingers that her hesitation hadn't raised his guard.

"Good." He rose, seeming to relax as he reached behind her. "Can I get your coat?"

"I've got it." She picked it up before he could. It wouldn't do for him to feel the weight of the Walther in her pocket.

She didn't look toward Sam, but she could feel his eagle-eyed stare anyway. He had her back. He wouldn't let her down. She slipped into her coat and walked outside with Richie.

The noise decreased abruptly. Out here, the music was a low roar and vied with the swoosh of passing vehicles, the far-off whistle of a train.

He gripped her arm proprietarily. "Where's your car?"

She fought off the impulse to jerk away. "I came with a friend. Can we drive yours?"

Suddenly suspicious, he stared at her. His eyes turned cold, eerily flat and for the first time, Dallas glimpsed the empty soul that would belong to a killer.

"I didn't see you with anyone in there," he observed quietly, taking her measure.

"Oh, Carrie disappeared with some guy right when we got here." Dallas infused her voice with just the right note of fond exasperation. "She always does that."

She held her breath, hoping he would buy her explanation.

After a second, he gave her a charming smile. "Well, then, we can take my car."

They walked across the parking lot to his Camaro. He opened the door for her, waiting until she was inside before he went around to the driver's side.

"I wish you guys were getting this," she muttered, knowing she was still too far away for the surveillance van to pick up any transmission.

As Richie climbed in, she smiled. "Coffee sounds good. Is there someplace around here that serves a good cup?"

He started the car and gave her a sheepish grin. "I was thinking maybe we could go somewhere a little quieter than a restaurant. Would that be all right with you?"

He followed their suspect's MO like a script. Despite the boyish tone of his request, Richie's eyes glittered with cunning. A shudder ripped through her and Dallas fought to keep her voice steady. "Sure."

"We could go to my place," he offered. "But I'm fresh out of coffee."

Why don't I just give you the key, buddy? she thought with a jolt of nerves. "How about my place?"

"Sounds great," he said.

As they drove out of the parking lot, Dallas caught a glimpse of Sam walking toward his truck. Hoping to keep

Richie's attention on her, she gave him directions to Sam's house.

Here we go. Steeling her nerves, she fiddled with the radio as her mind raced. Tension knotted her shoulders and it took all her willpower not to shrink into her door.

The combined comfort of her two weapons and the certainty that Sam was close behind were all that kept her from unraveling and pulling the Walther on this slimeball right now.

At last, she understood Sam's vehement resistance to her plan. For the next twenty-five minutes, she'd be out of contact with him, too far out of range for the surveillance van. If Richie became suspicious of her, there was no telling what he would do.

She was on her own.

Chapter 14

Tortured, his control strained, Sam followed them.

For almost the entire twenty-five-minute ride from Whiskey Joe's to his house, Dallas would be incommunicado. About two miles away from Sam's house, the surveillance van would begin to pick up her transmission clearly, but *he* wouldn't be able to hear anything.

Two teams waited in the surveillance van down the block from his house. One team was made up of Mace and his partner, O'Kelly. The other was comprised of Rock and Lieutenant Roberts, who was the only available officer due to that damn flu.

During the drive, Sam alternately prayed and cursed. He could only keep Lewis's taillights in sight and chafe at the imposed separation from Dallas. As long as nothing went wrong, they were okay.

Sam breathed his first sigh of relief when Richie took the correct exit off Broadway Extension. A few minutes later, Richie turned onto Sam's street. Even though his instincts protested, Sam slowed his truck to a crawl. He couldn't risk their operation now.

After several long seconds, he turned onto his street and drove toward his house. His porch light glowed welcomingly, showing Dallas and Richie already on the landing.

Sam drove past, fighting to keep to the residential speed limit so as not to draw attention. The van sat at the end of the street and Sam turned at the corner behind it, drove about fifty feet and parked. Heart thundering, he cautioned himself not to rush as he walked casually to the corner. Dallas and Richie had disappeared inside.

Sam sprinted across the street, knowing that when Richie made his move, it would go down fast. Sam wanted to bust in there right now, but they weren't one-hundred percent certain Richie was their guy, so he had to wait for the suspect to make a move on Dallas.

Clenching his jaw, he clambered into the van and took the earphones Mace shoved at him. "What's going on?"

"They just got inside," his brother whispered. "She's taking his coat."

Sam nodded, fitting the listening device onto his head.

"How'd she do?" Mace asked.

Sam gave a thumbs-up, closing out everything except the sound of Dallas's voice, trying to judge the next level of danger. The reception crackled in his ear, then cleared. He heard Richie compliment the place and Dallas thanked him.

The whole idea of her being in there alone made Sam's blood congeal, but he could reach her in ten seconds flat when the time came.

Nerves stretched taut, Sam perched on the edge of the seat, fighting the fear and murderous fury he felt at the thought of Richie Lewis laying one hand on her. She was his. His friend, his partner, his lover. *His.*

In some distant part of his mind, Sam realized he'd claimed her for the first time without guilt or shame or a thought of Brad. He wasn't sure he was free of Brad, but Sam wanted a future with Dallas. If she didn't want to stay in Oklahoma City, he'd go to Denver. He didn't care. He just wanted a chance.

As soon as this was over, he'd tell her. He narrowed his focus to what was going on inside his house.

As Dallas hung Richie's coat over the back of the recliner, she noticed the chain securing his wallet to his belt loop. It hung down to the middle of his thigh, a little longer than she'd seen teenagers wear them, but not too long for his height. Plenty long enough to strangle someone. *Her.*

He followed the direction of her gaze and frowned.

"That probably comes in handy." She smiled, moving around the couch toward the kitchen.

"Yeah." He fingered it and a dreamy look came over his face.

Dallas very nearly bolted right then. She wiped her sweaty palms down her jeans and pasted on a smile. "I'll start the coffee."

She walked into the kitchen, picking up the scuff of his boots on the carpet as he moved around Sam's living room. Pouring a potful of water into the automatic coffeemaker, she tried to ease the bow-tight tension in her shoulder. When would he make his move? Would she see him coming?

"Who's this?"

He spoke from the doorway and she started, resisting the urge to go for her gun.

He held out a photograph and she took it, startled to find the old picture of her, Sam and Brad at a summer cookout. Seeing the three of them together swamped her with nostalgia, but also gave her a small measure of reassurance. Sam was just outside. He wouldn't let anything happen to her.

Richie stared hard at her, waiting.

"My brothers." She tossed the photo onto the counter and turned to add the coffee.

She wished he would go back in the living room so she

could slip her Taurus out of the ankle holster. "Should be just a few minutes if you'd like to make yourself comfortable."

He eyed her curiously, then stepped back into the living room, but didn't turn away from her. He scanned the room, nodding toward the opposite hall. "Are the bedrooms that way?"

"Yes." Her throat went bone-dry and nausea rolled in her stomach. She noted that he kept his hand on the chain, stroking it intently.

During the nerve-knotting drive to Sam's house, Richie had told her he worked for a trucking company and how long he'd been driving trucks for them. There was no reason for him not to, she realized, since he was planning to kill her.

The coffee gurgled and streamed into the pot. From the corner of her eye, she saw him shift. Her hands shook. If he would turn away for one second, she could get to the gun. Would he immobilize her first or just whip out that chain?

The coffeepot hissed and he turned, giving a slow, predatory smile. "It's ready."

"Yeah." Her stomach dropped. She wanted to identify herself as a marshal. She wanted Sam to come busting in here with Mace and arrest this creep. But so far, Richie hadn't done anything to prove he was their killer.

She turned toward the coffeepot, taking one of Sam's black mugs from the counter. She felt Richie move. Her hand closed over the coffeepot handle.

Even halfway expecting the chain, she was still surprised when it silently whipped in front of her face and pressed toward her throat. She elbowed him in the stomach. Even though he grunted in surprise, the chain kissed her throat, then bit. Hard.

Reflexively her left hand clawed at the chain. She swung around with the coffeepot and caught him on the side of the head.

Glass shattered; hot coffee spewed out. He yowled in pain, loosening his hold for an instant.

She pushed hard and shoved her way past him, going for the door. He lunged and grabbed her around the hips, tackling her to the floor.

Hearing the faint thud of the chain on the carpet, she kicked and twisted, trying to knee him in the groin. He was wiry but strong, and his lower body pinned hers.

"Now, Sam! *Now!*"

She managed to squirrel her way up to the end table, grab the leg. He followed, struggling to his knees and trying to straddle her. She kicked out, caught him in the jaw. Bone crunched, but he kept coming.

"Bitch!" he screamed.

He got on top of her, pressed her spine into the floor, immobilizing her hips, her legs. Once again, he looped the chain around her throat and panic spurred her into a frenzy. She could only move her hands. She tried to scratch him, punch him in the throat, but she couldn't reach him well enough to deliver a blow of any power. His hips ground her into the floor.

Something hit the door. A man yelled. Sam! Fists hammered on the door and Dallas realized that Richie must have locked it when she had walked into the kitchen.

He pulled the chain tight and she choked. Spots danced in front of her eyes. She tried to reach for Sam's gun at her ankle, knew she didn't have time.

The door shuddered and Dallas registered that Sam was trying to kick his way in. She only needed a couple of seconds. She couldn't breathe. Her lungs burned. Her strength was fading. With the last of it, she boxed Richie's ears. He screamed and flinched.

She flipped to her side, trying to kick her way out from under him and clutching at the chain around her throat. Then the metal necklace yanked tight, catching two of her fingers beneath.

She knew what happened next was only a matter of split seconds, but it seemed as if each movement transpired as a freeze frame. Pressure squeezed like a vise around her neck, cutting into her skin, burning through her fingers. Her eyes bulged. She gasped, her throat on fire. She choked out a breath and felt herself fading. *Sam! Sam!*

She thought she heard the door splinter. The room swam. Blackness edged into her consciousness. Dallas was powerless to stay awake. Her last sight was of Richie Lewis staring down at her with empty focused eyes and sweat streaming down his face.

Garrett, where are you?

Sam kicked the door once more, his strength fueled by pure fury and dread. The door gave and he rushed inside, gun drawn. "Police! Freeze!"

At the intrusion, Lewis looked up and his eyes went huge.

Sam had the guy dead center as he took in the scene. Lewis had Dallas pinned to the floor, his hands at her throat. Chain winked in the light.

Sam lost it and charged. "Get off her!"

Lewis never had time to move.

Sam flew into the scum, knocking him off Dallas and rolling to the floor. He dropped his .45 and kicked it aside. Struggling to his feet, his vision hazed by a black rage he'd never experienced, Sam dragged the guy up with him, punched him in the face.

Behind him, he heard Mace and the others rush in. He slammed Lewis into the wall. Light fixtures shook. Pictures rattled.

"Stop!" Lewis screamed. "Stop!"

Sam punched him in the gut, then rammed his fist into the guy's mouth. Blood spurted, releasing satisfaction and spawning even more fury. He hit the guy again and heard his nose crunch.

Something hard grabbed Sam from behind. Steel wrapped around his arms, impeding his movements. Noise buzzed in his ears and he fought the enemy behind him.

Then he heard the voice. Mace's voice.

"Sam, get off! You're killing him, man. Get off!" his brother shouted, his arms like a vise around Sam's upper body. "Go check on Dallas. She needs you!"

It took a few seconds for Sam's brain to get the message to his body. His fists were clenched; his body braced and rigid. Breathing hard, covered in sweat, he strained against his brother's hold.

"Go, man. Dallas," Mace urged. "Dallas!"

"Okay. Okay." He shoved Richie Lewis against the wall and spun, hearing the guy fall.

Sam bolted for Dallas, still lying motionless on the floor. She was so pale, so still.

"Kittridge! Kittridge!" He slid to his knees, saw the chain loosely wrapped around her neck, the raw abrasions against her pale skin.

His heart stopped. Denial screamed through him. Reaching out with shaking hands, he pulled her to his chest, cradling her.

"Kittridge, don't you leave me," he ordered fiercely. Something wet and hot burned his eyes. "Don't you dare leave me now!"

Her eyes remained closed. The men behind him fell eerily silent. Panic clawed at him. He hugged her harder to his chest. "You're not leaving me, not when you finally came back."

Nothing.

He moved one hand to her throat, felt the thread of a pulse in her carotid artery. "Kittridge, can you hear me? Kittridge—"

"The whole town can hear you," she croaked. "You're yelling." Her eyes fluttered open, dazed, then focusing on him. "Sam?"

"We got him, Kittridge." His vision blurred. "*You* got him."

She dragged in a breath, then coughed. "We got him," she said in a raspy voice, wincing as she spoke.

Sam held her close. "I'm taking you to the hospital."

"I'm fine." She gingerly touched her throat. "I think."

"We're going," he said firmly, gathering her close and pushing to his feet.

She shoved weakly at his chest, coughing again. "Put me down. There's nothing wrong with my legs."

Gently, Sam slid her to the ground.

She wobbled at first, then straightened. "See?"

His gaze narrowed on her. "Lieutenant?"

Roberts stepped up, peered into her face. "I think you should have a doctor check you over, Dallas."

"Yeah, me, too," Rock added.

Carefully, still holding on to her with one hand, Sam stooped and picked up his weapon.

Mace had Lewis cuffed, facing the wall. He glanced over his shoulder. "We'll get this guy downtown for you, Sam. Make sure Dallas is all right."

Sam slid his arm around her waist. "Dallas—"

She didn't protest again, just laid her head on his shoulder and wrapped an arm around his waist for support.

He wasn't letting her out of his sight again. Sam stood beside her while the on-duty physician in Mercy's emergency room checked her over. He'd asked for Linc, but his brother was off tonight. Dr. Cline told Dallas the mild abrasions around her neck would fade in a few hours. Her throat might be sore for a couple of days, but other than that, she was fine.

The doctor dismissed her. Relief swamped Sam, but he couldn't dodge the image of Dallas lying limp on the floor of his house, that chain around her neck. Instead of taking her home and holding her in his bed all night as he would have preferred, they had to go to the station and finish up with Richie Lewis. But at least they were together.

When they walked into Homicide after leaving the hospital, it was after two in the morning. Lieutenant Roberts, Mace and O'Kelly had booked Lewis, then waited. They'd saved the suspect's interview for Sam to conduct.

As he and Dallas walked toward the lieutenant's desk, the other three men rose.

"Well?" Concern sharpened Mace's eyes.

"I'm fine," Dallas said carefully, her voice slightly strained.

"Good." Mace squeezed her shoulder.

Lieutenant Roberts extended a hand. "Fine job, Kittridge. If you ever want to leave the U.S. Marshals Service, look me up."

Surprise widened her eyes and she smiled.

"Glad you're okay." O'Kelly patted her shoulder, then shook Sam's hand. "Good job, you two."

"Thanks." Sam wanted to pull Dallas to him, hold her, reassure himself that she was indeed all right.

O'Kelly and the lieutenant said good-night and zigzagged through the double row of desks on their way to the door.

Dallas walked over to the watercooler and filled a cup.

Mace caught Sam in a brief hug. "You scared me there for a minute. I thought you were going to kill that guy."

"Yeah, I thought so, too." He'd never lost control like that. Ever.

"It shouldn't take you too long to finish up here," his brother said. "See you in the morning for Christmas?"

"Yeah."

Mace clapped him on the shoulder, then slipped on his coat, walking the few feet to Dallas. "I'm really glad you're okay, Dallas."

"Thanks to your brother." Over Mace's shoulder, she found Sam's gaze.

His heart squeezed. He'd come close to losing her. The realization still gripped him like a cold fist. He wanted nothing more than to take her home and hold her all night, but he still had to interview Richie Lewis. And they had paperwork to do.

"Merry Christmas."

Sam, his gaze still riveted on Dallas, heard Mace as if from a distance.

"Merry Christmas," Dallas returned, walking toward Sam.

He reached out and pulled her to him, his heart pounding in his throat. Since the bust had gone down, they hadn't had a minute alone.

Dallas laid her head on his shoulder and wrapped her free arm around his waist. "I'm okay," she said quietly.

His throat closed up. "That was a close one."

"Yes."

He couldn't voice the desperate fear, the paralyzing horror he'd felt upon seeing her lying motionless on that floor with that chain wrapped around her neck. It had flashed through his mind in a microsecond that God wouldn't be so cruel as to take her when she'd only come back into his life.

And that was when he'd known—she was his. He wanted her to stay. Somehow. They needed to work it out.

Resting his chin on her head, he closed his eyes and gave thanks that she was all right. The sweet scent of her hair and the spice of her perfume tickled his nostrils, reassuring him that she was here. That she was safe.

For a long moment, they simply held each other. Sam wanted to get her out of here. He pressed a kiss to her temple and drew back. "Let's finish this up and go home."

"Okay."

He left her sitting at his desk, starting on her report, while he went into Interview Room Three and talked to Richie Lewis.

It didn't take long to wring a confession out of the guy, who was blubbering like a baby.

Raised by a single mother who had been seduced and abandoned by his father, Richie had suffered from her rage over that. He'd been abused and neglected. By killing women and having sex with them, he'd been acting out his own rage against his mother. Sam didn't understand the twistings of the human mind, but a part of him felt some compassion for the man.

"Sick bastard," Sam muttered as he and Dallas finished up the last of their reports. Their empty coffee cups littered his desk. Looking up, he realized they'd been here all night.

Pink, watery dawn light streamed into the second-floor windows. Sam stood and arched his back, stretching out the kinks. He gathered up his paperwork and Dallas's, too.

She gave him a grateful look, massaging her shoulder.

"I'll be right back and we can leave."

"Okay."

He took the reports in and put them on his lieutenant's desk. When he returned, Dallas was on her cell phone. "Really, I'm fine, Mom. Yes, I'm still coming. I'll see you—" she glanced at her watch "—in about fourteen hours. My plane gets in just after eight."

Sam's heart sank. They'd worked straight through Christmas Eve. He hadn't asked her to spend Christmas Day with him, but he'd been hoping she would. Of course, she would make plans to be with her family. And then what? Sam didn't want to say goodbye to her.

She hung up, smiling at him as she slid her cell phone into the pocket of her coat. "Ready?"

"Yeah." He reached for his coat, slipped it on, feeling dissatisfied. The case was over, but how could he let her leave? Things were unfinished between them, because of him. At the possibility of her walking out of his life for good, emptiness consumed him. Different from what he'd felt when Brad had died, it was somehow even more bleak, more unthinkable.

He cupped her nape and rubbed a thumb over her soft skin. "I don't want you to go."

"To my parents'?"

"There. Denver. Anywhere."

"Sam—"

"I know things have been overwhelming the last twenty-four hours, but we need to talk."

"Yes." Her gaze, uncertain and expectant, held his. "I'd like to get out of these clothes and shower first. How about you?"

"Sounds good."

Invitation darkened her tired eyes. "Come with me."

His heart slammed into his ribs. "Carrie—"

Dallas glanced at her watch. "She's probably already at her mother's for the day."

They needed to talk, but he also wanted to hold her, feel her body come alive beneath his. "Are you sure?"

She nodded.

"And you're okay?" His thumb grazed the red marks on her neck.

She caught his hand and squeezed it. "Yes, Sam."

"Thank goodness," he said gruffly, relief stretching tight across his chest. And anticipation hammering low in his body.

"Won't your parents be expecting you?"

"I'll give them a call. They'll understand." She'd said nothing about staying, nothing about her plans at all. But he needed to tell her how he felt; needed to be with her, even if it was for the last time.

Once inside Carrie's house, Dallas turned into his arms. Early-morning sunlight slanted into the room, chasing away the shadows.

"I'm so glad you were there," she said against his chest, holding him close.

His arms went around her and he said hoarsely, "I was afraid I'd screw it up."

"I knew you wouldn't." She looked into his eyes, trusting, certain, sincere.

His conversation with Mace had initiated the process of sorting through the guilt, the shame, and separating those emotions from his feelings for Dallas. But her words helped him to finally accept that he hadn't been responsible for Brad's death.

Now he knew it was all right for them to be together. If only she would stay. "Dallas—"

"Shh, I know." Her eyes welled with tears and her voice was a papery rasp. "I know. Hold me, Sam. Don't let go."

Her lips touched his and he tasted the salt of a tear. His hands splayed on her back, pulling her closer and deepening the kiss.

Dallas clutched him to her. She was alive. She was safe. And she was with Sam. A sense of completeness spread through her and an ache bloomed in her chest. He kissed her tenderly, softly, with a hint of desperation. She understood that all too well. They'd come close to losing everything of themselves. They had a second chance. She wasn't going to blow it.

His lips moved over hers, seducing, giving, demanding. She felt his vulnerability in the quivering of his muscles. Felt it when he at last opened his heart fully to her. Another tear seeped out, then another.

She wanted to give him all of herself, too. Dragging her lips from his, she pulled away and looked into his beautiful, searing blue eyes. She took him by the hand and led him through her bedroom and into the bath. After turning on the shower, she faced him.

Soft morning light revealed the tender hunger in his gaze. They undressed each other slowly, savoring each second, each newly bared patch of flesh.

She peeled away his shirt, running her hands over his sculpted, well-defined chest, his rock-solid biceps. The feel of his smooth warm skin intoxicated her.

He unbuttoned her red-and-white shirt and pushed it to the floor. She was magnificent. A transparent satin-and-lace bra covered her full breasts, now flushed a delicate rose and quivering. His throat burned as he brushed a kiss on the swell of one breast.

She was his, really his.

She drew in a breath, her nipples peaking beneath the silky

fabric. A fierce tenderness crossed his features and her heart dropped to her stomach. Unhooking her bra, she let it fall, baring herself to him.

His eyes darkened with hunger and awe, touching something deep inside her.

"I don't think I can make it through a shower," he said roughly, his hands skimming up her rib cage, then cupping her breasts.

Loving the feel of his hands on her, she smiled and flicked open the button of his jeans. "Try."

She stepped toward him, her breasts brushing his chest. The sensation of her soft fullness against his crisp hair and hard muscle weakened her knees. She kissed him, pulling his bottom lip into her mouth and sucking gently.

His arms, hard and warm, went around her, and he took control of the kiss. She gladly let him. After a long, drugging moment, they parted. White heat pooled in her belly, between her legs. Dallas took his hand and led him into the shower.

His gaze burned into her, intense, loyal, forgiving. For the first time, she saw no shadows of the past, felt no hint of Brad. Or guilt. Or regret.

She took the soap and lathered her hands, starting at his shoulders, dragging her hands over the sleek lines of his belly, his legs, anticipating the moment when she finally cupped him tenderly. Her hand closed around him.

Desire slashed across his features, and muscles corded in his neck. "Be still," he whispered, reaching behind her for the soap.

Anticipation quivered in her belly and when his hands reverently cupped her breasts, she arched her head and gave herself over to the tender pleasure he worked on her body. He soaped her calves and up her thighs, moving gently between her legs, then over her bottom and up her back.

Her knees wobbled. His touch sparked a restlessness, a searing need to have him inside her. His hands returned to her breasts, slipping sleekly over their fullness, kneading them, plucking at her nipples.

She moaned and pulled his head down to hers. The soap hit the floor. Shower spray pounded her back as Sam pulled her against him. His arousal pulsed heavy and wet at the juncture of her thighs.

She needed him, desperately, wildly, immediately. He guided her toward the wall so the water sluiced down between them, washing away the suds. Cool tile met her shoulder blades. Warm, taut flesh pressed her front. His tongue delved deep into her mouth, stroking, claiming. She met him stroke for stroke, the languor of her body burned away by the rising need.

Suddenly he reached over, slammed off the faucet and shoved open the door. "Bed," he rasped.

She climbed out with him and each of them grabbed a towel, drying themselves, each other, not wanting to let go. Sam's hand was strong and damp in hers, his body magnificently aroused. Liquid fire curled through her.

They hurriedly toweled off, then came together in a heated, impatient kiss. Somehow he got her to the bed—she didn't remember taking the steps—and his weight pressed her back into the mattress. It was glorious. Still slick with water, she reached down and guided him to her.

"Now, Sam. I want you inside me."

Sunlight filtered through the curtains, softening the hard edge of his jaw. Pale gold light feathered his shoulders. His gaze burned into hers and he pushed inside slowly, prolonging the agonizing ecstasy for both of them. He filled her, huge and pulsing and hot. This time, their eyes were wide-open, locked on each other.

She looped her arms around his neck, her legs around his hips, and stared into his eyes. He began to move, in slow, sure, measured strokes, and she moved with him, her breath catching at each thrust. Her heart surrendered more completely with each movement.

The whole time, they held on to each other fiercely, the way they should have from the beginning. It was leisurely and deliberate; not making up for lost time, but promising a chance.

Her heart swelled and her throat tightened. This was Sam. He was hers—finally, really hers. And it was all right.

Tears stung her eyes and Sam's turned suspiciously bright.

His body pushed into hers, taking her higher, smoothing out the battered edges of her soul, bridging the past with love and surrender and forgiveness.

On his chiseled features, she read tenderness and a fierce possession. Even if he'd never said it, he loved her. And now he was claiming her, just as she was claiming him.

The measured movements of his body spurred an urgency in her. Sleek fire licked at her and she clutched him tighter, urging him on. They moved faster, straining together, fighting for the future with feelings they'd finally realized.

His gaze never left hers. Their hands grasped, twined over her head as she gave herself to him, as he gave himself to her. Binding, promising, cleansing.

When she climaxed, his name spilled out of her throat in a vow of trust and need and loyalty that made his gut cave.

"I love you," he panted against her mouth.

Her heartbeat skipped at the naked emotion in his eyes. Tears burned her throat and she whispered, "I love you, too."

His mouth covered hers and she felt him let go then. He pumped into her and she arched off the bed, meeting him. And when it was over, she held him close, tears rolling down her cheeks.

He buried his face in her neck, his breathing ragged, their bodies now misted with sweat. After a long while, he shifted to the side and pulled her against him.

"Don't go," he mumbled as he fell asleep. "Don't go anywhere."

She didn't want to, ever again. But as she lay there listening to the steady thump of his heart, she knew there was something she had to do before she could make that promise.

Chapter 15

Sam jerked awake suddenly. Bright sunlight streamed through the curtains. As he sat up in bed, he strained to hear a noise, something that would explain the abrupt prickling of his instincts, something strong enough to rouse him out of a sound sleep.

Then he registered the empty bed, the still silence of the room.

Panic squeezed like a vise around his chest. Where was Dallas? Even as he slid to the edge of the mattress and scanned the room, he wondered if what they'd shared had been a dream.

No. He could smell her on the pillow, smell the sultry scent of sex. Where was she?

He moved off the bed, jerked up one of the towels they'd dropped and wrapped it around his hips, striding out into the hall. "Dallas?"

There was no answer. The house was completely silent. She wouldn't just leave. She wouldn't do this to him. He knew that.

Even so, he couldn't halt the fear that she had. He'd told her he loved her, but there was more. How she was the only woman who completed him. Who challenged him to be better. Who anchored him. He should have told her all of that, he thought, as he realized the full impact of what they'd shared.

Their lovemaking had been profound and right and between them only. There was no more guilt over Brad, just a deep gratitude that he and Dallas had a second chance. *Where was she?*

Striding back into the bedroom, he dressed quickly. He glanced at the clock. It was just before noon. Her plane wasn't scheduled to leave until five-thirty. Where could she be? Why hadn't she woken him?

She'd surrendered completely to him during their lovemaking. Her beautiful eyes had held no shadows of Brad, no ghosts of regret or of the past. Surrounded by the mingled scents of their bodies, he stared down at the rumpled sheets.

And then he knew where she was.

Dallas set the potted poinsettia next to Brad's headstone and crossed her arms against the cold. She considered the gray granite for a moment, then squinted into the noonday sun. "It's time for me to move on, Brad. I'd like to do it with Sam."

Of course, there was no answer. But neither was there condemnation. Just a peaceful sense that she'd finally come full circle, finally come home. She knew that Brad, of all people, would be the last to deny her the chance at happiness.

After making love to Sam, she'd made a decision and she'd already taken steps to follow it through. All that remained was telling him.

He loved her. He'd admitted that. And while her heart warmed, she was reminded that he hadn't said he was ready to let go of the past.

She fished Brad's silver dollar out of her pocket and studied the coin in her palm. For a long time, she stood at his grave, feeling that old connection to him, but with a difference this time. It was a bond of love acknowledged and released, one of acceptance.

In the chill air, she felt a rightness she hadn't felt since her marriage to Brad. Being with Sam was right. Brad would want her to slough off the past, move toward the future.

She'd made her decision. How long would she have to wait for Sam to make his?

She closed a fist over the silver dollar. Pressing a kiss to her gloved knuckles, she touched the cold stone that represented her husband. "Bye," she whispered.

Head bowed against the cold, she returned the silver dollar to her pocket as she walked back to her car. She saw his boots first.

"I thought I might find you here." Framed by the sun, Sam leaned against her car.

She hadn't heard him drive up, but she wasn't surprised he'd found her. Her heart swelled.

"Saying your goodbyes?" His voice was rusty with uncertainty.

She stepped aside, half turning toward him with a smile and gesturing toward Brad's grave. "Did you want to—"

"I was here the other night." He jammed his hands into the pockets of his sheepskin coat. "I've come to some kind of peace with him. I don't blame myself anymore, but I might always feel some responsibility, because I'm here and he's not."

"I understand that."

He took a deep breath. "I was looking for you. There are some things I should've said—"

"Me, too."

Their gazes met, their breath curling like smoke in the chill air.

At his pause, she blurted out, "I've requested a transfer, Sam."

For a moment, he simply stared at her. Pain ripped through

him. And disbelief. And a raging bitterness that he didn't even try to disguise. "Another one? Where to this time?"

"Here," she said softly, her gaze searching his.

"Oklahoma City?" He blinked, taken totally off guard.

She nodded. "I want to come home. Maybe you're not ready to let go of Brad, but I am. And I want to do it here."

He cocked his head and his breath whooshed out in surprise. "Are you doing this for me?" he asked roughly. "Or for him?"

"For me," she said firmly. "I miss it here. And I miss you. I know you said you weren't ready to move on, but I think we're making progress. I'm not running anymore, Sam. And I'll be here when you stop."

Hope flickered. "That's what I came to tell you. I *am* ready."

"You are?" There was such longing in her eyes that Sam felt humbled.

He nodded, reaching for her hand. "Mace helped me to understand what was going on. So did you. When we made love a while ago, I knew. The last couple of days I've started to sort through things, separate my feelings for you from my sense of responsibility over Brad." He stared into her eyes, looking uncertain, then seeming to make a decision. "I wanted you the first time I met you."

Surprise widened her eyes.

"And I couldn't stand myself. It was bad enough to live with it while Brad was alive, but when he died, it made me feel even more guilty. He died by my gun, with me at his back. Then a year and a half ago, when you and I slept together, I thought—" He shoved an unsteady hand through his hair. "Somehow I thought that would put things in perspective. Instead, I felt more guilty, more responsible, more confused. But I've come to forgive myself for that night. And you, for hurting me."

Regret shadowed her eyes. "That's why, when we made

love, you felt like you'd wished Brad dead? That you'd allowed him to die so we could be together?''

''Yes.''

''Oh, Sam, I'm so sorry.''

''I figured I deserved to believe you'd used me. Hell, I couldn't do anything without thinking about Brad. How could you, when you'd been married to him?''

''That's why I ran. Because I thought I should be holding on tighter to him. With you around, I wasn't holding on to him at all.''

''We're quite the pair, aren't we?'' He stared into her eyes, putting the past to rest, trying to grasp the concept of a future with Dallas.

''At least we've got another chance. I don't want to blow it.''

''I don't, either. It scared the hell out of me when I woke up a while ago and you were gone.''

''I'm sorry. I thought I'd be back before you were awake.''

''So.'' Unable to look at her, he shifted his gaze to the horizon. ''Are you getting on that plane to Texas this afternoon?''

''Yes. I want to see my family.''

His gut caved in, even though he understood.

''You could come with me.''

He cautioned the hope that sprang to life inside him. ''And then?''

''My transfer will take a couple of months.''

''I guess I'll be making a lot of trips to Denver.'' He snagged her elbow and pulled her to him, cupping her face in his palms. ''I love you, Dallas LeAnn Kittridge.''

She covered his hands with hers as his mouth came down on hers, gentle and warm and possessive. She wrapped her arms around his neck and opened her soul.

When they came up for air, he said against her lips, ''Marry me.''

"Marriage?" She pulled away, sudden protest in her eyes. "Don't do this for me, Sam. I'm in no hurry."

"What kind of answer is that, Kittridge? Will you marry me or not?"

She tilted her head, her gaze narrowing on him. "You knew if you caught me in a weak moment, I wouldn't be able to say no."

He grinned that knee-melting grin she'd first fallen for. "I was hoping."

"You think you're so smart."

"Naw, you're the smart one. I'm the pretty one."

She laughed, kissing him hard. A slow smile spread across her face. "I love you, too."

"And?"

"Yes, Detective Charm," she said, laughing. "I'll marry you."

He caught her to him in a fierce kiss and when they drew apart, she laid her head on his shoulder. They stood with their arms around each other's waist, looking at Brad's grave.

"Do you think he knows?" she asked softly.

Sam stared up into the clear blue sky and the glittering ball of sun, and felt a subtle shift in the air. Peace. He felt peace. The day seemed somehow brighter, more complete. "I think he might."

He hugged her to him and murmured against her hair, crisp from the cold air, "Merry Christmas."

"Merry Christmas."

They shared a smile as Sam opened her car door. He glanced over his shoulder, overcome with a bittersweet nostalgia. *Merry Christmas, buddy.*

"I'd like to have your child, Sam," Dallas announced.

That got his attention. Jerking his gaze to hers, he stared. "You don't have to do this for me. You're all I'll ever need."

"I wouldn't be doing it for you. I'd be doing it because of us."

Humbled, he knelt beside the car and took her hand. "Then

I think we should get married tomorrow. At your family's home.''

"Tomorrow! Can't you wait until I at least live here?''

"No.'' He kissed her with all the promise and strength of their love. A love that had been tested and welded by fire. A love that completed them both.

That one night a year and a half ago had led them through regret and resentment and finally back to each other. Stronger. Better. Fulfilled. Their future had started with one silent night in the past.

*   *   *   *   *

Take 2 bestselling love stories FREE

Plus get a FREE surprise gift!

Special Limited-Time Offer

Mail to Silhouette Reader Service™

3010 Walden Avenue
P.O. Box 1867
Buffalo, N.Y. 14240-1867

YES! Please send me 2 free Silhouette Intimate Moments® novels and my free surprise gift. Then send me 6 brand-new novels every month, which I will receive months before they appear in bookstores. Bill me at the low price of $3.57 each plus 25¢ delivery and applicable sales tax, if any.* That's the complete price, and a saving of over 10% off the cover prices—quite a bargain! I understand that accepting the books and gift places me under no obligation ever to buy any books. I can always return a shipment and cancel at any time. Even if I never buy another book from Silhouette, the 2 free books and the surprise gift are mine to keep forever.

245 SEN CH7Y

Name	(PLEASE PRINT)	
Address	Apt. No.	
City	State	Zip

This offer is limited to one order per household and not valid to present Silhouette Intimate Moments® subscribers. *Terms and prices are subject to change without notice. Sales tax applicable in N.Y.

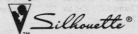

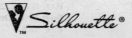

For a limited time, Harlequin and Silhouette have an offer you just can't refuse.

In November and December 1998:

BUY **ANY** TWO HARLEQUIN
OR SILHOUETTE BOOKS and
SAVE $10.00
off future purchases

OR BUY ANY THREE HARLEQUIN OR SILHOUETTE BOOKS
AND **SAVE $20.00** OFF FUTURE PURCHASES!

(each coupon is good for $1.00 off the purchase of two
Harlequin or Silhouette books)

....

JUST BUY 2 HARLEQUIN OR SILHOUETTE BOOKS, SEND US YOUR
NAME, ADDRESS AND 2 PROOFS OF PURCHASE (CASH REGISTER
RECEIPTS) AND HARLEQUIN WILL SEND YOU A COUPON BOOKLET
WORTH **$10.00 OFF** FUTURE PURCHASES OF HARLEQUIN OR
SILHOUETTE BOOKS IN 1999. SEND US 3 PROOFS OF PURCHASE AND
WE WILL SEND YOU 2 COUPON BOOKLETS WITH A TOTAL SAVING OF
$20.00. (ALLOW 4-6 WEEKS DELIVERY) OFFER EXPIRES
DECEMBER 31, 1998.

....

I accept your offer! Please send me a coupon booklet(s), to:

NAME: _____

ADDRESS: _____

CITY: _____ STATE/PROV.: _____ POSTAL/ZIP CODE: _____

**Send your name and address, along with your cash register
receipts for proofs of purchase, to:**

In the U.S.
Harlequin Books
P.O. Box 9057
Buffalo, NY
14269

In Canada
Harlequin Books
P.O. Box 622
Fort Erie, Ontario
L2A 5X3

PHQ4982

FORTUNE'S Children™

**The Fortune family requests
the honor of your presence at the weddings of**

FORTUNE'S CHILDREN™

The Brides

Silhouette Desire's scintillating new miniseries,
featuring the beloved Fortune family
and five of your favorite authors.

The Honor Bound Groom—**January 1999**
by Jennifer Greene (SD #1190)

Society Bride—**February 1999**
by Elizabeth Bevarly (SD #1196)

And look for more **FORTUNE'S CHILDREN:
THE BRIDES** installments by Leanne Banks,
Susan Crosby and Merline Lovelace,
coming in spring 1999.

Available at your favorite retail outlet.

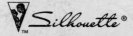

Silhouette®

Bestselling author

LINDSAY McKENNA

continues the drama and adventure of her
popular series with an all-new, longer-length
single-title romance:

MORGAN'S MERCENARIES

HEART OF THE JAGUAR

Major Mike Houston and Dr. Ann Parsons were in the heat
of the jungle, deep in enemy territory. She knew Mike's
warrior blood kept him from the life—and the love—he
silently craved. And now she had so much more at stake.
For the beautiful doctor carried a child. His child...

Available in January 1999, at your favorite retail outlet!

Look for more **MORGAN'S MERCENARIES** in 1999,
as the excitement continues in the Special Edition line!

COMING NEXT MONTH

#901 MURPHY'S LAW—Marilyn Pappano

Men in Blue

Detective Jack Murphy and psychic Evie DesJardien had been in love—until the night Jack was told she'd betrayed him. They were passionately drawn back into each other's lives when Jack enlisted Evie's help to catch a killer. Could the two learn to trust in their love again…before it was too late?

#902 CODE NAME: COWBOY—Carla Cassidy

Mustang, Montana

When Alicia Randall and her six-year-old daughter answered Cameron Gallagher's ad for a housekeeper, she knew that she could never let him discover the truth about her. Then she found herself immediately attracted to this sexy stranger. Was this the happiness she had been searching for, or would her past catch up with her and ruin her future?

#903 DANGEROUS TO LOVE—Sally Tyler Hayes

Sexy spy Jamie Douglass knew she was falling for her strong and irresistible instructor Dan Reese. He was a difficult man to get close to, but Jamie was determined to break down his barriers. Then a routine mission turned deadly, and Jamie was forced to admit just how much she felt for this tough, sensual man. She trusted him with her life…but did she trust him with her heart?

#904 COWBOY WITH A BADGE—Margaret Watson

Cameron, Utah

When Carly Fitzpatrick's determination to find her brother's killer brought her back to the McAllister ranch, she met Devlin McAllister, the son of the man accused of the murder. Torn between her growing feelings for Devlin and her desire to discover the truth, Carly found herself falling in love with this strong, sexy sheriff—but what would he do when he found out why she'd really come to town?

#905 LONG-LOST MOM—Jill Shalvis

Stone Cameron thought life was moving along nicely for himself and his daughter—until Cindy Beatty came to town. Deeply distrustful of women after his long-ago love abandoned him, Stone tried to resist her sensuous appeal. But there was something oddly familiar about this beautiful stranger that made her impossible to resist…and he knew that it was only a matter of time before he gave in to the attraction.…

#906 THE PASSION OF PATRICK MacNEILL—Virginia Kantra

Families Are Forever

Single father Patrick MacNeill's time had been consumed with caring for his son, leaving him no room for a social life—until he met Dr. Kate Sinclair. Suddenly he began to remember what it was like to feel…and to fall in love. So when Kate tried to deny the attraction between them, he planned on showing the lovely doctor his own bedside manner!